"Don't you want to teach?"

The vague feeling of discontent she'd been ignoring welled up inside her. "I certainly enjoy it. However, to be honest, it isn't really what I want to do."

He frowned. "Then what *do* you want to do?"

I want to have a family with a husband and children of my own. She sighed and leaned back against the stair railing.

"Helen?" Quinn's use of her Christian name for the first time drew her full attention. "I need to talk to you. I know this probably isn't the right time, but I can't hold it in."

"This sounds serious. Go ahead and tell me."

"My eldest nephew and niece are always going on about you and I've noticed that you seem to care a whole lot about them, too. That's true, isn't it?"

"It certainly is."

"Well, I'm doing my best for them, but anyone can tell that isn't good enough." He waved away her protests. "Now, that's just the plain truth and you know it. The fact is that they need a mother." She stared at him, wondering where this conversation was going before he spoke again. "I was wondering if you'd be willing to marry me—for the children's sake."

Noelle Marchand is a native Houstonian living out her childhood dream of being a writer. She graduated summa cum laude from Houston Baptist University in 2012, earning a bachelor's degree in mass communications and speech communications. She loves exploring new books and new cities. When she's not scribbling out her latest manuscript, you may find her pursuing one of her other passions—music, dance, history and classic movies.

Books by Noelle Marchand

Love Inspired Historical

Unlawfully Wedded Bride
The Runaway Bride
A Texas-Made Match

Bachelor List Matches Series

The Texan's Inherited Family

Visit the Author Profile page at Harlequin.com.

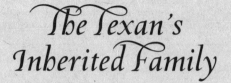

The Texan's Inherited Family

NOELLE MARCHAND

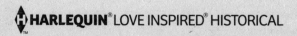
HARLEQUIN® LOVE INSPIRED® HISTORICAL

Recycling programs
for this product may
not exist in your area.

™ LOVE INSPIRED BOOKS

ISBN-13: 978-0-373-28304-0

The Texan's Inherited Family

www.Harlequin.com

Printed in U.S.A.

Instead of shame and dishonor,
you will enjoy a double share of honor.
You will possess a double portion of prosperity
in your land, and everlasting joy will be yours.
—*Isaiah* 61:7

This story is dedicated to my faithful friend Elizabeth Tisdale. Thank you for always listening, appreciating my love for Disney movies and encouraging me to have fun. Here's to all of the adventures we've had and all that are sure to come.

Chapter One

October 1888
Peppin, Texas

Quinn Tucker was not a smart man.

If he was, he would have realized he needed to get married as soon he'd found out he was going to be a foster father to a group of orphans. Three whole weeks had passed since then. Three weeks in which he'd struggled to be both father and mother to four children he hadn't even known existed until they'd been dropped on his doorstep by a stranger named Jeffery Richardson. The man had said the children had belonged to his brother, Wade, who along with Quinn's father, had gone off to seek a fortune for their poverty-stricken family. Quinn had been eight years old at the time, so he'd been left behind to be raised by and eventually take care of his ailing grandmother. Nana had died when he was fourteen. Quinn had been on his own. Until now...

Now, he was afraid to be on his own long enough to visit the outhouse for fear that one of the children would get hurt or wander off in his absence. Not that he regretted taking in his own kin. He didn't. Each of them had become real special to him during the short time that they'd lived with him. It was just that their entrance into his life had changed everything faster than he'd imagined possible.

He was still trying to get his bearings, which must have been why it had taken him seeing his friends Lawson Williams and Ellie O'Brien exchange vows yesterday for him to realize that he needed a wife. After all, a wife was supposed to be a helpmeet and he needed help—desperately. There was only so much bathing, washing, mending, braiding, baking and cooking a man could handle on his own with a farm to run.

Maybe he ought to ask Ellie for some advice on finding a wife. The town's newest bride was also its most successful matchmaker. Even as busy as he'd been lately, Quinn hadn't been able to escape hearing all the ruckus she'd caused over the past two months by gradually compiling a list of the town's most eligible bachelors and the ladies Ellie saw as their matches. Her intent had merely been to find her own match through the process of elimination. However, it seemed everyone had been hankering to get a peek at what had been deemed the "Bachelor List" to find out who their match was.

Quinn needed to know if he had one, but he wasn't sure what qualified a man to be considered "eligible." If it was looks, education or riches, he didn't have a chance. Women never seemed to get silly or swoony over him—at least not that he'd ever noticed.

Of course, that didn't mean one hadn't captured his attention.

Helen McKenna, the town's schoolmarm, caught him watching her from across the crowd of folks who'd gathered for a good old-fashioned shivaree at the ranch where the newlyweds lived. Her mahogany eyes seemed to sparkle in the lantern light as she tilted her head inquisitively and stared right back at him. A blush spread just below her high cheekbones, making him wonder just how long he'd been staring. He sent her a nod as if that's all he'd been trying to do in the first place, then glanced away.

He'd noticed her in church the first Sunday after she'd arrived in town, but hadn't met her until he'd enrolled his eldest nephew and niece in school. That first meeting had confirmed everything he'd feared about the schoolmarm. She was beautiful, refined, intelligent and far too good for him. Every time he looked at her, Nana's warnings rang in his ears. *Chasing after more than you deserve will only get you hurt or dead.*

Hadn't his pa and his brother proven her right? No need for Quinn to follow their example. He'd best stay far away from Miss McKenna—not that he actually had a chance with her, anyway.

Staying away from her tonight would have been a sight easier if she hadn't hung back to talk to him. The rest of the group followed Sheriff Sean O'Brien, who was the bride's brother and Quinn's closest neighbor, toward the cabin where the newlyweds lived. Quinn's grip tightened on the neck of his banjo in his left hand as Helen's generous smile set his heart thumping in his chest. Not wanting her to stumble in the dark, uneven field they traipsed across, he dared to place a cautionary hand near the small of her back. She angled closer to his side and chanced a whisper.

"I wasn't expecting to see you tonight. Who's with the children?"

"The groom's parents were kind enough to insist on watching them for me," he whispered back. "You can't get much better than the town doctor and Mrs. Lettie Williams for temporary caregivers. They even brought us supper."

Her lips tipped upward in a brief smile. "What about Reece? How is his black eye?"

"All right, I suppose, but it's turning an awful shade of green." Reece was Quinn's oldest nephew at nine years old and was the self-designated protector of the siblings. He hadn't taken kindly to one of the other schoolboys picking on his younger sister Clara. The seven-year-old was a true sweetheart and destined to be a heartbreaker with her rich brown curls and big blue eyes. "I'm not sure what to do. I don't want to encourage him to fight, but I don't want Clara to be bullied, either."

She nodded with understanding and concern written across her face in a frown. "I've already spoken to the other student's father about it. Hopefully, the teasing will stop. As for Reece, I'm sure he'll settle in soon."

"I hope so. He's been through a lot with his father and stepmother dying in that boating accident on their honeymoon only two years after his mother died in childbirth. Then he traveled thousands of miles to live with an uncle he'd never even met."

"It couldn't have been an easy transition for you, either." The empathy in her tone wrapped around him like a warm blanket.

"I manage well enough." At least, that's what he kept telling himself. Helen started to respond but someone shushed them, so she just nodded. He counted about twelve or thirteen people creeping along beside her to where a cozy cabin for two sat at the edge of the woods. Even the katydids stopped singing. A snicker sounded above the soft rustle of grass but was quickly drowned out by more shushes.

Sean lit the lantern he held and gave a single nod. A cacophony of sound shattered the stillness. Quinn's lightning-fast fingers picked an out-of-tune melody on his banjo. On his right, Helen banged an old frying pan with a mangled metal spoon while her good friend Isabelle Bradley rang the bell that usually sat on the Bradley Boardinghouse's front desk. On his left side, his best friend, Rhett Granger, played a jumbled assortment of chords on his harmonica before settling in on a single warbling note. Beside Rhett, Chris Johansen's fiddle screeched. Other folks added to the discordance by banging more pots and pans, whooping, hollering and whistling.

A cheer went up when the door opened a few seconds later. Lawson appeared, looking startled and drowsy but with a wide grin on his face. Ellie followed him out, laughing even as she covered her ears. In true shivaree fashion, the husband and wife were each made to sit in wheelbarrows. The ride ended on the banks of the farm's creek where the couple was finally allowed to stand. The noise and the music died down so that Sean's wife, Lorelei, could speak.

"Lawson and Ellie, this shivaree is to show you that your marriage has the full blessing of your family, friends and community." Lorelei gestured toward the creek. "As you take the plunge into married life, we take it with you."

Ellie eyed the creek then tilted her head and stared at her friends with calculating mischief. "Does that mean if we jump in, everyone else has to, as well?"

Quinn grinned at Ellie's exuberance. It was a pretty balmy night for mid-October. Of course, that didn't mean the creek would be anything but frigid.

Sean nodded. "That's the deal. Afterward, women will change in the cabin. Men will change in the barn."

Lawson gave a slow grin and winked. "Well, in that case…"

Ellie didn't seem the least bit surprised when Lawson lifted her into his arms and barreled into the creek with what could only be described as a war cry. Pandemonium broke out as folks tossed their noisemakers on the ground and men started picking up whichever woman was handy to follow their leader into battle. Quinn spotted Helen backing away from the melee as he set his banjo in the cushioned wheelbarrow with the other instruments. He cut off Helen's escape, swept her off her feet and plunged into the creek.

Rushing water muted the sound of Helen's shriek and the rest of the hollering until Quinn resurfaced, gasping from the cold. Helen pushed away from him and immediately headed to the creek bank. A wave of water rushed over Quinn's head. He soon found himself embroiled in a water fight with Rhett and Chris. Once they'd had all they could stand of the cold, they staggered to the creek bank to follow the rest of the party in the rush toward warmth and dry clothes.

Quinn didn't make it very far along the path before he realized he hadn't seen Helen head for the trees. She was probably on the path ahead of him, but even with only three weeks of experience in the role, the parent in him already knew not to leave the creek without making sure she wasn't straggling behind the group. Quinn doubled back to the creek bank. Sure enough, she was staring at the ground as she walked back and forth along the bank of the creek. "Miss McKenna, what are you doing?"

"I'm looking for something."

"Well, you aren't going to find it in the dark."

She sighed. "You're probably right."

"You should change before you catch cold. You must be freezing."

"I certainly am." Her gaze swept the creek bank one last time before she joined him at the edge of the woods. "Thanks to you."

His caught her elbow to escort her onto the path. "Aw, I just gave you a little help getting in the creek, that's all. You would have jumped in eventually."

"Yes, but not quite so enthusiastically." Her smile flashed in the darkness before she gave him a stern look she must have perfected on her students. "Is there a particular reason why you seemed to take such sheer pleasure in throwing me into that creek?"

He couldn't help but chuckle. "Maybe I don't like schoolteachers."

"What did they ever do to you?"

"Plenty." He tugged her onward, hoping his grim tone would put an end to her question. It seemed to have the opposite effect.

She stopped and looked up at him. "Now I'm intrigued."

The last thing he wanted was to delve into that, so he angled a grin her way as he helped her around a fallen branch. "Truthfully, I hoped you would come out looking as messy as the rest of us. Of course, you didn't. Look at you…prim, proper and perfect as usual. Not a hair out of place. How'd you manage that?"

"Is that what you think I am?" She didn't seem to realize that she was leaning into him to share what little warmth their bodies produced. Or maybe she was just too cold to care. "Prim, proper and perfect?"

A rush of heat tinged his face. It was too late to take back his words, so he just shrugged. "It sure doesn't seem like you're the type to ever let down your hair."

They reached the edge of the woods, but she didn't rush toward the cabin. Instead, she lingered with a hand on her hip. "I jumped in the creek, didn't I?"

"I thought you said I threw you." He winked as she seemed to scramble for a defense. "I guess I was just wondering what you'd look like a little mussed up, is all."

"Is that so?" She lifted her chin along with her brow. "Well, I've been wondering what *you'd* look like with a haircut and a shave."

He ran a hand over his thick beard. "That'll happen the day you let down your hair and enjoy yourself."

"Deal." She released his arm and started fiddling with the fancy knot of hair on the back of her head.

Alarm prompted him to take a few cautious steps back. "What do you think you're doing?"

"Letting down my hair."

"That isn't what I meant."

"No, but it's what you said, so you can't go back on our deal." She shook her head until her hair tumbled from its style then slipped her hand into her thick dark hair and teased it into disarray. "Is that mussed enough for you?"

He stared at the dark waves of hair that framed her face and slid past her shoulders to stop at her waist. The only other woman he'd seen with her hair down had been his grandmother. She hadn't looked anything like Helen. The schoolmarm seemed to capture the sparkle of starlight in her mahogany eyes while the glow from the cabin caressed her delicate features and stained her hair with a subtle dusting of gold. His hand reached out of its own accord to slide through the thick locks that were slick and heavy from their recent soaking.

The sound of her breath catching in her throat brought him up short. Suddenly realizing just what he was doing and to whom, he extracted his hand from her hair and restored the distance he hadn't realized he'd covered. "I'm sorry, ma'am. I had no right to do that. Guess I just wasn't thinking."

She deftly twirled her hair and pinned it into a simple style. "You get that haircut and shave and we'll call it even."

"You must think I need them awful bad to go through all this."

Her expression turned innocent, though her eyes were full of mischief. "Well, you do remind me a bit of a bear."

"A bear, huh?" He glanced toward the cabin as the door opened and Lawson walked out with a bundle of clothes in his hand. Quinn urged Helen into the clearing. "You'd better go on inside before you catch a chill."

She complied, greeting the bridegroom as she passed him. Lawson lifted a skeptical brow as he met up with Quinn and they walked across the field toward the barn. "Did you two get lost back there or something?"

Quinn shrugged. "I caught her dawdling by the creek, so I rounded her up and brought her in."

"Well, don't let her hear you describe her that way."

"What way?"

Lawson's eyes started twinkling. "Like a cow."

"I guess it did sound kind of bad." Quinn grimaced as Lawson laughed and clasped him on the shoulder. How was he ever going to find a wife at this rate? Lollygagging with a woman he didn't have a chance with then talking about her like she was a heifer. It wasn't a good start. He needed more than just an expert on love like Ellie. He needed divine intervention.

Being the last one into the tack room gave Quinn a moment alone to do what needed to be done. He bowed his head to whisper a prayer. "Lord, I might not be much and I may not deserve the finer things in life that other folks have, but I'm not asking for me. I'm asking for my children... All right, and maybe a little for me, too. Please send me a mother for them. Someone to be a helpmeet. That's all I ask, Lord."

"Quinn, everyone else has gone ahead," Rhett called through the door. "I'm going to head to the cabin. You'd better get your banjo out the wheelbarrow and come on."

"I'm coming." Quinn finished dressing, then left the tack room. Rhett waited at the barn door jumping up and down to get warm while looking longingly across the field toward the cabin. Quinn found his banjo resting right where he'd placed it. Whoever had been in charge of gathering the noisemakers from the creek bank hadn't been particularly careful in their treatment of his instrument. It had all manner of things piled on top of and around it. He pulled the instrument out only to find a stray piece of paper entwined in its string.

"Quinn, hurry up, will you? Lawson said Ellie was making some hot cider."

"Aw, stop your caterwauling. I've said I'm coming." Quinn tucked the folded paper into his pocket before joining Rhett. They ribbed each other all the way to the cabin, but Quinn's gaze kept rising to the starry sky that stretched above him. He could only hope that God had heard the pleadings of his heart and see fit to answer.

Fast.

Helen couldn't believe she'd lost the Bachelor List. That thought, along with the chill in the air, sent her snuggling farther into her covers the next morning. Amy, the oldest of the three Bradley girls at the boardinghouse where Helen lived, had begged off from the shivaree with a headache then entrusted Helen with a secret note for Ellie. Helen hadn't had any idea that note was actually the Bachelor List until she'd told Ellie about losing it at the creek. Hopefully, the matchmaker would have more success finding the list in the daytime than Helen had last night. She didn't understand why Amy hadn't just given it to Ellie herself later. Well, it was just one more thing that hadn't made sense about last night—like her sudden attraction to Quinn Tucker.

"Attraction" was the only explanation for why she'd lingered in the woods with him despite her drenched condition. But why would she feel that way? She'd been telling the truth when she'd said he reminded her of a bear. Just like the one she'd seen at the circus when she was a child; Quinn was big, hairy, arresting and more than a little intimidating. She couldn't help but wonder how he ate without getting things lost in that unruly-looking mustache and beard. His hair was also overly long. However, there was always that indescribable something about a man with hair that nearly reached his shoulders that made her want to chase after him... with a pair of scissors.

Raised in Austin's high society, she was used to polished gentlemen who were always perfectly groomed. But she'd learned her lesson about the cold hearts that could be hidden by gentlemanly exteriors.

As for Quinn, she couldn't stop thinking about the gentle, almost awed way he'd reached out to touch her hair. She ought to be outraged by his audacity, but then she'd have to be equally shocked by her own behavior. After all, she was the one who'd taken her hair down in front of a man who was practically a stranger. She ought to be ashamed of herself, but she wasn't. He'd made her feel comfortable, accepted and precious. It was unnerving. More than unnerving—it was dangerous!

It was dangerous because she might actually start believing what he'd said about her. Prim and proper she could handle since that was what every good school-marm should be, but she knew all too well that she was not perfect. Never perfect—especially not as a woman. Any doubts she'd had about that had been cleared away six months ago when she'd made the mistake of telling her fiancé, Thomas Coyle, that a riding accident she'd had at sixteen had left her unable to have children. Subsequently, their engagement had ended before the engagement dinner was over.

Helen had quickly studied to become a teacher then moved to Peppin in order to forget her humiliation. If only it was as easy to forget the dreams she'd cherished since she was just a child. Back then, she'd often been found playing house in her mother's dresses with at least one baby doll clutched in each arm. She'd thought being a teacher would be close enough to the fulfillment of that dream to keep her satisfied. Instead, it only fed the longing for the one thing she knew she'd never be able to have—children of her own.

No, Quinn wouldn't have called her perfect if he'd known the truth. Or, perhaps he wouldn't care that she'd never have children. He did have four of his own. She saw the two eldest every school day. She knew a teacher wasn't supposed to have favorites and she didn't let it show in the schoolroom, but the Tucker children's plight had paved their way straight into her heart.

She tossed the thoughts away along with her covers and dressed for the day. What was wrong with her? She knew better than to let herself think things like that. Hadn't she learned anything from her fiancé's rejection? Yet, she could almost hear the comforting tones of her mother's voice in the aftermath of that disaster. *I promise you, my darling, if Thomas loved you—truly loved you—it wouldn't have mattered to him that you can't have children.* As pretty as those words were, Helen wasn't entirely sure she believed them.

She grabbed her teaching materials then hurried out of her room. A quick glance at the grandfather clock in the main hallway told her that she'd better hurry if she planned to get that cantankerous schoolhouse stove going before class started. She popped into the kitchen only long enough to glean a muffin from a rather tired-looking Mrs. Bradley, before heading out the front door.

A whirlwind of yellow-and-brown oak leaves swirled around her as she hurried down Main Street toward the schoolhouse—their chaos an apt visualization of her nervousness, which increased the closer she got to the schoolhouse. There had been a few minor disturbances early in the school term while she had been adjusting to teaching and the students had been adjusting to her. The president of the school board, Mr. Etheridge, had warned her that another incident of any kind would warrant a discussion of her fitness for the teaching position with the rest of the school board. Sending the man's son home on Friday with a black eye and bloody nose courtesy of Reece Tucker couldn't have helped matters.

Helen took a deep breath to calm herself down. Surely Mr. Etheridge must have understood from her note that she'd managed to de-escalate the situation quickly. If nothing else, he had to appreciate the fact that she'd kept the boys from hurting each other further and had even gotten them to apologize.

Feeling a bit more confident, Helen unlocked the schoolroom door and got the fire in the stove going just as students began arriving. A few called jaunty hellos, but most just silently stored their dinner pails in the coatroom then rushed out to play until she was ready to call them in. She had the school bell in hand to do exactly that when Violet, the youngest of Mr. Bradley's three daughters, met her at the schoolhouse door. "Helen, why didn't you stay for breakfast? You missed all the excitement!"

She ought to remind Violet to refer to her as Miss McKenna during school hours, but technically the bell hadn't rung yet, so Helen allowed herself to be drawn in by the fifteen-year-old's exuberance. "What excitement? What's happened?"

"Amy eloped last night!"

"Eloped?" Her mouth fell open. "I don't believe it. How? With whom? Why?"

"With Silas Smithson, of all people! I don't think you've met him. He left town over a year ago. He stayed at the boardinghouse while he was here, which is how he and Amy became sweethearts. He tricked us all into thinking that he worked with the railroad when he was actually an undercover Ranger. I guess Papa's pride was hurt by Silas's deception, because he forbade us to have anything to do with him once the truth came out. That didn't stop Amy from corresponding with him in secret all this time. At least, that's what she said in the letter she left us."

Helen shook her head. "No wonder Amy asked me to give Ellie the Bachelor List. She wasn't planning to be around long enough to do it herself."

"*You* have the Bachelor List?" Excitement lit the girl's blue eyes. She caught Helen's arm. "What is it like? Where is it? Did you find out who your match is?"

"I *had* the Bachelor List. It was nothing grand—just a folded-up piece of paper. I didn't find my match because I didn't know the paper was the list until Ellie figured out what it must have been. By that point, I'd already lost it at the shivaree."

"You lost it? Oh, Helen. That's tragic."

Helen sighed. "It certainly is, and I feel horrible about it. Hopefully, Ellie will find it today. Meanwhile, I need to ring the school bell or we're going to start the day late."

"But I have so much more to tell you! This elopement is the most exciting thing that's happened to me."

"You'll have to tell me the rest at dinner. Now, hurry and put your things in the coatroom. I need to ring the bell."

Violet gave a dramatic sigh as she opened the cloakroom door then shut it immediately. She glanced back at Helen with wide eyes. "There's a man in there!"

Before Helen could do more than frown, Quinn Tucker emerged, hands raised as though he was a victim of a holdup. "I'm sorry, ladies. There just didn't seem to be a good time to interrupt."

Helen held back a laugh at the guilty expression on his face and crossed her arms. "Yes, well, there generally never is when you're eavesdropping. What were you doing in there, anyway?"

"I was bringing Clara and Reece the dinner I ordered for them at the café." He slipped his hands into his pockets then glanced at Violet. "I won't tell anyone what I overheard."

"Oh, half the town has probably heard the story by now and the other half will know soon enough. Tell whoever you want. I don't mind." Violet gave them a quick smile before disappearing into the coatroom.

Quinn opened the schoolhouse door for Helen then

gave her the same crooked grin Reece often used when he knew he was in trouble. "Does that square me with you, Miss McKenna?"

"I suppose it does." She glanced up at him when they reached the grass. "Of course, I'm still waiting for you to keep your half of the deal we made last night."

"I got suckered into that deal and you know it." He narrowed his eyes at the innocent smile she gave him and lifted a brow before setting his hat on his head. "Good day, Miss McKenna."

"Good day, Mr. Tucker." She rang the school bell as she watched him stride toward Main Street and wondered what it was about him that she found so attractive. In Austin, she'd preferred gentlemen with a certain level of suavity, affluence and ambition; but those very qualities were the ones that had left her ringless at her engagement dinner. Quinn seemed to be a different sort of man—honest, unassuming, devoted and a bit desperate in his attempts to be a good uncle. Perhaps that was what she found attractive.

A small hand tugged at her skirt. She dropped her gaze to find Reece's sparring partner standing before her with a greenish-yellow ring around his left eye. She knelt down. "How are you, Jake?"

He shrugged. "Aw, I'm fine, ma'am. Pa told me to be sure to give you this."

She took the envelope he handed her then thanked him and sent him into the schoolroom with the rest of the children. She tore open the letter, which was so brief it was almost a waste of good paper. She was to dismiss the children thirty minutes early so that an emer-

gency meeting of the school board could convene at the
schoolhouse that afternoon.

She pulled in a calming breath. No need to panic.
Despite all of her hopes to the contrary, she'd seen this
coming. Perhaps it didn't have to be a bad thing. After
all, this meant her job performance would be reviewed
by *all* the members of the school board—not just Mr.
Etheridge. The two other members had seemed nice
and welcoming when she'd met them at the beginning
of the term. But what if Mr. Etheridge was able to convince them that she was inept at her job?

She could always return home. Her parents had made
sure she knew their door was always open to her, but
she didn't want to leave Peppin. In this town, she was
known for what she did and who she was. In Austin,
people knew her for what her family did and who they
were in society. She'd received this teaching position
based on her own merit, not on the influence of her family. She meant to make the most of this opportunity and
that did not mean getting fired only five weeks into the
semester. If Mr. Etheridge thought it would be easy to
get rid of her, he had another think coming. She might
not be able to be a wife and mother, but she had no intention of letting her replacement dream slip through
her fingers without a fight.

Chapter Two

Please. Please. Please. Quinn's pleading matched the hurried rhythm of his steps as he left the schoolhouse behind. What were the chances that God had seen fit to answer Quinn's prayer for a wife only seconds after he'd spoken it? That could very well be the case if the paper that had gotten caught up in his banjo strings was the same one he'd overheard Helen saying she'd lost—the Bachelor List.

If Ellie had included him on the list, surely she would have matched him with someone who would be a good mother and wouldn't mind hitching up with the likes of him. Why, he might not have to do any courting at all if he showed the woman they'd been matched on the list. The children could have a mother by the end of the week if this panned out.

He waited until he could duck into the alleyway beside Maddie's Café then pulled the list from his pocket, grateful that his lack of time to do laundry meant he had on the same pants he'd worn the night before. He unfolded the paper and pressed it against the side of the building to smooth it out. It certainly appeared to be a list of some kind. He ran his finger down the column of script, looking for the circle with the line through the side of it that would signify the beginning of his name. There it was. Q-u-i-n-n. Quinn. The only word he knew how to read and write.

"Thank You, God! I'm on the list."

He threw a kiss heavenward to thank his grand-mother for giving him the skills to figure out that much. However, as usual, it wasn't enough. He knew from all the talk he'd heard about the list that the name of the woman he was supposed to marry should be right next to his. That looked to be true, but whose name started with a letter that looked as if he was staring straight at a beefy Longhorn bull?

Folding the paper back in his pocket, he blew out a sigh and pounded the side of his fist on the wall. He was going to have to ask for help. There was no way around it this time.

Two years. He'd been in this town for two years and no one knew that he was illiterate. Never once had he needed to set aside his pride and admit defeat until now. What else could he do? The children needed a mother. *He* needed them to have a mother.

He knew just who to go to for help, even if it would be a bit humbling. He walked into Maddie's Café and waved his thanks to the proprietress for keeping an eye on the two youngest children while he'd taken the elder two their dinners. Maddie offered him a distracted smile as she went about filling orders. Quinn realized it probably hadn't been a good idea to leave them with her since they were quietly drawing on *the table* with their colored chalk rather than the slates they'd been given. He wiped the evidence away with his sleeve the best he could before removing the chalk from their hands, which started Olivia wailing.

Quinn placed the eighteen-month-old on his hip then grabbed the hand of four-year-old Trent and hurried outside. The only blond in the family, Trent's brown eyes stayed as solemn as he'd been silent since soon after his parents' deaths. The boy's little legs chugged along as he frowned up at Quinn, who took that as a sign to slow down. Olivia stopped wailing long enough to push away from him and stare at a passing lady. The little girl reached out for the stranger. The woman saw her and smiled. It was a heartwarming moment until the girl's hand latched on to the fake red bird on the lady's hat. There was a struggle and when the woman finally managed to get away, she was missing the ornament. Quinn gently wrestled it from his niece's hand and offered it to its owner. "I'm sorry, ma'am."

The woman shook her head as she backed away. "She can keep it."

"Sorry!" Quinn called again then stared into Olivia's blue eyes as he gave the bird back to her. "The last thing I need is for you to start running off women."

The girl hugged the fake feathered ornament to her chest. Looking at him very intently, she said, "Doggie."

"No. That's a birdie."

"Doggie."

"Sugar, you can talk real good for your age, but most of what you say just isn't right. Maybe I ought to get Miss McKenna to have a talk with you." He reached down to grab Trent's hand again but came up empty. He glanced down. There was no trace of the boy. Panic rose in his throat. "Trent!"

Something landed on his boot—a little hand, which was attached to a pudgy arm. That was all he could see because the rest of Trent's body was underneath the raised wooden sidewalk. Quinn knelt down to haul the boy out of there. "What are you doing? How did you even fit under there? Now you're covered in dirt."

The boy didn't respond. He never did. Instead, he just frowned even harder and lifted a bright red feather that obviously belonged to the bird's tail. The sight melted Quinn's heart and it was all he could do to remain firm, when he wanted nothing more than to hug the boy close. "Thank you for picking that up for your sister, but you must not do that again. Do you understand?"

He waited for Trent to nod before wiping the dirt from the boy's face and combing the mussed blond hair into place. "That's good because you scared me. I thought I'd lost you. Hold on to my hand and don't let go. We need to cross the street. Are you ready?"

With Trent dutifully clutching his hand and Olivia on his hip, Quinn made it across the street into the blacksmith's shop. Rhett Granger glanced up from whatever he was pounding on at the iron. "Be right with you, Quinn."

Quinn put Olivia on the counter and set Trent beside her, caging them in with his arms and body. Olivia was too busy playing with her ill-gotten gains to care, but Trent immediately started wriggling. "Hold still, son. This will only take a minute."

Rhett tucked his work gloves in the pocket of the

leather apron he was wearing. He approached the counter with smiles for the children, who completely ignored him. "How can I help y'all?"

"Rhett, you're one of the most trustworthy men I know and a real good friend."

His friend's amber eyes lit with surprise. "Thanks, Quinn. I could say the same about you, but you didn't just come in here to shower me with praise, did you? Not that I mind if you did…"

"No, and I don't have the time or the patience to beat around the bush, so I'm going to come out with it." Quinn reluctantly allowed Trent to slide to the floor since the boy was trying to climb down his body, anyway.

"That's always a good policy."

Quinn looked around to make sure they were alone then leaned forward. He kept his voice low. "I have the Bachelor List."

"*You* have it?"

"Yeah, and I'm willing to give it you if you will just read it to me."

Rhett stiffened. "I've already been told who my match is. Since that woman ran away with someone else last night, I'm not particularly interested in the list."

"Amy? Your match was Amy? I didn't know. You didn't tell me. I mean, I knew you were sweet on her, but…" Quinn shook his head, searching his friend's face to see how hard the news of Amy's elopement had hit him. "I'm real sorry. How are you holding up?"

Rhett shrugged. "I don't know. To tell the truth, I didn't know her that well since our conversations mostly consisted of me tripping over my tongue like an idiot while she looked at me in confusion. Other than that, all we ever exchanged were a few looks and smiles. I guess my heart might not have been quite as involved as I thought it was."

"But you're disappointed."

"Yeah." Rhett sighed. "I'd hoped she was the one— especially since we were paired on that list."

"Well, this might not be much of a comfort, but I'm sure there's someone else out there. Perhaps someone you'll be able to talk to without being nervous around."

Rhett lifted a skeptical eyebrow. "I'm not sure how likely that is since my brain seems to abandon me anytime a relationship turns romantic. I'll tell you one thing, though. If there is another woman out there for me, I won't find her with the Bachelor List. You'd be wise to give it back to Ellie and find a woman on your own."

Quinn grimaced. "I hate to point this out, but Ellie has gotten every other match she's ever made right, so I'll take the chance. Please read it to me."

"Rub that in harder, why don't you?" Rhett narrowed his eyes and leaned against the counter. "If you're so interested, why don't you just read it yourself?"

"I would if I *could*." He stared Rhett in the eye and waited for confusion to turn to enlightenment then pity. The pity never came—only compassion—which was almost as bad, except it didn't leave quite as awful a taste in Quinn's mouth.

"I'll read it for you. Have you got it on you?"

"Yeah." Quinn laid the list on the counter between them and pointed to the only word he recognized. "My name is right there. I know that much, but whose is next to it?"

Rhett glanced down at the spot Quinn indicated before folding up the list and handing it back as if he couldn't get rid of it fast enough. "Ellie put you with Helen McKenna."

The words reached his brain then fell flat as the pancakes he'd tried to make that morning. "Come again?"

"The schoolmarm. Helen McKenna."

"That isn't funny." Quinn tried to give the list to Rhett again. "Read it right."

Rhett held his hands up and refused to take it. "I'm telling you, Quinn, it says Helen McKenna. I wouldn't joke about this."

Quinn closed his eyes and lowered his head in defeat as the hope that had flared in him burned out like a faulty matchstick. What had Ellie been thinking? Helen McKenna was far too good for him. She'd been nice to him—friendly, even—but she'd never consider him as a marriage prospect. He had nothing to offer a woman like her.

A tiny forehead braced against his. He opened his eyes to see Olivia blinking up at him from inches away, her big eyes nearly crossing in the effort. He kissed her tiny nose then straightened to his full height. He may not be Helen's first choice in a man. However, judging by the way Reece and Clara talked about her nonstop, she'd probably be the children's first choice in a mother. That was enough for him. "She might not love me, but I dare her not to fall in love with my kids. She'll marry me, if only because of that."

Rhett looked dubious. "Are you sure that's best for them? For you to marry a woman you don't love?"

"A mother is what's best for them. She'll be a good one. Ellie must have thought the same thing. Otherwise, she wouldn't have matched us up." He put the paper back into his pocket. "I'll need this as proof. I promise I'll give it back to you as soon as possible."

"Don't bother. I have no use for it. Besides, I've had enough woman trouble to last me a good while." Rhett gave him a nod of silent encouragement. "I'll be praying for you, man."

"Thanks. I'll need it." He scooped Olivia back onto his hip, reached down for Trent's hand…and came up empty. He pulled in a deep breath. "Trent!"

A head poked out from beneath a bench in the waiting room. Quinn strode over and held out his hand. "We just talked about this, son. You are not allowed to crawl under anything that puts you out of sight without letting me know first. That includes benches."

Quinn opened the door with his shoulder then stood outside trying to figure out what to do next. He should probably get the haircut and shave that Helen seemed so particular about. He'd need to find someone to watch the children for an hour or so to get that done. Maybe the doctor's wife? He hated to impose on her again so soon, but she had said she'd be happy to help if he needed someone to watch the children again.

He frowned as he rubbed a hand over his thick beard. He could hardly expect a schoolmarm to accept the proposal of an illiterate man who reminded her of a bear. While he couldn't do anything for his lack of book learning, he *could* get rid of some of his wildness.

He shook his head. Helen McKenna. He might as well be reaching for the moon. He might not deserve her, but his children did and that's exactly who they were going to get.

Mr. Etheridge reminded Helen of a thundercloud with his snapping gray eyes, prematurely silver hair and commanding voice that filled the schoolhouse with a confidence that dared anyone to disagree with him. "Miss McKenna, you have demonstrated a concerning inability to maintain proper discipline during school hours. The school board overlooked the troubling pranks that took place at the beginning of the school term, but now our students are brawling in the schoolyard."

A frown etched across the face of Mr. Johansen, whose youngest son was in the fifth grade. "I heard there has been fighting."

Mr. Etheridge's pacing steps in front of her desk seemed intended to slowly, deliberately sever any connection between her and the two other members of the school board. "My son, Jake, finds himself in constant need to defend himself from the aggressions of his fellow student Reece Tucker, who is treated with blatant partiality. While my Jake was sent home from school on Friday with a black eye and bloody nose, Reece was allowed to stay at school for the remainder of the day."

Nathan Rutledge's gaze locked on Helen's. The final member of the three-person school board was Ellie's brother-in-law and the father of a little boy in the same class as Reece Tucker. "Is it true that you only sent Jake Etheridge home, Miss McKenna?"

Helen forced herself to adopt a more pleasant look as she straightened her back and lifted her chin. "Yes, but—"

"You see?" Mr. Etheridge turned to face the other members. "I think it is quite obvious that Miss McKenna lets favoritism get in the way of good discipline. Despite her high recommendations, her inexperience is detrimental to the welfare of our students."

The indignant flush rising in her cheeks from Mr. Etheridge's interruptions and the urge to defend herself faded into confusion. "High recommendations?"

Mr. Johansen nodded, though he didn't take his gaze from Mr. Etheridge. "He means the letter from the governor."

Her hands tightened into fists. "The governor recommended me for this position?"

"Yes," Nathan agreed. "It was the deciding factor that led us to choose you over the local candidate—Mr. Etheridge's daughter."

Everything suddenly became clear. No wonder she'd been placed at a school so quickly after taking the teaching exam despite having no former experience. She'd thought it was a sign from God that she'd made the right decision in giving up on the impossible to focus on the attainable. Instead, it was simply a sign that her loving, overprotective parents had asked a favor from the governor, who had been a friend of the family for years.

"My daughter was unable to find another position and would be willing to replace Miss McKenna should the need arise."

She stared at Mr. Etheridge, finally able to understand the reason for his attitude toward her. No doubt he saw her as the interloping city girl who'd stolen the position that rightfully belonged to his daughter. Maybe that's exactly who she was. Maybe she'd stolen some other girl's dream. She had no right to do that just because she wasn't woman enough achieve her own. She shook the thoughts away and forced herself to focus on the situation at hand. Nathan Rutledge was watching her with concern. "Is there anything you would like to say in your defense, Miss McKenna?"

She swallowed and tried to remember the charges Mr. Etheridge had laid against her. "I think any teacher would have been subjected to the same pranks I was at the beginning of the semester. They were harmless and I put an end to them as soon as I could. I can't deny that Reece and Jake have been fighting. Jake seems to have a bit of an unrequited crush on Reece's sister Clara and often teases her to the point where Reece feels compelled to defend her."

"That isn't true." Mr. Etheridge interjected.

"I'm afraid it is, Mr. Etheridge." Turning back to the other members of the school board, she continued, "I didn't send Reece home on Friday because I thought he lived too far out of town to walk home alone in his condition. If that's showing favoritism and poor discipline, then I suppose I'm guilty."

Mr. Johansen gave a weary sigh. "Will you please step outside so that the board may talk privately?"

She nodded and stepped down from the platform. The rustle of her skirts was the only sound that filled the room until she stepped outside and closed the double doors behind her. Only then did she hear the muffled sound of men's voice rise inside. She stared at the schoolhouse door. That had not gone at all the way she'd planned. She'd practically given up. What was wrong with her?

"Miss McKenna?"

Startled, she spun toward the deep voice. A steadying hand stilled her forward momentum in time to keep her from tumbling down the schoolhouse steps. Words of gratefulness stalled on her lips as she glanced up to the stranger who'd lunged up the stairs to catch her. Her gaze slid from the chiseled angles of his jaw to the thick golden-brown curls of his close-cropped hair before settling on his vibrant blue eyes. Everything else went blurry as a strange weakness filled her knees. He steadied her once more. She shook her head, blinked and refocused. "Mr. Tucker?"

He didn't release his hold on her arm but stepped closer, his brow lowered in concern. "I'm real sorry, Miss McKenna. I sure didn't mean to scare you like that. You didn't hurt yourself, did you?"

"I'm fine." She eased back slightly as she allowed her gaze to trace his features again. "You look…nice."

A sheepish grin flashed across his lips, carving a shallow set of dimples into his cheeks. "Thank you. My own kin didn't recognize me when they saw me like this, so I reckon you were right and I was overdue for a shave and a haircut. I picked up some new duds, too, but that isn't important right now. What's going on in there?"

"In where?"

He pointed to the sign hanging from the doorknob that read Private Meeting. "In the schoolhouse."

Land sakes! How could she have forgotten about

that? A sinking sensation filled her stomach so she sank along with it to sit on the top step. She rested her chin in her hand with a heavy sigh. "It's possible that I might be getting fired."

"Fired?" Quinn frowned at the door then sat one step below her. "Why would they want to fire you?"

"Apparently there are several reasons."

"But you're a great teacher."

She gave a short laugh. "You still say that after your nephew went home with a black eye last week?"

His eyes narrowed. "Is that what this is about? I'll go tell them it wasn't your fault."

He moved to stand but she placed a stilling hand on his shoulder then lowered her gaze to avoid his questioning look. "No. Don't. Perhaps it's for the best."

"The best?" He stared at her then shook his head. "Why? Don't you want to teach?"

She shrugged as the vague feeling of discontent she'd been ignoring welled up inside of her. "I certainly enjoy it. However, to be honest, it isn't really what I want to do."

He frowned. "Then what *do* you want to do?"

I want to have a family with a husband and children of my own. She sighed and leaned back against the stair railing thinking about how foolish she'd been. Of course, teaching school wasn't anything like having children of her own. She'd been reminded of that at the end of each day when the students all rushed out the door, leaving her behind.

"Helen?" Quinn's use of her Christian name for the first time drew her full attention. "Do you mind if I call you that?"

Surprised, she offered a quizzical smile. "I suppose you might as well. Many of the other students' parents do."

"I need to talk to you. I know this probably isn't the right time, but I can't hold it in much longer."

"This sounds serious." She crossed her arms on top of her knees and nodded. "Go ahead and tell me. We may have a few moments before they call me back in."

He sent a speculative look toward the door. "My eldest nephew and niece are always going on about you and I've noticed that you seem to care a whole lot about them, too. That's true, isn't it?"

"It certainly is."

"Well, I'm doing my best for them but anyone can tell that isn't good enough." He waved away her protests. "Now, that's just the plain truth and you know it. The fact is that they need a mother."

She stared at him, wondering where this conversation was going as he unfolded a piece of paper she hadn't realized he was holding. He handed it to her. She didn't bother to look at it. She couldn't have if she'd tried for his gaze held hers captive with its intensity. "I prayed for a helpmeet and God sent me the Bachelor List. It says you're my match. I was wondering if you'd be willing to marry me—for the children's sake."

Her gaze finally dropped to the paper unseeingly as she tried to make sense of what he'd just said. "Will you repeat that please?"

His hand covered hers. "You're my match. My nieces and nephews need you. I need you. Will you please marry me?"

The schoolhouse door opened startling them both as

Mr. Eldridge stepped outside. "We have reached a decision, Miss McKenna. Please, come in."

Quinn helped her stand murmuring, "I'll wait here."

She gave him a brief nod then stepped inside. The grim faces of the school board members spelled out her not-so-surprising fate. She glanced down at the paper she held. Her attention caught on the sight of her name printed as clear as day next to the name of the man who was waiting for an answer to his proposal.

"Miss McKenna," Mr. Etheridge began in a cadence that seemed unnaturally slow juxtaposed by her racing thoughts. "On behalf of the school board and the citizens of Peppin—"

Quinn was offering her exactly what she'd always wanted. Well, not exactly—but the closest she was likely to get to the marriage and children she longed for.

"—I would like to thank you for the kindness, energy and time you have devoted to the children of this community."

Quinn hadn't mentioned love in his proposal. Of course, she could hardly expect him to since they barely knew each other. Who was to say that it wouldn't turn into love eventually? Her parents had an arranged marriage and they'd grown to love each other deeply.

"I would also like to apologize for any behavior on our part that would make you doubt our gratefulness—specifically my own."

Most important, there were the Tucker children to consider—children to whom she could give so much love and care. She and Quinn wouldn't be able to have children of their own, but she'd learned her lesson and would keep that bit of information to herself. What could it hurt? With four little ones of his own already, he might not have time to notice.

"We would be happy to have you stay with us through the rest of the school year per our original agreement."

Quinn wanted her. Quinn *needed* her. She had a chance with him—with *them*—that she might not have ever again. She wouldn't walk away from that. She *couldn't*.

Her gaze snapped up from the Bachelor List as Mr. Etheridge's words finally registered in her brain. "You want me to stay?"

"The school board has concluded that I might have been a bit hasty and overprotective as the matters concerned my own children." The poor man looked as if he'd swallowed a marble. "We will honor our original agreement with you concerning the position."

"That's wonderful!" Her smile was returned by the other members of the board then she bit her lip. "You did say that your daughter is willing to start immediately, though. Didn't you, Mr. Etheridge?"

"Well, yes, I did."

"In that case…" She took a deep breath then couldn't stop the smile that spread across her face or the way her chin rose with pride. "I resign."

Chapter Three

Quinn paced in front of the schoolhouse steps waiting for Helen to return. He felt nervous and even a little light-headed. Of course, that might be from the haircut and shave he'd just had but it was uncomfortable nonetheless. He rubbed his hand over his clean-shaven jaw as he remembered the shocked look on Helen's pretty face at his clumsy proposal. He'd done the best he could. That didn't mean it would be good enough. It certainly didn't mean she'd agree to marry him. Why hadn't she just outright told him no and put him out of his misery?

He stopped pacing long enough to stare at the schoolhouse door then across the schoolyard to where his children were playing with the Rutledge boy. Reece's eyes had been as wide as plates when he'd seen Quinn with his new haircut. Clara had turned downright shy. Olivia had started crying. Even now, Trent kept sending him suspicious looks. Helen couldn't refuse him after he'd alienated his children just to please her. Besides, there wasn't any other woman in town he'd have a chance with. Not that he personally had a chance with Helen, but the children did.

Please. Please. Please, he prayed again. *I know I don't deserve her, but she isn't for me. She's for them.*

He jumped when the schoolhouse door opened. Helen was nowhere in sight as the members of the school board clomped down the steps. A grin flashed across Mr. Etheridge's face and he reached out to pump Quinn's hand up and down. "May I be the first to congratulate you? What a wonderful surprise!"

Quinn could only respond with a confused grunt.

Mr. Johansen winked. "She's waiting for you inside."

Nathan Rutledge clapped him on the back. "I wish you and Helen all the happiness in the world."

"Me and Helen—" Quinn stopped breathing. His heartbeat pounded in his ears. He stammered some sort of reply though what it was he'd never know. The men left him at the bottom of the stairs staring up at the schoolhouse door. Could it be possible? It certainly seemed likely. What else could they have meant?

He grabbed hold of the banister and took a tentative step up, then surged up the rest of the stairs into the schoolroom. Helen stood at the front of the room cleaning the day's lessons from the blackboard. His noisy entrance caused her to turn and meet his gaze with a smile. Quinn swallowed, cleared his throat and jerked his thumb toward the door. "They said— I mean, they told me…congratulations. Does that mean that you're saying yes? That you're going to marry me?"

Her mahogany eyes sparkled. "I suppose it does."

"You mean it? For real, now?" He strode forward

until he stopped at the edge of the teacher's platform. "You aren't joking, are you?"

Her voice turned gentle as she met him there. "Quinn, I'd never joke about something like that."

"You're going to marry me." It wasn't a question this time. It was a statement even if his tone did hold a hint of disbelief. Trying those words on for size, he found that he liked the way they fit in a terrifying sort of way. He stepped back a little just in case a bolt of lightning struck him in holy retaliation for daring to marry a woman so far above him in every respect. He wouldn't want it to hit Helen by mistake.

"Yes, I am." She stepped down from the platform and lifted her face to stare up at him. "Well, isn't there anything you'd like to say or do about it?"

His attention honed in on her lips which offered a smile far more tempting than anything she could have intended. He'd never kissed a woman before and today wasn't the day to start him. He'd already pushed the Almighty far enough in asking for what he had no right to claim. Besides, she wasn't for him. She was for the children. That's what he'd promised God and he'd be smart to remember that if he wanted to have any chance of actually marrying her. Realizing he was leaning toward her, he pulled himself back. He took her hand to pump it up and down in a fair impression of what Mr. Etheridge had done earlier. "I'm real glad about it, Helen. Real glad."

A hint of confusion marred her brow as she glanced down at their hands before she pulled hers free with a funny little frown. "Good. I have to finish out this week of school, but we can be married anytime after that."

He watched her gather papers and books from her desk. "I reckon I'd better talk to the preacher about performing the ceremony."

"And the judge. We'll need to start the paperwork for the marriage license right away."

He held back a groan. The marriage license. He'd completely forgotten about that part of the process. Anxiety rose in his gut. "Do we have to do that? I mean, wouldn't it be all right if we just let the preacher hitch us up?"

She set the stack she'd gathered on her hip and cocked her head at him. "Not if you want it to be legal."

"Of course, I do." He ran his fingers through his close-cropped hair, hating that he'd made himself look foolish. "Guess I'll talk to Judge Hendricks tomorrow then."

"We can go together."

"Great!" Even to his own ears, his reply was a little too enthusiastic to sound genuine. He couldn't help it. With her along, he wouldn't be able to ask for help with the reading and writing even if he had a mind to humble himself enough before the judge to do so. She'd be right there watching, expecting him to know something when he didn't know much of anything.

"I'm sure it won't be too laborious and, after all, it must be done."

Looking into her intelligent eyes, he couldn't help wondering if he was making a mistake. They had to be the most mismatched pair in town. However, they *were* a pair and they were going to stay that way as long as he could help it so he took the load from his intended's hands and followed her outside. He stashed her things on the seat of the wagon he'd parked nearby. "I'll drive you to the boardinghouse after we tell the children."

"Oh, it isn't far. There's no need—" Her eyes widened. "You mean we're going to tell them right now?"

"Sure we are. You don't want them to hear it from someone else, do you?"

"No. I just…" She glanced over at the children, smoothing her hair as if she could make herself look more perfect than she already did in her cranberry colored gown.

Somehow her nervousness set him at ease—mostly because it meant he wasn't the only one feeling that way. His shoulders relaxed, his breath came a bit easier and he felt more like himself than he had all afternoon. Catching her hand in his, he smiled. "I'm sure they'll be as pleased as I am."

She sighed when he tugged her forward. "I certainly hope so."

He stopped at the fenced-in lawn that was shaded by a large oak tree. His nieces and nephews were the only ones left in the school yard, but they didn't seem to mind a bit for they were completely involved in playing kick the can. Quinn waited, not wanting to interrupt as Reece held Trent back and Clara helped Olivia take a turn at kicking. A squeal erupted from Olivia once her little foot set the can spinning a short distance and Quinn couldn't help but grin at the sight. "Good job, Olivia! Y'all come on over here now. Miss McKenna and I have something important to tell you."

Helen stepped a bit closer to his side as the children approached. Trent arrived first, huffing and puffing from all his misplaced exertion. Clara came next with her sister in tow. Finally, Reece joined them with apprehension dogging each slow step. "I didn't do it, Miss McKenna. Honest."

Quinn glanced over at Helen for explanation. She shrugged in confusion before turning back to the children. "You didn't do what, Reece?"

"I don't know, but I've been trying hard to be good so if something's messed up, it wasn't me."

Amusement warmed Helen's voice. "Reece, you aren't in trouble. Your uncle has an announcement to make, that's all."

Clara tilted her head, her wide blue eyes ripe with curiosity. "What kind of announcement?"

"Miss McKenna and I are going to be married."

Clara gasped. Reece frowned. Trent's brow furrowed. Olivia stuck her thumb in her mouth and leaned into her sister's side. The three eldest exchanged glances then their expressions settled into varying degrees of confusion, fear and sadness. Their reaction stunned him. They must not have understood him correctly. Quinn tried again. This time he used more enthusiasm. "That means she is going to be your aunt! Isn't that exciting?"

Reece crossed his arms. "Does that mean she won't be our teacher anymore? I like having her as my teacher."

Helen placed a gentle hand on the boy's shoulder. "Oh, but being an aunt is so much better than being a teacher."

Clara looked nothing if not doubtful. "Why?"

"Because, I am going to live with y'all so that I can love you, and laugh with you and help take care of you."

Helen caught Clara's free hand. "Don't you see? Having an aunt is kind of like having a Ma—just like having an uncle is kind of like having a Pa. I want to be that for you more than anything in the world."

Longing filled the children's eyes for an instant before Reece shook his head. "I still think you'd better stay our teacher."

"Me, too. Besides, Uncle Quinn takes care of us really well. He doesn't need help." Clara looked to him for confirmation. "Isn't that right, Uncle Quinn?"

"No, it isn't right, Clara." He frowned at them out of confusion and concern more than displeasure. "I don't understand. I thought you would be pleased. You *should* be pleased. I am. I want what's best for you and that's Miss McKenna, which is why I'm going to marry her."

Trent bowed his head as his shoulders shook in silent sobs. Before Quinn could blink, Helen was on her knees in the grass with his youngest nephew cradled in her arms. She looked up at Quinn with a myriad of emotions darkening the usual spark in her eyes. "Oh, Quinn, maybe we shouldn't—"

"Yes, we should." He sat in the grass beside her then gave a gentle tug to first Reece then Clara to compel them to do the same. His arm tightened around Olivia as she scrambled into his lap. He split his focus between Clara and Reece. "Do either of you know why Trent is crying?"

Clara scooted a little closer into their huddle. "He just a little upset seeing how y'all are going to die and all."

"What?" he and Helen exclaimed together.

Reece pulled at a blade of grass beside his boot. "Getting married is what killed Pa and our new Ma."

Clara nodded. "We don't want that to happen to you and Miss McKenna, too."

Nonplussed, he gladly let Helen handle that one. She hugged Trent tight. "Oh, darlings, nothing bad is going to happen to your uncle and me just because we are getting married. Tell them, Quinn."

A single nod was all he could manage. He wasn't worried about Helen. She would be fine. She didn't know how far below her due in terms of status, intelligence and sophistication she was marrying. He wasn't going to tell her, either. Not now. Not ever if he could help it. He wasn't afraid of facing the consequences of his decision to reach for far more than he deserved— not since he knew how much it would benefit the children. If something did happen to him as a result, at least they would have her.

"What happened to your folks was an accident." Helen wiped Trent's tears away with a soft-looking handkerchief. His brown eyes watched her intently as she spoke. "We may not know the reasons why it happened. However, we do know getting married doesn't mean you're going to die immediately."

Reece's face was full of cautious hope. "How do we know that?"

"Look at all the married people still alive just in this town—not to mention the whole world. There's nothing for y'all to worry about." She placed a hand on Quinn's knee as her eyes sent a silent encouragement for him to assure them. "Is there, Quinn?"

"Not a thing." He made sure to look the children in the eye as he said it. All the while, he tried to ignore the warmth spreading from Helen's hand into his knee.

"Your uncle and I are going to be perfectly fine. We'll be better than fine, actually, because we're all going to be a family...if you'll have me."

Reservations gone, Clara gave Helen a hug including Trent out of necessity. "Of course we will."

Quinn cleared his throat. "What do you say, Reece? Are you going to make your aunt feel welcome?"

"Yes, sir!" Reece's enthusiasm was reflected in his grin.

"Trent?"

The silent boy gave a grave nod.

"Good. Now, let's drop off Miss McKenna at the boardinghouse and get ourselves on home." He set Olivia on her feet so that she could toddle toward the wagon with the other children. "Helen, I sure am sorry about how they responded at first."

"It ended well and that's all that matters."

"I reckon you're right." He stood and reached down to help Helen to her feet. He made sure to release her as soon as she was steady. He'd told the children that there was nothing for them to worry about. There wouldn't be so long as he remembered that he was marrying Helen to be his children's mother—not his wife. That would be a whole lot easier if he kept his distance.

Helen waved goodbye to the Tuckers. Quinn tipped his hat and sent her a quick grin before leaving her behind on the sidewalk in front of the boardinghouse. She barely resisted the impulse to break into a jig right then and there. Wonder of wonders! She was getting married! Not to just anyone, but to Quinn Tucker—a man with a ready-made family. It felt as if she had wandered into her favorite daydream. She could only hope to be lost in it forever.

"Who was that?"

Helen yelped at the sound of Isabelle Bradley's voice. She'd been staring after the Tuckers' wagon so fixedly that she hadn't heard her friend's approach. "Where did you come from?"

"The post office." Isabelle's narrowed green eyes didn't waver from the retreating wagon. "Was that Quinn Tucker? I heard he got a haircut, but goodness me who knew it would make such a difference. He actually had a face under all that wild hair and a handsome one at that! It was nice of him to drive you home. Violet told me about the school-board meeting. What happened?"

Helen leaned against the cold rod iron of the Bradley's waist-high fence to push it open for her friend. "The other members of the board made Mr. Etheridge apologize."

"Good for them." Isabelle trotted up the porch steps and opened the door for Helen. "So does that mean you no longer have to worry about keeping your position?"

"Yes and no. I resigned." She had time to place her schoolbooks on the front desk and her coat on the rack before Isabelle's shock wore off.

"Why," Isabelle began, extending that one word into several syllables, "did you do that?"

Helen shrugged. "You have to resign if you're going to get married."

Isabelle's mouth dropped open then curved in an incredulous smile. "You're getting married? To whom?

When? Why do I never know about these things? Helen!"

She laughed. "Yes, I'm getting married. On Saturday, I think. You're the first to know besides the school board and his children."

"His children?" Isabelle's eyes widened and flashed in the direction Quinn's wagon had gone. "Quinn Tucker's children?"

She nodded. "All four of them."

"But, I didn't even know the two of you were courting."

"Well…" She leaned against the front desk, straightening the stack of books she'd brought home. "We didn't court…exactly."

Isabelle sat on the stool behind the desk. "What does that mean?"

Helen rolled her eyes. "It means we didn't court at all, but it doesn't matter. There will be plenty of time for that after we marry."

"Well, then." Isabelle lifted a brow. "Would it be safe to guess that this isn't a love match?"

She shrugged. "It is in a way. I love his children."

"But you don't love him."

"I could. I will…one day. I'm certain of it. He's kind, Christian, hardworking—"

"—suddenly handsome—"

Helen laughed. "I was attracted to him even before the haircut and shave. Besides, he makes me feel…"

"He makes you feel…?"

Whole. He makes me forget that I'm a little bit damaged. She smiled and settled for, "Pretty."

"You are pretty."

"Thank you. Besides, what *is* love, anyway? It isn't just a feeling. It's a commitment. It's endeavoring to understand and appreciate someone for who they are. Even if it was just a feeling, feelings are controllable." She shrugged at Isabelle's doubtful look. "Perhaps I come at it from a different perspective than most. You see, my parents had an arranged marriage and they love each other very deeply now. I don't see why I should expect anything less."

"What can I say to that? As long as you're sure, Helen. I'll support you."

"I'm sure, and I'd like you to be my maid-of-honor."

"I'd love that."

Suddenly realizing that retrieving and sorting the mail was normally Amy's job, Helen froze. "Oh, Isabelle, Violet told me about Amy. Have y'all had any more word from her?"

Isabelle shook her head. "Nothing as yet. Father has gone to search for them mostly to assure himself and Mother that Amy's new situation is suitable—whatever that means. Mother seems hurt that one of her daughters would do such a thing—hide a relationship and then run off like that. Violet is all aflutter thinking she's in an Austen novel or some such nonsense."

"I never should have lent her my copy of *Pride and Prejudice*. All through dinner she explained to me the parallels between this situation and Lydia's with Wickham. I believe Violet has convinced herself she's Kitty." She laughed at her friend's grimace then regarded Isabelle seriously. "And how are you dealing with all of this?"

"To be honest, I'm more than a little annoyed with

Amy, as much as I love her." Isabelle sighed. "Amy's elopement isn't a problem for Amy. It's a problem for me. My parents are determined not to make the same mistake twice, so I'll be the one facing more restrictions and tougher discipline. In the meantime, I'm trying not to be offended by mother's suspicious looks."

"You really had no idea?"

"Amy didn't confide in me on this one at all." Isabelle shrugged. "What's done is done. It's a good reminder that each decision we make not only effects ourselves but may have unintended consequences in other's lives. I suppose we just have to pray about our options, follow God's leading and be ready to live with the consequences of our choices whether good or bad."

"You have a good head on your shoulders, Isabelle. I'm sure your parents will recognize that once the excitement dies down."

"I hope so." Isabelle frowned as she went back to sorting the mail.

"I guess I'll see you at supper." Helen hurried from the foyer down the hall to her room. She closed the door behind her, but couldn't shut out the wisdom of Isabelle's words.

Pray about our options…follow God's leading…be ready to live with the consequences. She hadn't prayed about the decision to marry Quinn. How could she have with everything happening so quickly? That didn't mean she wasn't following God's leading. After all, how many times had she prayed for a husband and children of her own? Well, not that many because she hadn't thought it possible. However, this was a blessing—an undeniable, pure, simple blessing. She'd be a fool not to run full speed toward it and Helen McKenna-soon-to-be-Tucker was no fool. She'd be more than happy to live with the consequences of her decision. They could only be good ones even if she didn't know her husband very well yet. Or, have much experience running a home. She'd been a teacher for almost half of a semester. How much harder could it be to be a wife and mother?

Chapter Four

"Dearly beloved, we are gathered here in the sight of God and in the presence of these witnesses to join together this man and this woman in holy matrimony..."

Those sure were some highfaluting sounding words. Thankfully, all Quinn had to do was make sure he said *I do* at the right time and he'd be married to a woman too sweet, too intelligent and too attractive for his own good. He swallowed against the nervousness roiling in his stomach. He pulled at the fancy shoestring tie that went with the rest of his getup.

He wished someone had prepared him for how expensive it would be to buy a ready-made suit. Of course, that was only a drop in the bucket compared to what it would cost to feed and clothe four children until they were grown up and on their own. And it could be even more than that if he and Helen added to their brood.

He winced, hoping God hadn't heard that last thought. How could he and Helen have children if he was half afraid to touch her hand for fear of making the Almighty angry? The deal was that Helen would be a mother—not a wife. The distinction was already blurring in his thoughts and the ceremony wasn't even over.

Maybe he ought to have gotten a better handle on that before he asked Helen to marry him. Maybe he ought to have figured a lot of other stuff out, too. Like how to read. Fat chance of that happening, though.

He'd managed to get her to fill out the paperwork for the marriage license by pleading poor penmanship. He'd even put off signing the license in front of her so she wouldn't see that pitifully written signature comprised of only his first name. That didn't bode well for the future. What if he got too comfortable around her and let his secret slip? How would she react if she found out the truth about him?

He shook the thoughts from his head. He didn't even want to consider such a thing happening. Especially not in the middle of the ceremony. But it was already too late. His heart started racing. His palms began to sweat. Maybe he'd keel over right now and be done with it. Helen would take care of the children even if they hadn't been officially married.

He slowly became aware of the oppressive, awkward silence filling the church. Pastor Brightly cleared his throat. "You *don't* wish to take Helen to be your wife?"

"I—" He stopped and stared at the preacher realizing that wasn't the question Quinn had prepared himself to answer. "What?"

"You shook your head. I thought…"

"Oh, no." Quinn waved his right hand dismissing the action he'd done during his lapse of concentrate.

Helen's left hand slipped from his as the preacher's brow furrowed in confusion. "'No' what?"

Quinn frowned at Helen and took her hand in his again as a nervousness seemed to spread from him to the folks gathered in the chapel. Helen wasn't going to leave him at the altar, was she? "Where are you going?"

"I'm not—" Her words stumbled to a halt. She looked flat out bewildered. "Quinn, are you going to marry me or not?"

"Well, I'm trying to, honey. The preacher here can't seem to get the question right."

A chuckle sounded from the audience. Quinn turned in time to see Ellie Williams smack her husband on the shoulder for the outburst before glaring at her sister-in-law, Lorelei, who sat on her other side shaking with silent laughter. Quinn glanced at his best man for help. Rhett just shook his head. Helen leaned into Quinn's side to whisper, "Pastor Brightly already asked you once."

"Oh." He almost admitted he'd been distracted then stopped himself in time to keep from getting into more trouble. He nodded at Pastor Brightly. "I reckon you'd better ask me again."

Pastor Brightly looked decidedly nervous as he cleared his throat. "Will you take Helen Grace Mc-Kenna to be your wedded wife—"

"I will."

"—to live together after God's ordinance in the holy estate of matrimony—"

"I will."

Pastor Brightly took in a deep breath and somehow managed to say the rest without pausing even a second for Quinn to answer. "Will you love her, comfort her, honor and keep her, in sickness and in health, and forsaking all others, keep yourself only unto her, so long as you both shall live?"

Finally, realizing he'd been interrupting the minister, Quinn hesitated before adding one final. "I will."

It was Helen's turn. She answered Pastor Brightly only once and not until the end, but the surety in her voice was worth the wait. Then it was time to exchange rings. He made sure to pay close attention so that he could say *I do* at the right time to endow all of his worldly goods upon Helen—such as they were. Quinn's heart had managed to calm down somewhat by the time Helen slid the ring he'd picked up at the mercantile onto his finger...until he realized there was only one thing left to do.

"I now pronounce you husband and wife. Quinn, you may kiss your bride."

He froze in panic. Sending a quick glance heavenward, he turned to his bride. *What else is a groom to do? It's expected.*

He glanced down at her smiling lips and wished more than anything that he'd kissed her in the schoolhouse first, lighting bolt or no lightning bolt. Now he had an audience and no idea how he was supposed to do this. He leaned down slowly to make sure he had the right trajectory. He brushed his lips across hers. That didn't seem quite right. He tried again, lingering this time. She tilted her head and did the rest.

A lightning bolt hit him, all right. It traveled from his lips down to his soul. It blocked out everything in a flash of light and heat except for the woman before him. He pulled away to stare down at her. A hundred questions battled for answers within him. Had she felt the lightning, too? More important, who had taught her to kiss like that and how soon could he get his hands around that man's neck? Finally, maybe if Quinn was real good about everything else, would God mind if he tasted lightning at least one more time before he died? He wasn't anticipating a long wait seeing as he had not only chased after but caught more than he was entitled to.

Nope. A wedding kiss was acceptable. He'd better play it safe from here on out. That's what a smart man would do. He'd never professed to be one before, but he'd married the schoolmarm. He had to at least try to use his wits if he wanted to keep her.

And he did. For the children. *Only* for the children.

Sean and Lorelei O'Brien had insisted on keeping the children at their neighboring farm overnight. Helen sorely missed their company, for the evening seemed to stretch on interminably without them. She tried to present a picture of unselfconscious comfort by tucking her feet under her and snuggling into the settee with a copy of Jane Austen's *Persuasion*, but an undercurrent of unease seemed to crackle in the air along with the soft roar from the logs in the fireplace. Even the crisp notes of Quinn's banjo couldn't drown it out, though he wasn't above trying—bless his heart.

After announcing that he hadn't had much of a chance to practice lately, he'd settled on the rug-covered floor across from the settee and started playing…and playing…and playing. It seemed as though he'd been strumming for hours, pausing for only an instant between songs, if that. At first, she'd enjoyed it. He was a very talented musician, after all. He'd even gotten her toe tapping a time or two. Now, she was getting concerned and a bit frustrated.

It was their wedding day, for goodness' sake! Didn't he even want to talk to his new wife? She certainly wanted to talk to him. She'd been counting on this time to get to know the acquaintance she'd just married. She'd be downright mad at him for ignoring her if he wasn't so attractive while doing it.

Book abandoned, she stared at him, since he wasn't paying her any mind, anyway. The firelight caressed his jaw with golden fingers that swept up to his cheek and back down again as he bobbed his head in time with the music. His strong arms curved around the instrument while his left hand slid back and forth across the neck of the banjo and his nimble fingers coaxed music from the strings. His brow furrowed slightly in concentration. She bit her lip to hold back a sigh. *Talk to me.*

He glanced up and caught her watching. His fingers stalled. She smiled her entreaty. His lips curved upward in response. He went back to playing. She closed her eyes in annoyance then opened them to find his gaze fixed on her again. Progress! She'd better do something while she had his attention. His piercing cobalt eyes rendered her mind a complete blank. She reached for something sensible or meaningful to say then dared to speak over the music. "This is a nice room."

Really? That's the best that I could come up with?

It seemed to take Quinn off guard a little, too, for he glanced around as though with new eyes. The furnishings of the living room weren't fancy, but they were comfortable and of good quality. The floors were the same rather worn oak that seemed to stretch through the entire house. The burgundy rug on top of it reflected the red brick of the fireplace, which was cooled down by the hunter green and dark blue in the settee and matching chairs. Having finished his inspection, Quinn offered her a nod. "I'm glad you like it."

Her mind scrambled for something else to say. What could she talk about? The ceremony? She wasn't eager to discuss the fact that he'd made her a nervous wreck by originally accidentally refusing her. The children? All she could think about was the fact that they wouldn't return until tomorrow. Leaving her alone. With her husband. Who had only just discovered that she was in the same room with him.

Realizing they hadn't stopped staring at each other while he played, she wanted to look away but was afraid she wouldn't get his attention again. To be honest, she was tired of trying. It had been such a busy few days with her finishing up at school, packing her things and moving them into her new home. She was worn out. Perhaps she ought to just call it a night and hide until the children returned. She stood.

The music stopped. Quinn looked up at her expectantly. Her mouth opened then closed as she realized that, though she was ready to turn in, she had no idea where to turn in *to*. She'd been so distracted by laying out the wedding supper their friends had sent home with them that she hadn't seen anything of the house besides the kitchen and living room. After supper, Quinn had been too involved with his banjo to offer a tour. He stood, watching her with a concerned frown. "Something wrong?"

"No." Without her permission, her gaze strayed to the banjo which he still clung to rather tightly. "I'm just tired, that's all. I'm ready to go to bed, but I'm not sure where I'm supposed to sleep."

He carefully laid the banjo in its case. "I already put your trunks in my room. It's the first door you'll come to in the hallway."

"*Your* room?"

Her words were infused with just enough panic and disconcertion to jerk Quinn's head up. His eyes were already widening when they connected with hers. A flush spread just above his well-shaven jaw. "I didn't— I mean—I'll be sleeping in the boys' room from now on."

"Oh." A wave of relief washed over her, but ebbed with confusion. He'd asked her to marry him because he needed a mother for his children. However, since he'd never specifically said that their marriage would be in name only, she'd assumed it would become like any normal marriage after they fell in love. Was he ruling out that prospect? If so, did that mean he was also ruling out the far more important possibility of falling in love with her?

She really ought to ask him to clarify the issue. After all, she had a right to know exactly what she'd gotten herself into. She paused with the question on her lips. Did she want to know the truth? Absolutely. Did she have the nerve to ask? Certainly not.

Instead, she wished him a good night and easily found the right bedroom. The door was heavier than she'd expected so she pushed it open only far enough for her slim frame to slip through. Readying herself for bed, she tried to sort through the myriad emotions tangling in her chest. This marriage had not started out at all as she'd imagined it would. Even the ceremony had been a bit flubbed. She had to admit that Quinn had been rather frustratingly adorable in that moment. He'd been so serious, so confused, so desperate to make things right. He'd even called her "honey." Then he'd kissed her and she'd felt a sensation similar to the one she'd felt at the circus when she'd placed her hand on a glass ball that conducted static electricity—only more powerful. Of course, he'd followed all of that up by ignoring her the whole evening.

One labored sigh later, she slid under the covers of her new bed. At least, she tried to slide in. Her legs would only go so far. She kicked and pushed and wiggled to no avail until one overenthusiastic effort sent her careening toward the floor. She landed with a loud thump, clamping her lips shut a second too late to smother a startled scream. She groaned in a mixture of pain from her soon-to-be-bruised hip and pure, honest-to-goodness frustration. The pounding of bare feet sounded in the hallway. The door flew open, setting off a popping sound as an avalanche of rice covered her concerned husband.

Helen burst out laughing. Quinn ignored the sticky rice clinging to his body in his hurry to kneel by her side. "Are you hurt?"

She shook her head even as she winced at the stitch in her side that came from laughing too hard. "I just hit the floor a little hard."

He helped her up. "How did you end up down there?"

"Try to get in the bed."

He glanced from her to the bed then down at himself. "But I'm covered in rice."

"Doesn't matter. Go ahead and try." She smirked as she watched him lift the covers as though they were going to bite him. "Scaredy-cat."

He narrowed his eyes at her then jumped under the covers. His long legs had nowhere to go. He fell out of the bed, but managed to control his fall with catlike grace. He grinned up at her from the floor. "Helen, I reckon we've been shivareed."

"I hope that's the extent of the troublemaking." She shook her head. "Interesting how it isn't quite so fun when you're on the receiving end. I think I'd better get a broom."

"You can put the rice in the slop pail for the pigs. Meanwhile, I'll see how they rigged up the bed and undo it."

By the time she returned, he'd pulled back the quilt completely from the bed to reveal their saboteur's handiwork. The fitted sheet seemed untouched, but someone had tucked the top sheet into the head of the bed so that it looked like the fitted sheet. They'd then doubled it over so that it also appeared to be a normal top sheet. Lastly, they'd tucked in the sides so the sheet became sort of an impenetrable envelope.

Quinn quickly remade the bed correctly, shaking his head the entire time. "I made this bed myself this morning with new sheets and all. It kind of gives me an eerie feeling to know someone was prowling around the place, causing mischief when I was gone. I've a mind to go into town on Monday and get a better lock for the doors around this place. There. All fixed. I'll take the trash you have with me when I leave."

"Thank you for coming to my rescue." She swept the last of the rice into the dustpan and emptied it into the slop pail.

"I'm just glad you aren't too badly hurt."

She watched him plump the pillows for her as she sat on the edge of the bed. "You don't have to do that."

He shrugged. "I'm done now. Good night."

"Good night." She moved to the head of the bed as he grabbed the slop bucket, broom and dustpan. She'd just blown out the lamp when the sound of him softly calling her name made her turn to find the silhouette of his broad-shouldered, slim-hipped frame lingering at the door. "Yes, Quinn?"

"You looked beautiful at the wedding today. I hope I told you that."

He hadn't and she hadn't realized how dearly she'd missed the compliment until now. The sincerity in his voice caused a small smile to curve at her lips. "Thank you."

"I'll let you get some sleep." He stepped away from the door.

She moved to the far end of the bed. Clutching the footboard, she called his name. He reappeared in an instant. She bit her lip. Somehow the darkness helped her find her courage. It didn't stop the blush from rising in her cheeks. "Quinn, I think it's only fair of you to explain what you meant when you said you'd be sleeping in the boys' room 'from now on.' Does 'from now on' mean forever?"

His shoulders tensed as she spoke, and his gaze dropped to the path of light that led toward her. "I don't know, Helen. Maybe. Probably."

She nodded then waited for him to close the door behind him before sliding under the covers. She even went so far as to pull them over her head. It wasn't enough to shelter her from the doubts that stalked her thoughts.

She'd married Quinn thinking that it would be easy to fall in love with him one day. However, she hadn't considered the possibility that he might not be inclined to return the favor. Judging by tonight, that might very well be the case.

It would be wise to guard her heart and not place too much faith in love making the difference. If he did fall in love with her and they decided to have a normal marriage, how long would it be before he figured out there would be no baby coming? Would he realize she'd known she was damaged all along? That she'd hid it from him?

It didn't matter. It *wouldn't* matter. Quinn had married her to take care of the four children he already had. Surely her worth as his wife was secure in that. She didn't need to think that far ahead, anyway. Right now, their marriage was only a matter of convenience to him—no matter how much more it might mean to her.

Chapter Five

The dusky-blue light of dawn crept down the hallway where Quinn paused outside what used to be his bedroom. He tapped on the door and listened for any sounds of his wife stirring. Hearing none, he tapped a little harder. Still nothing. With a frown, Quinn eased the door open and immediately wished he hadn't. Something just didn't seem decent about being in a lady's bedroom while she was sleeping. Yet, he couldn't take his eyes off her as he rounded the corner of the bed and knelt beside it.

She was cuddled under the covers with her hand resting beside her cheek on a hunter-green linen pillowcase. The color complemented the roses in her cheeks and lips. Her rich brown waves tumbled over her shoulder. Quinn felt his brow furrow in confusion. How on earth had he convinced this beautiful creature to marry him?

He'd be a lot more comfortable with this situation if she were a little more plain, slightly dumb or just flat-out boring. She wasn't, though. He'd never been more aware of that than when he'd found himself alone with her for an entire evening. He wasn't completely dense. He knew that his banjo playing had bordered on excessive. He'd felt the annoyance rolling off his bride in waves. He just hadn't known what to do about it. He was afraid to talk for fear that she'd realized she'd been bamboozled into marrying a man so much dumber than her. He was afraid to look at her because that made him forget he didn't deserve her. Touching her was completely out of the question.

He'd lain awake for hours with his thoughts spinning in circles inside his head. They mostly revolved around the fact that he barely knew the woman he'd just given his last name. He knew plenty *about* her, but he didn't know her personally. He could count on one hand the number of times they'd spoken to each other and most of those conversations had occurred within the past week. That should make for an interesting married life, especially since he had little idea about what one was supposed to be like. His mother had died when he was Trent's age and his father hadn't remarried, which meant Quinn had never seen a marriage modeled in his own home. Townsfolk in Peppin seemed pretty fascinated by making matches and marrying people off, yet no one ever said anything about how to build a good marriage after the match was made.

He wasn't sure how long he'd been kneeling beside the bed thinking and watching Helen sleep before her sooty lashes began to flutter. He suddenly realized how close he was to her and tried to move away, but he was too late. Her eyes opened, locked on his and widened. Gasping, she bolted upright in bed and scrambled away from him. "Were you watching me sleep?"

Quinn figured his best tactic was evasion. "I was just about to awaken you. We've got chores to do."

"Chores?"

He nodded. "I need you to milk the cow, feed the chickens and gather the eggs. We'll have to hurry to get everything done, dress, pick up the children and still be on time for church."

She blinked. "Milk the chickens?"

She must be one of those folks who was slow to wake up. He didn't even try to hide his grin, though he quickly rubbed it away. "I'd like to see you try that."

"Try what?" She corralled her hair so that it pooled over one shoulder.

"Milking the chickens."

The teasing in his voice must have gotten through her sleep-fogged state, for a dangerous glint of humor warmed her brown eyes. "I bet you would. Repeat the list for me again."

He braced his elbows on the edge of the bed and ticked off each chore on his fingers. "Milk the cow. Feed the chickens. Gather the eggs. The milk pail and egg basket will be on the worktable in the barn with the bin of chicken feed beside it. All of that will be on your left side as soon as you walk in. You can't miss it."

She nodded. "Right."

"No, left." He pointed to his left, which he realized too late would be her right.

She tugged his hand down with a laugh. "No. I meant, 'right,' as in 'I understand.'"

"Oh, right." He glanced at her hand still covering his and wondered how the deal he made with God applied when she was the one reaching out. Yes, sir. He and God had some things they needed to hash out. Until then, he'd better not chance it. He disengaged his hand from hers as he stood. "Better get moving. The animals don't like to wait."

The man had no shame. It was obvious that he'd been watching her sleep for some time, yet he didn't even have the grace to look the slightest bit embarrassed at being caught. Then, as if she hadn't been disoriented enough by awakening in an unfamiliar place, he'd knocked further off balance with his teasing before delivering the final blow to her sensibilities. Chores.

She should have known that living on a farm would mean that she'd have farm chores. She'd just gotten so wrapped up in the idea of being a mother and having her impossible dream come true it hadn't crossed her mind. That and the fact that chores had never really been something she'd ever had to consider before. Growing up, she'd been responsible for keeping her room tidy. However, the maids had taken care of any real cleaning. And there had been no animals to care for.

Her move to Bradley's Boardinghouse hadn't necessitated any real change on her part since the Bradley family handled most of the mundane responsibilities for their boarders. Of course, she'd been in charge of keeping the schoolhouse in order. That had consisted of encouraging the children to clean up after themselves, giving the floor a good sweep and cleaning the chalkboard. There was nothing too strenuous or demanding about that.

Still, how hard could it be to take care of a few basic farm chores? She was an intelligent woman, after all.

Surely she'd catch on to her responsibilities quickly. She tied her hair back with a ribbon, put on a light coat and buttoned up her boots. There would be time to dress later. The important thing was to heed Quinn's admonishment to hurry.

The sound of Quinn splitting wood behind the house rang through the brisk autumn air as she stepped outside. She gave a little shiver and gathered her coat closer before setting off across the open field toward the barn. Her right hip reminded her of last night's unfortunate tumble out of bed by protesting each step she took with that leg. It didn't help that she continually had to jerk the heels of her kid-leather boots out of the thick grass. By the time she arrived at the door of the large red barn, the hem of her nightgown was wet with dew and clinging uncomfortably to her bare legs. Next time, the animals would have to wait for her to dress more warmly.

The smell of the barn stopped her in her tracks. It was a mixture of sweet hay, musk from the animals and the sharp, acrid scent of dung. She rubbed her cold nose. It wasn't so bad. Surely she'd get used to it in a few moments. Since she was already in the barn, it made sense to milk the cow first, so she grabbed the milking pan. Two horses neighed as she passed their stalls. She couldn't tell whether it was a welcome or a warning. Finally, she found the right animal.

Whoa. She'd seen cows from a distance before, but she'd never gotten this close to one. She hadn't realized they were quite so…large. The animal swung its head toward her and stared. Not threatening exactly—just slightly intimidating. Helen bent her knees to get a look at the teats attached to the bulgy sack on its stomach.

In theory, that's where the milk came from. She knew that. She just wasn't entirely sure what was required to procure the milk from that into the bucket. Oh, well. What had she told her students? Learning begins with the decision to try.

She unhooked the gate, closed it behind her and did exactly that. She tried...and tried...and tried to milk that blasted cow. It wasn't as easy in reality as it was in theory. That was for sure. Even when the cow stood still long enough for Helen to set up the stool and reach under its belly to get a hold of its bulgy contraption, nothing came out. Out of breath from the chase as much as the struggle, Helen decided that the cow just didn't want to share her milk today, so she traded in the milking pail for the chicken feed and egg basket.

The chicken coop was on the right side of the barn, closer to the house. She walked into the caged-in yard with confidence. The chickens would be far more manageable than the cow, if only because they were smaller. Plus, there was no fancy equipment on a chicken. It would all be very straightforward. Feed them. Gather the eggs from their nest. No problem.

At her approach, six hens and a rooster rushed out of their little house like children after a long day of school. Helen benevolently spread the feed across the yard as the clucking hens gobbled it up. The rooster seemed far more inclined to follow her around crowing and pecking at the feed that fell near her feet. Sometimes he missed the grain completely and accidentally pecked her boots. He was a pretty thing with his iridescent red-orange body and black-feathered bottom. He seemed to know it, too, from the way he strutted and crowed. The more she watched him, the more he began to remind her of her ex-fiancé in Austin.

She was just throwing the last of the feed when she realized that the rooster either had consistently bad aim or his target had, in fact, been her foot the whole time. She took a large step away from him. The next thing she knew, the rooster was hopping, flapping its wings and chasing her around the closed-in yard. The chickens squawked their disapproval. That caught the rooster's attention and he veered toward the loudest complainer with dubious intentions.

Helen ducked for cover inside the chicken coop, closing the door firmly behind her. With a sigh of relief, she surveyed her surroundings only to find that she was not alone. Two chickens had not left their roosts. Soon all the eggs lay safely in the basket except for the ones the hens were hiding. She approached the white one first, crooning, "Sweet little chick. Aunt Helen needs you to move aside. That's a good girl."

The white chicken clucked her sad tale and backed farther into her nest to let Helen take the precious egg. Helen couldn't help beaming. "Thank you. Now, don't let that mean old rooster scare you. You go on out and eat when I open the door. *If* I open the door. Maybe you could cause a diversion for me so I can get out of here."

She turned to the red chicken. "Time's up, honey. You need to move out the way."

Helen edged closer, but the hen didn't move or stop watching her with beady eyes. Helen extended her hand toward the nest. Perhaps she could just slide her hand under the seemingly frozen bird and... The bird launched out of the nest right toward Helen's face in a flurry of feathers, squawking and screeching. Helen let out a scream that sounded a little too similar to what was coming out of the hen as something scratched her cheek. She tried to ward it off with the feeding pan but only ended up hitting herself in the face. All of a sudden she realized the hen was gone. She'd been fighting the egg basket swinging from her arm.

Her panic faded, leaving her gasping for breath. She searched for her assailant, only to find the red hen clucking at the door as though it would open by her command. Helen gritted her teeth. She plucked the egg from the nest and placed it beside its rattled counterparts, then let the hens out the door. Helen peered out in search of the rooster and found it eating placidly near the door of the chicken coop—waiting for her, no doubt. She braced herself then ran for the exit.

Her peripheral vision told her the rooster was hot on her trail. The red hen appeared in her path, blocking her way out. Helen shifted to the right. Her hip protested. She stumbled. Glancing back, she saw the rooster go airborne with his claws outstretched toward her. Suddenly, she left the ground, too. The world spun. She landed firmly on her feet—unharmed, with her eyes clenched shut. Opening them, she saw the most beautiful sight.

Quinn was waving his arms at the rooster and chasing it into a corner away from her. His strident voice was music to her ears. "Back off! You know better than that!"

She didn't stick around to see the rest. She slipped out of the chickens' yard to await her husband out of harm's way. Her cheek was stinging from its encounter from the basket. Her lip was starting to fatten where she'd walloped herself with the feeding pan. She anxiously sifted through the eggs in the basket, looking for damage. She was so involved in her task that she didn't hear Quinn approach until an instant before he lifted her chin with a gentle touch. His gaze explored her face as a frown marred his. "What happened to you?"

She felt her eyes flash with indignation. "Your chickens attacked me. That's what happened."

"My chickens did this?"

Her gaze dropped from his for an instant. "I might have helped them out a bit. Still, they were the cause."

"I'm not sure what that means, but you'd better wash your face. This scrape on your cheek is bleeding." The concern in his tone, without even a hint of mockery, was just the balm she needed for her wounded pride.

She found herself leaning closer to him, hoping he'd wrap her in his arms if only for a moment. "Thank you for saving me *again*."

"Glad to do it." He chuckled. "I was on my way to the barn to feed the livestock and muck out the stalls when I heard you scream. Did you get a chance to milk the cow yet?"

"I tried, but there's no milk."

That frown was back. "No milk?"

She shrugged. "I guess the cow didn't want to give any today. Maybe there'll be some tomorrow."

A strange look appeared on his face. Confusion? Suspicion? Disbelief? She couldn't quite tell. He ran his fingers through his short hair. "I'll deal with it. You go on inside and take care of yourself. I should be in by the time you have breakfast ready."

"Breakfast. Right. That sounds good." She backed away, smiling and nodding the whole time. She could fix breakfast. No problem. After all, how hard could it be to scramble a few eggs?

Quinn had married into trouble. The knowledge had come upon him gradually at first. Now, with the day drawing to a close, he could no longer deny the truth. He'd suspected it when he'd found his wife running from the rooster, but he'd been willing to give her the benefit of the doubt because it was a fact that roosters could be territorial, especially with new people. As soon as she'd said that piece about the cow, he'd known he had a problem. The cow wasn't dry. She couldn't be. In fact, he had to milk her twice a day just to keep up with her production. However, it wasn't until the disaster of a meal she'd called breakfast that realization had come hard and swift like a knee to the stomach.

His wife knew nothing about housework. What was worse, he wasn't sure she was aware of the fact of just how little she knew. She attacked everything with an optimistic vivacity that remained unfazed despite her missteps throughout the day. It truly boggled his mind how a woman so obviously intelligent could be so clueless about the most basic things. He needed to talk to her. He'd been trying to all day but hadn't managed it yet.

It wasn't that he'd been speechless. He could think of a lot of words to say. He just knew that saying them was going to get him into trouble, which is why he'd initially kept his mouth shut. Then they'd picked up the children from the O'Briens and hadn't had a moment alone since.

Having completed the evening chores, he heaved a sigh and trekked from the barn into the house. Sunday had become the night when he put everyone to bed early—including himself. A fact he realized he'd forgotten to mention to Helen when he found the three older children enthralled by the book she was reading to them in front of the fire. Olivia had long since succumbed to sleep and so had Quinn, though he'd somehow managed to stay on his feet. He waited until Helen paused to take a breath before interrupting. "It's past time for bed, you three. Go on now."

Clara, usually the only one he could count on to obey and enforce his rules on the others, rebelled with a groan. "Please, just a few more minutes, Uncle Quinn."

"I'm almost to the end of the chapter." Helen smiled as if that should solve everything.

The boys added their pleas, Reece verbally and Trent with his puppy-dog eyes. Quinn wavered—not because of their resistance but because he was contemplating the idea of going to bed now and leaving Helen up to put the kids to bed alone. She ought to be able to manage that since Clara and Reece knew what to do even if she didn't. Quinn would talk to her in the morning. After all, the situation wouldn't change before then.

Quinn nodded. "All right, then, but morning comes early and we don't want to be late for school, so y'all had better finish up soon. Good night."

He ignored the hint of surprise in their voices as they returned his farewell. The bedroll he stretched out on in the boys' room was no worse accommodation than it had been during the two years he'd traveled from ranch to ranch helping with brandings and roundups in Texas cattle country, saving up money for his own spread. It was comfortable enough for him to drift to sleep immediately…until a pint-size foot landed square on his chest. Quinn opened his eyes to find Reece grimacing down at him. "Sorry, Uncle Quinn. I slipped. Just trying to blow out the lamp."

"No problem. I'll do it," Quinn murmured with a sleepy slur as he stood and glanced over to make sure Trent was in the bed that the boys shared. The boy's small form was burrowed completely under the covers in preparation for the coming darkness. Quinn wasn't sure what to do about the boy's fears, since leaving a kerosene lamp burning all night would be a safety hazard. He could only hope that eventually Trent would realize he was perfectly safe.

The lamp had only been out a few seconds before Reece's voice broke the quiet. "Why are you sleeping in here and not in your own room?"

Quinn slid back into his bedroll. "It's your aunt's room now. That's why."

"That's not fair!" The boy leaned over the edge of his bed. "It was your room first. She ought to share. I share with Trent, and Clara shares with Olivia."

"Get back in bed before you hurt yourself."

Reece obeyed, then there was a thoughtful silence that could only mean trouble. "How come we have to share with you if she doesn't?"

Oh, boy. He needed to play his cards right or he'd find himself sleeping in the barn. "It isn't about sharing. Ladies need privacy."

"For sleeping?" Reece's tone said he wasn't buying what Quinn was selling.

The barn was getting more attractive by the second. "Yes. Now, go to sleep."

"But why?"

Quinn rolled onto his side, feeling the hardwood floor through the thin padding. "I'm tired, Reece. If I don't get some sleep tonight, I'll be dragging the whole week. Now, I don't want to hear any more questions from you tonight."

"What if it isn't a question?"

Quinn smiled even as he rubbed a shaking hand over his face. He should have known better than to try to go to sleep before the boys were dead to the world. He stood and edged toward the door. "Go to sleep. I'll be back in a minute."

He passed the door to the girls' room then Helen's, but he didn't stop at either of them. He kept going until he walked out the front door, down the porch steps and toward the wooded hills. He made it to the middle of the clearing before the invisible weight pressing on his shoulders dropped him to his knees. He battled the urge to pray. What good would it do to cry out for help? He'd done that once. Now it seemed that he had even more of a challenge on his hands than before.

He lifted his confused gaze heavenward then couldn't look away. The dark sky was clear, showing off the innumerable stars shimmering above. It was an awe-inspiring sight. More than that, it was fearsome. It served as a blatant reminder of his insignificance and the power of a God big enough, calculating enough, to create it all. Pastor Brightly had preached about it at church this morning. "And he is before all things, and by him all things consist." Of course, the pastor had tried to put a positive spin on that verse, but Quinn knew the truth about God's power. Nana had made sure of that.

Her body may have been growing weaker during those last few days of her life, but her fervor for sparing him from the fires of damnation had been stronger than ever. He could almost hear her wispy voice as clearly now as he had when he'd knelt at her bedside. *You've got to work out your salvation with fear and trembling, boy. You hear me? Your father and brother succumbed to that heathen greed and left me to die. I don't want to be the only one from my family in heaven. You've got to make it there, too.*

She'd spent the last of her strength instructing him on how to do that as if she hadn't drilled it into him long before that. Then the woman who'd been so afraid of being alone had left him behind. He'd been fourteen. Twelve years later, he was still doing his best to follow her advice. That's why he'd lived life hoping that if he left God alone, God would let him alone. Then he'd gone and messed everything up by asking for help.

"Quinn?"

He closed his eyes at the sound of Helen's soft voice. "I'm fine, Helen. You can go back inside."

She didn't move. Silence stretched between them until it broke with her whisper. "I know you aren't fine, Quinn. Just as surely as I know I'm at least one of the reasons why."

He finally turned his head to look up at her. She was bathed in moonlight. Her dark hair fell to her waist, a shiny backdrop to the turquoise Sunday-best gown she still wore. Forgetting for a moment that all of heaven was watching, he caught her hand and guided her down to the grass in front of him. "Why didn't you tell me that you didn't know anything about living on a farm or doing chores?"

"I thought you knew that I hadn't lived on a farm before."

He shook his head, realizing again just how little he actually knew about the woman he'd married. "Even so, some things like cooking don't require a person being on a farm to learn."

"Breakfast was terrible, wasn't it? I can see why you accepted the O'Briens' invitation for dinner and insisted on cooking supper yourself." He could see her blush even in the moonlight. "I'm afraid there's a lot I didn't learn growing up. You see, my family had servants to handle pretty much everything regarding the household."

"Servants?" The word was foreign to him, like something out of a fairy story he couldn't read. How wealthy did a person need to be to have everything done by servants? He couldn't even fathom it. He stiffened. "Wait. What do you mean *everything*?"

She gave a hapless shrug. "I mean the housework."

"Like cooking, cleaning, washing clothes, mending…" Her every nod filled him with more trepidation and confusion. Why had God sent Helen if she couldn't be the helpmeet he needed?

The question must have shown on his face, for Helen reached up to cradle his jaw with her hand, riveting his attention back to her. "I'll learn, Quinn. I promise you that."

"I'm sure you will." They didn't have a choice. She had to learn—and as quickly as possible. He caught her wrist and gently tugged her hand away so that he could think clearly as he made his own promise. "I'll show you what little I know. What I don't know, we'll have to find someone to teach you."

She smiled. "I already asked a couple of my friends for help at church. They agreed to give me a few lessons this week. See, Quinn? It will turn out all right."

He was relieved that she seemed to be eager to learn. Did that mean God intended her to turn out to be a helpmeet, after all? Or a hindrance? Or just plain temptation? Maybe all three options were right. Perhaps He'd sent Helen as some sort of test. If so, Quinn wouldn't falter. He wouldn't start caring about her as anything more than the helpmeet she was supposed to be. Not that he'd ever had a chance with her, anyway. That much had been made even clearer tonight for, despite her frustrating lack of practical skills, she was so far beyond him on every other level, it made his proposal and subsequent marriage almost laughable. Somehow he didn't find it funny—only confusing. He'd prayed for a helpmeet and God had given him a princess. How in the world could Quinn even endeavor to deserve that?

Chapter Six

Helen drew back the faded curtains from the window in her room the next morning to see the orange haze of daybreak stealing across the tops of the farm's eastern hills. That was the only sign of morning as she gave herself one last cursory check in the mirror. The reflection of determination on her face couldn't replace the memory of seeing Quinn sink to his knees on the fog-covered ground last night. She wasn't ignorant about the frustrating lack of skills she'd exhibited yesterday. Nor had she been unaware of the gradual strain it had seemed to be placing on her husband. However, she hadn't realized its true impact until that moment.

She was prepared to put her best foot forward today. The shadows under her eyes spoke of how much thought she'd put into doing exactly that last night. She grabbed the short stack of index cards she'd had the foresight to take to church with her yesterday and tiptoed across the hall into the living room. She stopped short at the sight of Quinn sleeping in a bedroll near the hearth where a banked fire dimly glowed in the fireplace. When he'd said he would be sleeping in the boys' room, she'd assumed that meant in a bed. Apparently not. He worked too hard to be relegated to the floor. Something would have to be done about that. She just wasn't sure what.

She stoked the fire in the cookstove, silently thanking Nathan Rutledge for teaching her how to manage the cantankerous stove in the schoolhouse. Next, she turned to the first index card, which happened to be written by Nathan's wife, Kate. It was entitled, How to Make Coffee. She followed the directions carefully and quietly. She taste tested the resulting brew and was pleasantly surprised to find it quite tasty. She closed the stove's damper to keep the brew warm for Quinn. Now to conquer the chickens...

A few minutes later, she set the egg basket near the door to the chicken coop and laid out most of the feed in one area of the yard before opening the door. A couple of tosses showed the chickens where the feed was, which freed her to ward off the aggressive rooster with a few nudges of the broom, as Ellie Williams had suggested. He soon grew bored and left her alone. Confidence growing, she picked up the basket and entered the coop to find the red hen stubbornly sitting in her roost.

Helen made sure to keep to the side as she reached under the troublemaker. This time when the hen launched from the roost, Helen was out of its trajectory. She gathered the rest of the eggs and was soon headed back to the barn unscathed. She was standing outside the cow's stall with a rope and the milking bucket contemplating her next move when Quinn's deep voice eased into her thoughts. "What exactly are you planning to do to Bessie?"

She turned around to find him standing behind her with his arms crossed and a half amused, half concerned smile on his face. She lifted a brow in response. "I'm going to milk her, of course. The rope is to keep her from moving around the stall."

He frowned. "She is usually pretty content to stay in one place when I milk her."

"Well, I was probably doing something wrong."

"Probably." He gave her a wink then returned the rope to the tack room before setting the milking pail and stool in place for the chore. He beckoned her into the stall with a quick tilt of his head. He crouched down beside her once she was seated. "First thing you want to do is to prod or rub the udder so she'll know it's time to let the milk down."

"Down from where?" She tried to follow his example, but the cow sidestepped at her touch. "See? That's what happened last time."

He narrowed his eyes thoughtfully. "Give me your hands."

"What? Why?"

He took one of her hands in both of his and began to rub it. "They're too cold. That's something you have to watch out for the closer we get to winter. Although, I've been thinking that I should keep doing the milking since dealing with the chickens, cooking breakfast and getting the children ready for school is a lot for anyone to handle in the mornings."

She spoke over the sound of her heart thundering in her ears. "You did all of that and more before I got here."

"Which is why I know it's a lot to handle. Besides, it will go faster if I do it." He switched his ministrations to her other hand. "You should still learn how to milk the cow, though. It's an important skill to have on a farm."

"Did you find the coffee I made?" She asked the question to the top button of his shirt, which she discovered was a far easier feat then looking into his eyes at such a close distance.

"Sure did. It was nice and hot. Thanks for making it. I also saw that you collected the eggs. How did the rooster treat you?"

She shrugged, wishing he'd hurry up and finish with her hands. "I handled him."

"I don't doubt it." He chuckled then lifted her hands to his cheeks to test their warmth. "Better."

She froze. Her gaze drifted upward to meet his. How could he be so completely unaffected by her when she could hardly even think? It didn't seem fair. Her thoughts must have shown in her face, for his eyes widened then deepened. She felt his jaw tighten beneath the day-old stubble. He abruptly released her hands. His words seemed directed more to the ceiling than her. "Sorry. I guess you could have done that yourself. I wasn't thinking."

"It's fine." She turned to face the cow. "What now?"

She nearly winced at the sound of her breathless voice. She was embarrassing herself. He'd made it clear that he wasn't interested in her as anything more than a mother for his children. There was no need to turn into a ninny just because he deigned to warm her hands. Quinn's arm brushed hers, jolting her from her reverie as he demonstrated the proper hand position for milking. "You're going to want to squeeze from top to bottom to draw out the milk. Don't pull or you could stretch out the teat. Stay alert. You don't want the cow to kick you or the milk pail."

"No, I certainly don't." She copied his movements and jumped when a stream of milk hit the ground. "I did it!"

He grinned. "You sure did. Just try to get the next one in the pail. Once you're comfortable, try milking two teats at once by alternating."

After two or three minutes, she'd developed a slow rhythm. She glanced at Quinn, who still hovered a bit too close for comfort. "Quinn, I thought you had a real bed to sleep in."

He seemed a bit taken aback by the sudden change of conversation. "A bedroll will do just fine for me."

"You work too hard to be relegated to the floor. Can't something be done about it?"

He rubbed his jaw. "I was thinking about expanding the house. I could add another bedroom. I also thought a room for the kitchen might be nice instead of just a corner in the house. Then we could put the table in there and have more room in the living space. What do you think?"

She paused to glance up at him, both surprised and impressed by how much thought he'd already put into solving the problem. "You know how to do that? Build part of a house, I mean?"

"Sure I do. I traveled around Texas doing whatever honest work I could find until I saved enough to buy my own piece of land." He shrugged. "It made me one of those jack-of-all-trades folks are always insulting."

She laughed. "I guess you must have seen a fair bit of Texas with all that traveling."

"That's a fact. Of course, nothing beats this place." His lips stretched into a lazy grin. "Want to know why?"

"Why?"

"Because it's mine."

She smiled. "That's a good reason."

She focused on the milking again and was proud that she seemed to be picking up speed. "After all that traveling, how did you end up settling down here?"

"I was passing through Peppin in between jobs and heard that the man who owned this place was looking for a farmhand. He was an older widower who was having some trouble running the place by himself, so he hired me on. About a year later, he decided to move a few towns west of here to live with his older son. I bought the place and most of the furnishings from him." His gaze turned curious. "What about you? You didn't need to work, so why did you leave home to become Peppin's schoolmarm?"

Her mind blanked then raced into action. What could she tell him? That she'd fled the embarrassment of a broken engagement? What if he asked who'd broken it off and why? "Helen?"

She blinked, focused a blithe smile on him and lifted one shoulder in a shrug. "I became a teacher for the joy of it. This is where I was placed. I think I'd better go start breakfast and awaken the children."

A furrow appeared on his brow. She wasn't sure if it was a result of her abrupt explanation or the idea of her fixing breakfast. She didn't stick around to find out.

Mrs. Helen Tucker was hiding something. At least that's what Quinn believed after their conversation yesterday morning. He didn't doubt she was telling the truth about why she had become a teacher, but the flash of pain in her eyes and the flush of pink on her cheeks had told him there was more to the story than she was letting on. He was actually kind of glad that she'd kept whatever it was to herself for the moment since he was still adjusting to that last revelation of his wife living the life of a fairy princess story. Until she'd married him, that is.

He had to hand it to her, though. Whatever she had written on those little cards of hers sure seemed to be making a difference. It helped that as a rule she was eager to learn and willing to take initiative. Each meal she'd made over the past two days had been an improvement over the last. That was a good thing, since she'd moved the spices out of the order he'd created for them in the cabinet. He'd lost all hope of being able to tell one identical-looking package from the other without a taste test first. How odd would it look if she caught him doing that?

It had occurred to him belatedly that hiding his illiteracy was probably worse than her failing to mention she didn't know how to do housework. However, that didn't make him any more eager to divulge his secret. He'd done a fair job of hiding it so far. Of course, he'd nearly had apoplexy the first time he'd walked into the house to find Reece reading a recipe aloud to her while she cooked just like the boy had done the few times Quinn hadn't been able to avoid trying a new dish. Thankfully, Helen hadn't seemed to think there was anything out of the ordinary behind Reece's efforts to be helpful. That was all Reece thought it amounted to as well so Quinn's secret was still safe.

Quinn's horse stumbled slightly, reminding him that he was supposed to be paying attention to his surroundings. Today, he'd been riding the fence line of his property fixing any areas with sagging barbed wire. This was the first time he'd been able to survey the state of his farm since the children had come. Having Helen to watch the young ones while the older ones were in school was a huge help to him. Yesterday, he'd gotten more work done in the field than he usually did in a week. The winter wheat was growing steadily though the lack of rain lately had become a concern.

Upon returning to the house, he wasn't too surprised to find that his wife had company since she'd told him that several of her friends had agreed to teach her some household chores. He just hadn't realized that the author of the Bachelor List, Ellie Williams, would be Helen's instructor today. The women's quiet voices and soft laughter told him that Olivia and Trent must be taking their afternoon nap. How the children could sleep with the lingering sweet, spicy smell emanating from the kitchen was beyond him. His stomach gave a rumble almost loud enough to wake them in the other room.

Ellie was the first to spot him. Her green eyes lit up with a calculating gleam that told him he'd be wise to walk right back out the door. "Quinn, you're just the man I was hoping to see."

Uh-oh. His gaze slid to Helen for some clue to what he was in for, but she gave him a guileless smile that set him at ease. Or perhaps it was the smudges of flour on her cheeks and all down the front of her apron that made him think perhaps he could handle himself with the two forces of nature before him. "Good to see you, Ellie. Did Lawson come with you?"

"No. He had to stay and work with the horses." She tapped her booted toe looking downright impatient to skip the preliminaries and get the bee out of her bonnet. "I rode Starlight over here by myself then set her up with some water and a stall in your barn. I hope you don't mind."

"Certainly not."

Helen must have seen him eyeing the door for she stepped forward with a plate of golden cookies that were sprinkled with some kind of red powder. "Try a snicker doodle cookie. The children helped us make them."

"Thanks. I don't mind if I do." He selected two large misshapen cookies and sat down to await his fate. Hopefully it would involve more cookies. He couldn't remember the last time he'd had one. It had to have been at a church picnic or barn raising because he'd certainly never tried to make them on his own. He was starting to think there was something to be said for this marriage deal, after all. Catching Ellie's narrowed eyes on him, he lifted a brow. "Something on your mind, Ellie?"

She nodded as she wiped her hands on her apron. "I was talking to Rhett the other day. He seemed to be attributing your marriage to the Bachelor List, which is ridiculous because Helen lost the list. Right?"

Helen exchanged a glance with him. "Yes, I lost it. The funny thing is…Quinn found it."

Quinn nodded. "Sure did."

"I see." Ellie swallowed. "But, y'all didn't get married just because of a silly list I made."

Quinn bolted upright. "*Silly* list?"

Helen hushed him with a furtive glance toward the hallway that led to the bedrooms. "If you wake the children too soon they'll be cranky the rest of the day."

"Well, I'm sorry, but that list isn't silly." He frowned at Ellie who seemed to grow a bit paler with each word from him. "It's one of the main reasons I married Helen along with the fact that she loved the children."

"And because you love each other…?" When Ellie's hopeful prompt was met with uncomfortable silence, she grabbed onto the table for support. "Oh, dear. I had no idea people would take my list this seriously when I made it. I don't like the idea of people following it so unquestionably. It isn't infallible, you know, and neither am I."

"It doesn't have to infallible for God to use it to bring people together." Helen pulled out a chair and urged her friend to sit down. "Now, there's no need to get in such a dither about things. Quinn and I know what we're doing."

Ellie bit her lip. "Well, I suppose if y'all are happy then I'm happy. I would like the list back, though. Y'all certainly don't need it anymore."

"If that's true, then I guess you don't need it, either." He leaned his chair back onto two of its legs. "Seeing as you're married and all."

Helen's mouth dropped open. "Quinn, the list belongs to Ellie. She should be able to have it back if she wants it."

"It seems to me that since it's called the *Bachelor's* List it belongs to the bachelors who need it."

Ellie lifted her chin. "It's the *Bachelor* List—as in

a list of bachelors. There is no apostrophe *s* to make it belong to anyone but me."

A pasta—what? That thought nearly spilled into words until a quick glance at Helen told him he somehow ought to know what Ellie was talking about. He settled for an ineloquent, but less revealing, "Huh?"

"Will you give me back my list?"

"I'm afraid not."

"Helen, talk some sense into your husband."

Helen looked purely ticked as she crossed her arms and gave him a look that somehow mixed a glare with puzzlement. "We haven't been together long enough for me to know how to do that yet."

Quinn grinned at Helen then gave Ellie's hand a quick perfunctory pat. "I'll take good care of it until the next fella is ready to receive it, and I've got a good idea who that man will be. I believe the list fell into my hands as a result of divine intervention. There's nothing you or anyone else could say to convince me otherwise. Anything good or bad that comes from it is God's responsibility—not yours."

Ellie sighed. "Well, if God's in it, it's bound to turn out good."

For whom? He wanted to ask, but kept his mouth shut because he believed every word he'd spoken. Of course, he'd questioned why God had sent Helen at first. He still wasn't sure he entirely understood all of the reasons. One thing he did know was that, after a few days of marriage, Helen was beginning to be downright helpful. Between the chores, children and ladies visiting he hardly ever saw her alone. That suited him perfectly because it helped him remember that she didn't belong to him so much as she did to the children. He'd be just fine if they could keep this up for another twenty years or so. After that…well, he wasn't sure what he'd do.

Chapter Seven

"Well, darlings, let's hope that's the last of it," Helen said the next day as she entered the living room where she'd left Olivia and Trent a few moments ago to gather the laundry. She'd discovered that the children had come to Quinn with a relatively large wardrobe of good quality clothes. Of course, that meant more work for her because all of them were dirty. She glanced up as she began to separate the clothes into piles. She found Olivia sitting on the rug playing with a doll. However, Trent's watercolors and paintbrush sat abandoned near his latest masterpiece on the kitchen table. "Trent, come back here and show me your painting!"

Silence—thick and suspicious—permeated the house. That didn't mean the boy wasn't close by. She hadn't heard Trent make a sound since she'd arrived. From what she'd heard from his siblings, Trent's silence was a relatively new development and one that she found greatly concerning. Quinn had told her that Doc Williams had examined the boy but hadn't found anything physically wrong. The doctor also said the silence was probably induced by the stress of losing his parents and was most likely a temporary condition. That left room for hope, which was far more than her family's doctor in Austin had given her after her riding accident.

She froze realizing that another minute or two had passed without any sign of Trent. She left the clothes on the floor once more to search for the boy. She went through each room, searched every potential hiding place and concluded that Trent was not in the house, after all. Reining in her mounting panic, she set Olivia on her hip and headed outside to the only logical place for him to have gone in such a hurry. The outhouse door was wide open showing an empty interior. She spun to scan her surroundings causing Olivia to squeal in excitement at the sudden motion.

"There's no need to panic. He couldn't have gotten far. He's probably just in the barn with those gentle and mammoth animals like Bessie who could step on him or kick him or..." She shook her head to stop the flow of thoughts. "Quinn will find him if I can't. Of course, I'd have to find Quinn first. Only I don't know where he is because he's been working on the fences. How long can it take to fix fences?"

Trent wasn't in the barn. She ran outside and glanced toward the wheat fields. The burgeoning stalks weren't tall enough to hide a four-year-old. Perhaps he'd gone back to the house. She trotted from the barn toward the house which set Olivia giggling. Helen started up the porch steps calling, "Trent?"

"He's right here." Quinn's deep voice stopped her in her tracks. She turned to find Trent holding on to Quinn's hand as they rounded the far corner of the house—the one area she hadn't been able to see during her frenzied search. "I was breaking sod for the new addition and he must have seen me through the kitchen window. He was sitting on a nearby log watching me work. I didn't even see him there at first."

"I only left the room for a few minutes. When I came back he was gone. I knew he couldn't have gotten far but still…" She shook her head and covered her heart as she walked down the porch step.

Quinn rubbed his jaw, the look in his eyes slightly guilty. "I guess I should have warned you this fella has a talent for disappearing at the drop of the hat."

She glanced down to find Trent watching her with his deep brown eyes. She set Olivia down then kneeled over to wipe the smudged of dirt from his face with the hem of her apron. "You must have had quite an adventure before sitting on that log to be so messy, young man."

A reluctant little quirk of his lips was his only response.

"He has a talent for that, too," Quinn admitted.

She lifted her brow at the men. "A talent for having adventure or for getting messy?"

"Both."

Helen sank to her knees in front of her nephew so that she could look him in the eye. "Well, I'm all for having adventures and even for getting messy once in a while. However, when you're with me, you are not to go off by yourself without my permission. Is that understood?"

He understood. She could see that in his eyes. He just didn't agree. She could see that, too. She was narrowing her eyes, trying to figure out how to handle it when a shout ruined the moment. "Hello, the house!"

She stood in time to see Rhett Granger wave at them as he drove a wagon practically onto their front porch. Isabelle sat beside him, her hands gripping the sides of the conveyance. Helen couldn't tell if she was hanging on for dear life or preparing to jump out. Apparently, it was the latter because her friend stepped out of the wagon almost before it stopped. "Helen, never let your children ride with that man. He cannot drive."

Rhett set the brake and hopped down to join them. "Now, that's gratitude for you. There I was shoeing a horse next to the livery when I overheard Miss Adventure here trying to convince the livery owner that she should be allowed to take out her father's buggy by herself. Quinn, ask her how many times she's driven a team of horses."

Quinn frowned. His tone was unnecessarily grave. "How many?"

"Father let me take the reins a few times."

Rhett nudged Quinn in the side with his elbow. "Ask her how she planned to move these heavy boxes she brought with her."

"How did—" Quinn must have seen Helen shaking her head at him for joining in his friends' antics for he stared down at his boots as though they were the most interesting things in the world.

"For your information, *gentlemen*, I was going open the crates and carry the books in stacks to the buggy then get Quinn to help me carry them into the house when I got here." Isabelle popped the top off the crate on the back of the buggy. Taking the first book in hand, she tested its weight as though preparing to throw it at Rhett. "Now, I'm getting a better idea of what to do with them."

Rhett quirked his brow. "Ladies and gentlemen, I give you the gentler sex."

Quinn did a very poor job of hiding his laughter which only made Rhett's grin broaden. Helen frowned at them both. "Rhett, I'm beginning to think you're a bad influence on my husband. Let's get these things inside—although I don't really know why you're giving them to me, Isabelle."

"These are from your parents. The postman dropped the boxes off at the boardinghouse. He said he didn't want them taking up room in his office forever and a day which they surely would since Quinn never checks his mail."

Everyone looked at Quinn who flushed a nice shade of red. He shrugged. "Only family I've got is right here. No one else would have cause to write so why bother?"

"That isn't true, Quinn." Helen smiled at his befuddlement. "When we married I didn't just become part of your family. You became part of mine. You have in-laws and they're pretty lovely people if you ask me."

"In-laws. Now, isn't that something? I reckon I could stop by the post office now and again if they'll be writing you."

"Not just me—us."

"Us," he repeated. A flash of worry crossed his face. Before she could question it, he was lifting a crate from the wagon and carrying it toward the house. "Rhett, I can take Isabelle back to town when I pick up the kids from school."

Rhett followed suit with the last crate. "I'd appreciate that, Quinn. I have a lot of work to do back at the smithy."

The men deposited their burdens in the living room before Rhett said his goodbyes. Quinn took the children with him to "help him dig" the foundation for the addition. Helen was pretty sure that just meant they'd be playing in the dirt, but appreciated him watching the children while she learned how to wash clothes. First, though, she and Isabelle delved into the crates of books to see what treasures her parents had sent. "Thanks for bringing these out, Isabelle."

"You're welcome." Isabelle stacked a few children's books on the table.

Helen gave her friend a sideways glance. "It was nice of Rhett to drive you."

Isabelle grimaced. "He just wanted a chance to ask about Amy."

"He asked about Amy?"

"No, but he would have if I hadn't been complaining about his driving the whole way. The more I complained the worse he drove." Isabelle pursed her lips and narrowed her eyes. "This seems highly suspicious now that I think about it."

Helen's smile quickly sobered. "What is the latest on Amy?"

"Father wired home to say he found her in a small town near Dallas where her husband is from. Violet said she wanted to visit them so mother forbade us to leave the house. Thankfully, I was able to convince her that wasn't practical. Stop laughing. It isn't funny and I have nothing further to say on the matter." Isabelle glanced around the living room. "Where should I put these books?"

Helen followed her friend's gaze. "Hmm. I hadn't realized that there aren't any bookshelves in this room. Or, anywhere else in the house now that I think about it. We'd better put these back in the crate for now. I'll figure out what to do with them later. I have some water heating in the stove's reservoir for the wash."

"We'll probably need a pot or two more. It looks like you have quite a few loads to do." Isabelle put the last of books back in the case. "So Quinn isn't a big reader then?"

"I suppose not." Helen found her largest pot and pumped the faucet to fill it. "He's more interested in his music. Besides, he stays so busy that he'd hardly have a chance to read if he were so inclined."

Isabelle leaned onto the large farm sink beside Helen. "I thought farmers had more free time in the winter with harvest over and planting season not until the spring."

"Well, he has a crop of winter wheat in the ground. He's also working on an addition to the house."

Isabelle took over the pumping for her. "Really? What is he building?"

"Another bedroom and maybe an extension on the kitchen." She carried the heavy pot to the stove, careful not to slosh it.

"Another bedroom? Are y'all planning to add to your family immediately?"

Helen lost her grip on the pot. Thankfully, it was close to the surface of the stove so it settled with a loud bang and only a small splash. Like unexpected pressure on a bruise, pain made her eyes well and prompted her to answer honestly. "The bedroom is for him."

Isabelle was quiet for so long that it seemed Helen could almost hear the thoughts racing through her friend's head. "That sounds...permanent. Are you all right with that?"

"Yes." She blinked away her unshed tears as she mopped up the water on the stove with a clean rag.

Isabelle squeezed her arm. "This from the girl who was certain she'd fall in love with her husband without a problem?"

"I forgot to factor in the possibility that he might not be willing to fall in love with me."

Isabelle's mouth dropped open. "Did he say that to you?"

"He might as well have." Helen reached for the cookie jar. "Take one. The children and I made these yesterday."

"You can't shut me up with a cookie even if they do smell delicious. Why does Quinn get the final word on this? You have every right to fall in love with your husband and seek his love in return. In fact, I'm pretty sure y'all promised to love each other before God and a handful of witnesses not even a week ago."

"I can't control his feelings."

"Perhaps not, but you can't give up, either."

Helen felt her temper rising so she forced herself to take in a deep breath and calm down. She usually wasn't a short-tempered person, but this had been a trying week. As in she had been trying really hard to be who she needed to be for the children and Quinn. She was suddenly realizing that some things had fallen by the wayside during that process. Important things, too. Things like Trent's silence and the fact that her husband was building for a future that didn't include her. Meanwhile, he didn't even have a bed to sleep in.

Isabelle had made an erroneous assumption. That's what made Helen so mad. She hadn't given up on her marriage such as it was. She just hadn't had time to think about it. That needed to change. First, she had to figure out how to do the laundry. Second, she had to cook supper. After that, she had to help the children with homework and put them to bed. Then, once all of that was done and Quinn was avoiding her as usual, she'd come up with some sort of solution to at least one of these problems. She just had to.

Late that evening, Quinn watched the flames in the fireplace abate with grim satisfaction. Something about watching a fire dance always brought to mind things like damnation, the coming judgment and a lake of fire. Nana had become more concerned about those things after his father and brother had gone searching for "fool's gold" as she'd called it. As a child it had terrified him. Eventually, he'd learned not to show that fear for it only seemed to prompt her to add more detail to her descriptions. If the fear of the Lord was really the beginning of all knowledge, those formative years should have left him a lot smarter than he'd ended up.

He speared the wooden logs with a metal poker and a bit too much force. His arms, sore from breaking ground for the new addition, protested the motion. He'd known he was overdoing it at the time, but he couldn't seem to slow down once he'd started—not when every splice of sod was meant to demonstrate his acceptance that he wasn't good enough for Helen. Surely, God would appreciate his efforts.

Satisfied with the glow of the banked fire, Quinn set the poker aside to lay out his bedroll. He found it wasn't where he'd left it that morning or anywhere else in sight. He'd been married less than a week but already knew that nothing was truly lost unless his wife couldn't find it. He went to knock on her bedroom door only to discover someone else had already beaten him to it. Helen's voice sounded through the partially open door. "And just what are you doing out of bed, little lady?"

Clara's giggle induced him to peer through the gap in the door just as Helen swept the seven-year-old onto her lap. Clara tilted her head back to use what Quinn called her "pleading doe eyes" on Helen. It was hard to deny the child anything when she pulled that weapon from her arsenal. "I was hoping you might read a little more of *Treasure Island* to me. It's so exciting."

Quinn barely quelled a groan that would have given his hidden position away. Books. Why was his whole family suddenly fascinated by books? It used to be they were happy if he had time to play them a few songs after supper. Now, the three older children weren't satisfied unless Helen read about pirates and buried treasure. It was a wonder they settled down to sleep at all with that nonsense filling their heads. Yet, they enjoyed it so much that he couldn't speak against it. It would have been highly suspicious for him to do so, anyway. More suspicion was the last thing he needed after Helen's discovery that there was not a single bookshelf or book in the house besides the ones that her parents had sent. There was his Nana's Bible, of course, but if he mentioned that she might wonder why she never saw him reading it.

Clara's lips pouted slightly. "Please Aunt Helen? I like to hear you read."

The girl was being a scamp, but he couldn't argue with her choice of flattery. Helen was a good reader. No, she was a *great* reader. She made a person feel like they were part of the story. So much so that he'd found himself caught up in the fantasy, too. That scared him a little. He didn't want to find books interesting because that just meant there was more that he was missing out on. As if the notification he'd originally received about his brother's death, his own marriage certificate and any letters from his in-laws weren't enough.

"Thank you, darling. I'm glad you're so eager to hear more, but you know I can't do that. It wouldn't be fair to the others." Helen lifted an eyebrow and added a hint of mystery to her voice. "There's another reason, too. I'll tell you what it is if you can keep a secret."

"I can keep a secret. What is it?"

Helen whispered rather loudly. "It's past your bedtime."

"That isn't a secret!"

Helen placed a finger over her own mouth. "Perhaps if you're very quiet, Uncle Quinn will carry you back to your room."

Caught, Quinn could do nothing but smile as Helen met his gaze. Clara, at least, was surprised at his presence so he winked at her. "Say good night."

"Night." Clara kissed Helen's cheek then rushed toward him. He lifted Clara into his arms and carried her down the hallway to the girls' room.

Clara automatically started to whisper once they entered her room so as not to wake Olivia. "Uncle Quinn, I don't want to go to sleep. I want to stay awake with you and Aunt Helen."

"But we're going to sleep, too," he whispered as he pulled back the covers and set her on the bed.

Her mouth scrunched into a sideways pout. "It isn't fair. I don't get to see Aunt Helen as much as Olivia and Trent do because I have to go to school. It isn't nearly as fun there without her."

"Well, tomorrow is Thursday. Starting on Friday, you'll have the whole weekend to spend with her." He knelt beside her bed and tucked in her recalcitrant form. "The fastest way to get to tomorrow is to sleep."

"But I'm not finished with today yet." Her long dark lashes closed in a drowsy contradiction.

"Oh, yes, you are." He leaned over to kiss her forehead. "Good night, Clara. Snuggle in tight and tomorrow will be here before you know it."

Her words came out more as a heavy sigh than a whisper. "Good night."

He closed the door behind him quietly and found Helen waiting in the hallway. "Did she settle down?"

"Yeah, she's practically asleep already. By the way, I seem to be missing my bedroll. Have you seen it?"

"I took it apart and washed all of the blankets for you. I was about to bring them out to you." She led the way into the bedroom and grabbed the stack of blankets from the top of the dresser. "You know, Quinn, I still don't like the idea of you sleeping on the floor. This room is plenty big enough for the both of us. We could fit another bed in here across from mine. Perhaps under the window? We could put up a changing screen for a bit more privacy. That way you'd have a real bed to sleep in until the addition is done. Or, if it worked out well enough, you may not have to build anything extra. What do you think?"

The idea of having his own bed and a little privacy again was more than enticing. To tell the truth, sleeping on the floor was getting old fast. It was cold—not to mention uncomfortable—and he had a long way to go on the addition to the house. He'd broken the sod, but that was only step one. He'd need to dig down to the house's foundations, gather stones to lay a new one, build the frame for the floor and the floor itself, the framing for the wall... The list went on and on. It would be expensive, too. He'd known that from the get-go and had been willing to put down the money to secure Helen's place as the mother to his children. Or, had it been out of self-preservation? For his own protection against whatever penance the Almighty might demand for such a blessing? Whatever his motivation, he'd still be building onto the house if he accepted her offer. He just wouldn't have to sleep on the floor while doing it.

He nodded. "I reckon we could try it out, Helen. It will probably take me the weekend to make the bedframe and stuff a new mattress. My first night in here would probably be Monday. Does that work for you?"

"Certainly."

He took a step back toward the door. "Well, I guess I'd better get on back to the floor for now. Thanks for washing these for me. Have a good night."

Quinn determinedly pushed away his misgivings as he reconstructed the bedroll in the living room. God would understand the change of plans. As he drifted to sleep, Quinn repeated that assurance to himself until he began to believe it.

Chapter Eight

After Quinn left her room with the blankets, Helen finally had the time and privacy she needed to read the letter Isabelle had brought from Helen's parents. She picked it up from her nightstand and sat at the small desk Quinn told her had belonged to the cabin's original owner. She'd never seen him use it so she doubted he'd mind if she did. She opened the lone drawer in search of paper and ink. All it held was a dusty Bible and a jumbled assortment of papers so she shoved the drawer closed, gathered writing materials from her trunk and settled back at the desk to read the letter.

From the start of her parents' letter, it was obvious they were shocked by the announcement of her marriage. She'd sent the news by letter, telling them that the wedding had been planned so quickly that she hadn't had time to invite them. She grimaced. That wasn't entirely true. She hadn't told them until after the fact because she hadn't wanted to take the chance that they might try to discourage her from going through with it. They might have humored her by helping her get the teaching job; however, they hadn't hidden their belief that she'd soon tire of it and come home where she belonged. Instead, she'd gotten married.

She was somewhat relieved to find that their only protests seemed to be directed not at the marriage itself, but rather the fact that they hadn't been notified in time to attend the ceremony. Her father didn't try to hide his disappointment at not being able to walk her down the aisle. Her mother, on the other hand, tried to disguise her hurt and confusion at not being invited by offering cautious congratulations. Helen grimaced, feeling downright guilty as those words became more genuine as the letter progressed.

I know that only the deepest love could have moved my daughter to act so quickly to secure it.

"More like the deepest desperation," Helen whispered. "And fear. Fear that I'd never have the chance again."

I remember all too vividly the night your first engagement ended.

Helen froze, seeing the memory play out even as her mother described it.

While your father sent the guests home, I held you and you cried as I have never heard you cry before. It was only then that I realized how deeply that riding accident had scarred you—not just physically, but emotionally.

Helen rubbed her hand across her lower abdomen. She hadn't realized it until that moment, either. Thomas's rejection has confirmed what she'd known since the accident. As normal as she looked on the outside, she was broken on the inside in ways that could never be fixed. Tears filled her eyes as the emotion of that night rushed back to her. She blinked away the blurriness to keep reading.

> *Oh, how feeble my attempts to comfort you seemed then when I told you that he existed—the man who would love you for everything that you are. I cannot express how satisfying it is to see my words come true.*

The words hadn't come true. Not yet. The room partition she and Quinn had decided on was a step in the right direction. He would be physically close by, but what good would that really do? They'd shared a house for a week and were still closer to being acquaintances than they were friends or sweethearts, let alone spouses.

> *I am so proud of you, my darling, for being a woman of integrity. It would have been so easy not to tell Thomas Coyle the truth. Yet, you did. God saw that and blessed you for it by giving you what you truly desired all along—a husband and children whom you love and are loved by. What an amazing testament to His goodness!*

Helen stared at those words until a heavy tear fell and landed on the paper and caused one word to blur. *Integrity.*

She'd always thought of herself as what her mother had described "a woman of integrity," but could she really make that claim now? While she might have told Thomas the truth, she hadn't extended that same courtesy to the man who actually mattered—her husband. Why should she when everything she'd longed for was finally within her reach?

Perhaps because the secret had begun to weigh on her soul. She was so afraid that her faults might make her undesirable as a woman or undeserving of being a mother. No matter how hard she tried to suppress it, it was always lurking in the back of her mind.

Suddenly, she knew. She was going to have to tell Quinn the truth. Her heart slowed to a steady rhythm. For the first time all week her mind cleared. Her eyes widened as she realized what she was experiencing. Peace. She couldn't remember how long it had been since she'd felt this way. Perhaps not since she'd agreed to marry Quinn.

She swallowed hard at the implications of that. She knew that marrying him had been the right thing to do. She *knew* it. Of course, she hadn't exactly asked for God's input or help since then. Now, she was freely admitting she needed help. She might need to tell Quinn the truth, but she didn't want to be foolish about it. She'd pick the opportune time and place for that to happen. To her way of thinking, a few things had to happen first—like them falling in love. And...well, that was pretty much it.

She set her parent's letter aside then dipped her pen in the ink well and began to write out her response. She thanked them for their congratulations before telling them truth about her marriage—that it was a matter of convenience not love. At least, not yet. She carefully blew the ink dry as she contemplated how to finish it.

Quinn doesn't know about the accident and I don't plan to tell him until I'm certain he loves me. I'm sorry if I've disappointed you by sharing this. I just wanted you to know so that you might pray for me—and for Quinn and the children. I have a feeling this road may not be an easy or a smooth one. However, I am holding on to the hope that it will be worth it.

She signed the letter and couldn't help noticing how much better she felt having confessed everything to her parents. Somehow in doing so, it made the task before her seem less insurmountable.

She'd figured out the household chores this week. Maybe she wasn't doing them all perfectly but it was enough to build on. Now was the time to enjoy her family and past time to get to know the man who had become her husband. The man her mother had talked about in the letter. The one who would love her for everything she was—in spite of what she wasn't. Once she knew he did, she would tell him everything. She would. Even though the mere thought of it made her want to run back to the safety of her parents' arms.

Monday evening, Quinn paused outside door of the room he was supposed to share with Helen for the first time. He wasn't at all sure what to expect from her since they'd hadn't been alone with each other since they'd come up with the idea of sharing quarters. He'd made sure of that—not wanting to give her, himself or God the wrong idea about what this move would mean for their relationship. If the perplexed looks she'd been sending him lately were any indication, she'd certainly taken note of the increased distance between them. Hopefully, that distance would make things easier for them both tonight.

The sound of his knock seemed to echo through the heavens as thunder rolled in the distance promising some much needed rain for Quinn's crop of winter wheat. His misgivings swelled as Helen bid him enter, but he did so, anyway. There was no sign of her until he spotted a hint of movement behind the changing screen.

"Quinn, is that you?"

"Yep." He felt heat crawling up the back of his neck. He chanced a glance over his shoulder to find her watching him with a lifted eyebrow as she belted her dark pink dressing gown at her waist. He offered what he hoped was a passable smile. "Are you done in there?"

"It's all yours."

"Thanks." He grabbed his sleep shirt then waited for her to move aside before he slid past her and behind the screen. These things weren't meant for men. He could tell that by the flowery fabric and the fact that it barely came up to his chin. Feeling a little foolish, he changed clothes before leaping under the blanket of his bed as nonchalantly as possible. He stared at the ceiling for a long moment then couldn't resist peeking at Helen again.

She was brushing her hair with a frown on her face. Perhaps she was as ill at ease with this situation as he was. He cleared his throat. "If you're uncomfortable with me being in here, I can leave."

She set the brush aside and turned to face him. "Why should I be uncomfortable? You are my husband, aren't you?"

He felt his jaw tighten. "I reckon so."

"Do you? That's funny. You've been acting more like a stranger than anything else."

There was no way he was going to get into that with her. Not even if she was right. Obviously, this sleeping arrangement had been a mistake. He could only hope that God wouldn't hold it against him. Mindful of Helen's watchful gaze, he grabbed his pillow and a blanket. He only got halfway across the room before she caught his arm. "Where do you think you're going? We aren't finished with this conversation."

"Yes, we are." He shook his head, unable to reconcile the woman standing before him in defiance with the sweet-tempered woman he'd married. "*What* has gotten into you?"

She blinked her long dark lashes then loosened her hold on his arm until it became gentle and disturbing for an altogether different reason. Her tone softened though it retained an underlying strength and thoughtfulness. "I don't know, Quinn. Maybe it's the way you've been avoiding me for the last three days. Even before that, we hardly ever had any real conversations. And now… now, you can't even look at me."

All the charges she laid against him were true except one, so, of course, he needed to focus on that one. "What are you talking about? I'm looking right at you."

"No." She slowly shook her head. "You aren't looking *at* me. You're looking *through* me. You aren't really seeing me at all."

He wished he could say that she was speaking in riddles, but he knew exactly what she meant. He'd been trying to block her out of his senses. It had worked moderately well so far... Well, except for the fact that it had eventually made his normally even-keeled wife madder than a cat caught in a rainstorm. He needed to smooth things over, but how? He could apologize. However, that would probably require a subsequent change in his behavior, which would make it a whole lot harder to stay on the straight and narrow concerning his arrangement with God.

"You're still doing it." Helen crossed her arms and tilted her head. "You're still looking through me."

"Right." He searched his mind for something to say that would make her happy. Thinking wasn't really his strong suit. It was even harder now with her looking at him like that. "Let's sit down and, uh...talk."

He led her to the nearest object, and then hopped back up when he realized that object happened to be her bed. He settled on her vanity stool. That was still closer to her than he wanted to be, so he stood and started to pace. She must have mistaken that for an attempt to escape, for she dashed to the closed door and pressed her back against it to thwart him. Panic tightened his shoulders as she narrowed her eyes at him and seemed to be waiting for something to happen. *Oh, what does it matter? Either way, I'm not getting out of this unscathed, so I might just as well be done with it.*

He let out a short puff of air, braced his feet shoulder width apart and closed his eyes. His ears filled with the sound of the rain's rhythm drumming against the house. That's when he became aware that the scent of his room had changed. It smelled like her. It was a mix of the spiciness of snicker doodles, the clean scent of soap with an underlying trace of some kind of exotic perfume. No doubt it was expensive.

The rain drove harder against the house as he pushed that thought away.

Opening his eyes, he saw the caution in hers. They weren't just ordinary eyes, though. They were the kind he could stare into for hours and still not fully discover all of the mysteries they hinted at. His gaze fell to her lips, so often curving into a smile when she interacted with the children. Now they were pursed slightly to one side in challenge. Her delicately arched eyebrows lifted in a silent reminder that she was waiting on him.

He shook his head. "You're wrong. I may not have been looking, but I couldn't help seeing you…in glimpses."

"Glimpses?"

He stepped toward her. "I've seen your determination and persistence when it comes to the chores."

"You have?"

"Yes." He stepped closer again. "More important, I've seen love, compassion and patience with the children."

Her gaze clung to his. "I do love them."

"Yes, you do, and every day you make life better for them—for me, too." With most of the distance erased between them, he figured he was close enough— probably too close for his own good—so he stopped moving. "I *have* seen you, Helen."

She tucked her hair behind her ear. "Then why don't you show it?"

He frowned. "How do you want me to show it?"

"Let us get to know each other, actually have a relationship."

Thunder crashed above them. It couldn't drown out the sudden aloofness Quinn heard in his own voice. "We agreed to marry for the children's benefit not our own."

"Why do those two things have to be mutually exclusive? It would be to their benefit to have a healthy marriage modeled in their home."

Everything within him quieted at that. He tried the idea on for size and liked the way it fit. It wouldn't work, though. He hadn't asked God for a healthy marriage. He'd asked God for a helpmeet and hadn't even deserved to get that. He glanced up at the rafters shielding them from the storm raging overhead. "What we have will be enough. Mutual respect, shared goals, our love for them…" He trailed off as she began to shake her head. "What, Helen? What more do you want from me?"

"Exactly what I thought I was getting when I married you. A chance for companionship and caring. Perhaps one day even love." The hope that filled her eyes was destined to be disappointed.

No matter how much he found himself longing for the same thing, it couldn't happen. "I can't give you that."

She paled slightly then covered his mouth with her fingers. "Please don't say that, Quinn. You can't mean it. Leave me a little bit of hope."

He took both of her hands in his so that she couldn't keep him quiet. "I do mean it. The truth is I'm n—"

—not worth hoping for, he would have finished if she hadn't kissed him square on the mouth. The rest of the world faded away until it only comprised Helen, him, this moment. Yet, in the back of his mind, he *knew* she was only doing it to shut him up. That frustrated him to no end. Their kisses shouldn't be like this. They ought to be real and true and meaningful.

When she would have ended it, he gathered her closer and kissed her back, the way she *should* be kissed. She caught her breath in surprise then melted against him as the kiss turned into something far warmer, sweeter and gentler than she could have intended it to be. He pulled away once they were both good and breathless. "Look at me."

He waited until her dark lashes swept upward and her eyes focused on his. "Maybe I've no right to tell you what you can and can't hope for, even if I'm certain you'll be disappointed. However, I do have a right to tell you something else, so I want you to listen to me." He lowered his voice and kept his tone gentle yet firm. "This isn't a game between us. If you ever kiss me again, you'd sure as shooting better mean it. Understand?"

That infernal light of hope leaped into her eyes again. That's when he knew he'd done something wrong. It came to him as a flash of lightning illuminated the room. First, he shouldn't have kissed her back. Second, after kissing her he should have backed away, apologized and repented. He hadn't done any of that. Instead, he'd implied that another kiss was inevitable and acceptable. To make matters even worse, he'd done it out loud for God to hear and take notice. He groaned, "What have I done?"

A loud pop and the sound of shattering glass exploded

through the room. Reflexively, he shielded Helen's body with his own until he determined that the danger had passed. He turned in time to see something roll across the floor toward him in the candlelight. He knelt down to find it was a clear orb of ice the size of an apple. His gaze reversed its path to the broken window above his bed while the popping sound surrounded the house. "Hail. It's a hailstorm."

Pounding sounded on their bedroom door. Helen opened it to reveal Reece and Clara standing hand in hand. Clara threw her arms around Helen's legs. "We're scared!"

Reece rolled his eyes then jumped at a crash of thunder. "I'm not scared, but Trent is curled up in a ball and won't move. I promised to get a grown-up."

"I'll go." Quinn put the hailstone in Helen's washbasin before grabbing his blanket and pillow that had fallen to the floor at some point in their exchange. He handed them to Reece. "Hold on to these, son. Helen, get Olivia. We'll wait it out together in the hallway where there aren't any windows."

Quinn found Trent just as Reece had described him. The window was on the opposite side of the room from the bed, which put Trent in the direct trajectory of anything that might burst through it. Quinn situated himself between the boy and the possible danger before rubbing Trent's back. "Hey, cowboy, we're all going to camp out together in a safe place until this nasty ol' storm blows over. We're going to sing some cowboys songs, too. Would you like that?"

The little boy managed to nod.

"How about pretending I'm your horse so we can

ride on out of here?" Quinn let out a sigh of relief when Trent uncurled himself to latch on. They cantered out of the bedroom into the hallway where Helen was getting everyone comfortable and warm. Olivia sat on her hip with eyes alternately widening and drooping from loud noises and sleepiness. Quinn sat down with Trent in his lap. Reece huddled closer to them. Clara moved closer to Reece. Helen and Olivia snuggled in next to Clara.

Helen leaned forward to look down the line. "Is everyone warm enough?"

Reece nodded. "We're getting there."

Trent threw his head back to look at Quinn expectantly. "Trent wants us to sing. What'll it be, folks?"

Clara reached for his hand. He was pretty sure the other one was holding Helen's. "'Old Chisholm Trail,'" she said.

Quinn cleared his throat and began to sing over the sound of the storm. "'Oh, come along, boys, and listen to my tale, I'll tell you all my troubles on the ol' Chisholm trail.'"

Reece and Clara immediately joined in on the chorus. Helen soon caught on and sang in a rich alto that blended nicely with his baritone. The song ended up being a great choice because there were many verses to it. It kept the children so distracted from the storm that they didn't seem to hear the window break in the kitchen or the living room. However, as five minutes turned to ten then twenty without any letup from the hail, Quinn found it increasingly hard to sing.

The wheat crop had been destroyed for sure. There was no doubt about it; and he had only himself to blame.

Chapter Nine

Helen leaned her head back against the wall in the hallway to listen to the hail peter out a good thirty minutes after that first ball of ice had crashed through the bedroom window. This night had not gone at all as Helen had hoped it would. She'd envisioned that she and Quinn would have a nice heart-to-heart chat then go to sleep in a companionable silence. Instead, all the emotions she'd stored inside from her talk with Isabelle, her mother's letter and Quinn's avoidance had swirled together to create a storm that had rivaled the one raging outside. The tension in that room had been palpable, leading up to the argument. It was then that everything Helen had wanted to say for days tumbled out in all the wrong ways.

She could hardly believe she'd been foolhardy enough to try to kiss him into silence. But in the moment, she'd been too desperate to think of anything else. And if she hadn't, she was certain she would have heard him proclaim that he could never love her. She refused to believe that. Besides, *never* was such an ugly word. It

ch as I wish I could turn down
u out of the weather, I'll need
ards in place while I nail them.
s from the barn and meet you

ght to sweep up the glass first. If
they'll come looking for us again
."
eeping while I get the supplies. In
slipped past her into her bedroom
ng his mattress, which he used to
en's rooms. "That should slow them
yell for us. Since they slept through
torm, hopefully they'll sleep through
nails. Besides, this won't take long."
nd that was a good thing because the
for a moment while she held the boards
. With the broken windows sealed up,
ck toward the front door. Helen sud-
Quinn wasn't behind her anymore. She
he'd stopped halfway up the steps of the
Quinn?"
to check the fields."
idened. "Now? Can't that wait until morn-

know." His gaze dropped to the porch
d to know what we're up against, if there's
ft."
he stared in the direction of the fields as
washed over her. How could it never have
er mind that all of Quinn's hard work and

created a life empty of hope—one that was filled with desperation and fear. She knew that firsthand. Her fingers slid toward her abdomen only to encounter Olivia's slightly rounded tummy instead.

A smile tugged at Helen's lips as she leaned down to place a kiss on the sleeping child's head. She peered down the line to find that the children had all fallen asleep curled up together like a litter of newborn kittens. Her focus shifted past them to her husband. He sat with his head in his hand and his elbow braced on a propped-up knee. Her gaze traced the strong lines of his profile. She'd been trying to ignore it since he'd laid down the ground rules for their marriage, but the man was far too handsome for her peace of mind.

He turned his head slightly and pinned her with his cobalt stare. She ought to be embarrassed at getting caught staring at him. She wasn't. After all, what was there left for her to be ashamed of? She'd already all but begged him to give love a chance and had been turned down flat.

His gaze trailed down to her lips before returning to her eyes. She couldn't help remembering that, while she may have started their kiss, he'd finished it with an intensity that her left her breathless. She'd thought he'd experienced the same thing, but that was before remorse had filled his eyes and he'd muttered those simple words of regret. *"What have I done?"*

She kept her voice low so as not to awaken the children. "The hail may be over, but the storm doesn't seem to be letting up. Rain may be getting into the house through the broken windows in our room."

Our room. His slight wince at those words told her

all she needed to know about his intentions of sharing it with her after their argument. He pulled in a deep breath, ran his fingers through his close-cropped brown curls and nodded. "Stay put. I'll inspect the house for damage."

She waited while he checked the children's rooms first then knelt beside her. "It looks like their rooms were spared because their windows didn't face the brunt of the storm. Let's get them back to bed and go from there."

After somehow managing to get all the children tucked in without waking a single one, Helen peered around Quinn's broad shoulder to stare into *her* room. The lantern he held aloft revealed the gaping black hole where the window should be, while a deluge of rain angled through the opening. "Oh, Quinn, your new mattress!"

She rushed forward to save it from being rained on. Quinn's arm snaked around her waist, lifting her off her feet and back to the threshold. "The floor is covered in glass. The last thing we need tonight is for someone to get cut."

She glanced down at her bare toes planted right next to his. "Shoes. They're in the living room by the front door."

"Stop." He caught her arm as she tried to dash away. "Let me check it out first. I think I heard a window break in there, too."

The living room window had shattered completely. Large pieces of glass mixed with rainwater, leaves, broken branches and hailstones to litter the floor from the

their family's livelihood was at stake? What would the impact of this be if the winter wheat crop was indeed lost? She had no idea where they stood financially. She should know. She should have asked. Here, she'd just criticized Quinn for not trying to get to know her, but had she truly taken an interest in anything that mattered to him beyond the children?

"Helen?"

She glanced back at him, saw the worry wrinkling his brow and nodded. "Go. I'll check on the children."

He returned her nod then hurried into the night. Helen found the children still sleeping, seemingly undisturbed by the activity around them, so she changed out of her sodden clothes and built up the fire in the stove to replace the heat that had been lost through the open windows. Her teeth had just stopped chattering, when a blast of cold, wet air announced Quinn's return. He closed the door behind him and leaned against it as rainwater dripped off his clothes and puddled around him. He had to see her standing near the fire, for she'd lit both of the lamps in the living room, but he seemed reluctant to look at her.

Silence stretched between them. It didn't matter. The grim look on his face said it all. They'd lost the crop.

She crossed the living room to meet him at the door. "You must be soaked and frozen through. You should change before you do anything else."

She hesitated only a moment before removing the slouch hat from his head and setting it on the hat rack. She felt his gaze on her as she unfastened the metal buttons of his slicker. He caught her wrist and she glanced up to find regret, guilt and even a hint a fear in his eyes. "I'm sorry, Helen."

"Why? None of this is your fault."

His lips firmed into a straight line. She recognized that look as the one she'd seen on Trent's face when she'd told him not to wander without her permission— stubborn disagreement. He released her wrist to shrug out of his yellow slicker and hang it on the coatrack. "I'll put on some dry clothes."

When he returned, he sat on an armchair near the fire, so she sat on the footrest in front of him. "Tell me."

He ran his fingers through his damp hair and sighed. "It took most of my savings to buy this property and fix it up to the standard it's at today. I invested what was left in the ground with the wheat I planted last spring. It wasn't a big crop, but the fall harvest was good. I reinvested much of the profit from that into the winter wheat. It's gone. All we have is what's left from the fall harvest."

"Will that be enough to last us until the spring?"

"I'll only be planting in the spring. We won't have any real income until I harvest the crop in the fall."

"I see." Her gaze shifted to the fire in the fireplace as she tried not to let her alarm show on her face. "Will we have enough until the fall then?"

"If nothing else goes wrong, if we're thrifty, if we have no other major expenses, we should be fine."

"That's a lot of *ifs*."

"Well, one thing is for sure, there won't be any additions built to this house. At least, not this year. And tonight's arrangement isn't going to work. I'll put the new mattress on the floor out here at night and back in the room during the day."

She'd expected as much so she signaled her agreement with a nod even though he didn't seem to be asking for it. "So we should be fine *if*..."

"Pretty much." He rubbed his stubbly jaw. "I know you aren't used to dealing with anything like this. I don't want you to worry. I'll do whatever is necessary to take care of this family."

"I know you will, Quinn."

He seemed to soak in her confidence before surprising her by reaching down to squeeze her hand. "Good. My family may never have the fancy things in life, but we won't ever have to go without the basics like food, clothes or a solid roof over our heads. I've kept that promise to myself ever since I got my first job working as an errand boy. I'm not going to break it now."

Her eyes widened as compassion filled her heart at the possibility of Quinn as a little boy being hungry or cold. He must have read the questions in her eyes, for he bristled. His jaw tightened as he released her hand. He warded off any comments with the shake of his head. "Forget I mentioned that."

She didn't want to forget it. However, she didn't want to make him uncomfortable, either, so she lifted her brow and offered a smile to ease the moment. "You may be glad to hear that I know a sight more about finances than I did about housework. My parents may be wealthy but they're still careful with their money. They make a budget each month that allows them to run the household, factor in all their expenses and set money aside for—" She froze, blinked. "Me. They set money aside for me. Quinn, I'm such a fool!"

"What? Why?"

"My dowry. It's quite extensive. I need to remind my parents to send it. Our marriage happened so fast and I've been so busy that I forgot about it completely. I guess they did, too." She grinned up at him. "I do believe that solves our problem, Quinn."

"A dowry?"

She narrowed her eyes. "Please, tell me I didn't lose you all the way back there."

"No, it's just…I don't want us taking any handouts from your parents."

She straightened her back and lifted her chin. "It isn't a handout. It's the money my parents have been saving for me since I was born. When we got married, what's mine became yours. So legally it belongs to you, too. We have every right to use it, especially if it's to help take care of the children."

He paused, seeming to consider this. "Well, I reckon if it already belongs to us, it's all right, then."

She opened her mouth to argue, only to close it upon the realization that he'd agreed far easier than she'd expected. Finding him watching her with a slow smile tugging at his lips, she lifted her chin. "Why are you laughing at me?"

"I'm not laughing." The statement was ruined by his chuckle. "I'm just coming to the realization that I married a woman with some fire in her bones. I wasn't really expecting that from you since you're so—"

"Prim, proper and perfect?"

"Yeah." He smiled at the reminder of the interaction

that seemed so long ago now, though it had only been about two weeks.

"Well, I don't know about that. However, I suppose I can get fired up about certain things—like my family." She wanted to add, *And I might even be able to get fired up over you, if you'd let me,* but didn't dare. She'd already pushed him too far too fast during their conversation before the storm. That didn't mean this was over. She wasn't giving up. Somehow she'd get to know her husband, secure her place in his heart and tell him the truth. Right now, however, they had another obstacle to overcome. "I'll write to my parents about the dowry. In the meantime, we'd better finish cleaning up if we want to get any sleep tonight."

Helen was so sure her dowry was the answer to all their problems. Quinn understood that their problems went deeper than that. Or rather, higher. He glanced up at the sky that was still gray and foggy after last night's thunderstorm. Quinn slapped the reins to urge the team down the field. The pressure of the plow caused the matted remnants of his wheat crop to give way to moist brown dirt beneath it, covering the signs of what he suspected might very well be God's punishment for Quinn's impetuous decision to kiss Helen.

He also had a feeling the effect of that kiss on his relationship with Helen would not be so easily or neatly buried beneath the surface as the ruined wheat was. Something essential had change between them. There was a new awareness...connection...openness... He wasn't entirely sure how to describe it, but he was certain that it was going to get him into more trouble. He couldn't afford that. Financially, Helen may have found a way to ease things for their family. Spiritually, Quinn figured he had a lot of work to do to get back on the Almighty's good side. Otherwise, it would all come to naught in the end.

"God, I'm sorry for kissing her." He frowned, realizing that wasn't entirely true. He might as well be honest since God knew his thoughts, anyway. "Well, let's just say that I'm sorry kissing her made me go back on our deal. I repent. If You'll forgive me, I'm more than willing to go back to our agreement."

"What agreement?"

Quinn choked on air at the sound of Helen's voice. He turned to find her trailing after him with Olivia on her hip while Trent lagged a good distance behind, hopping across the upturned mounds of dirt in a game of his own making. Quinn suddenly realized he was no longer holding the reins, so he rushed around the horses to grab their bridles. He gathered the reins and tied them to the plow before turning to face his wife. "You shouldn't sneak up on a man working with horses. It's dangerous."

"I'm sorry." Her lashes lowered innocently. "I would have spoken sooner if I hadn't heard what you were saying."

He squared his shoulders as he sized her up, sass and all. She looked unapologetically feminine in a purple dress with little lacy black bows down the front. Her hair was half up and half down, which seemed to fascinate Olivia, since the girl's tiny fingers were tangled in the shiny brown locks. The wonder on the child's face told him Helen was in trouble. He stepped forward just in time to stop Olivia from giving a mighty yank to the hair in her grasp. "That was a private conversation between me and God."

"About kissing me."

Quinn stared down at her, then cleared his throat nervously. "Did you need something, Helen?"

"Dinner is ready, but I need you to answer my question." She narrowed her eyes and stepped even closer. "What agreement do you have with God and how exactly does it concern me?"

He ought to just go ahead and tell her. In fact, it would probably make things easier for him if she knew. Maybe she'd stop thinking the future could be any different than the present. Since he'd promised to stop ignoring her, it would be great if she could stop being so frustrating, attractive and inquisitive. "I've always done my best to be a good man, to fear the Lord, to make as little trouble for myself with the Almighty as possible. The children came and I found out that it wasn't enough. *I* wasn't enough. I needed something that I had no real hope of getting on my own. I asked God for a helpmeet. He gave me you—and because I knew I didn't deserve you, I promised in exchange that you would be here for the children and only for the children. I went back on that promise by kissing you."

He gestured to the desolate field around them. "You see? All of this *is* my fault. It happened because I was weak. I gave in to…"

"Temptation," she finished for him.

He felt the color rising in his face and he glanced toward the house. "I reckon I should have told you all of this before. I just didn't realize how high the stakes were."

She was quiet for a long time—a really long time. At least, it seemed that way while he was waiting in silence. When she spoke, her words were not at all what he expected to hear. "Quinn, you need to read the Bible."

Everything within him froze. His heart pounded in his ears. "What makes you think I don't read the Bible?"

"Pretty much everything you just said."

Stay calm. Just because she figured out you haven't read the Bible doesn't mean she's figured out that you can't read at all. He swallowed hard. He'd gotten quite adept at tuning out preachers over the years. A habit he'd picked up from so many Sundays trapped in the pew during the fire-and-brimstone sermons his grandmother's favorite minister had preached. Still, he made the only claim that might help at the moment. "I go to church."

Helen touched his arm. "I know you do, but that doesn't replace the need we have as believers to read the Word for ourselves. Why don't you?"

He carefully picked his words. "It's a little hard for me to understand."

She nodded. "That King James English can seem a bit antiquated at times, I will give you that. I have an idea, though. How about we read it together?"

How about let's not? He gritted his teeth to keep those words inside. "I don't think so."

"Please, Quinn. You need to hear the truth about God. He isn't anything like what you described. He isn't trying to punish you. He loves you. I can prove it to you with the Bible. Besides, I haven't been as connected to God lately as I should be, so this would benefit me, too."

He rubbed his jaw as he considered her words. Was it possible that Nana and her minister had been wrong? He didn't like to think so. Nana hadn't always been the easiest person to live with. However, she'd been pretty much all he had growing up with his mother dead, his father and brother gone, and the teasing he'd received for being slow at school leaving him without many friends. Her opinions had been the deciding factor in his life. Was he supposed to abandon all of that because Helen said it was wrong?

Then again, if he was being honest, Helen wasn't the first one to make him question his perspective on God. The few times he'd paid attention in Peppin's church, he'd heard things that hadn't lined up, either. He'd just attributed it to the difference in denominations. What if it was something other than that? Something more important?

"Quinn, what do you say? We can read the Bible this evening after the children go to sleep. Although, it would be nice if we included them in it once a week."

Oh, boy. She had it all planned out now. However, that bit about the children gave him an idea. He watched her carefully to see if his words aroused any suspicion in her. "I suspect you might be able to make it more exciting if you read it out loud like you do those adventure books."

"Then that's what I'll do."

He took a deep breath then nodded. "I suppose we could do it, then."

A slow smile blossomed on her lips and she threw

one arm around his neck in a hug. He started to wrap an arm around her waist to pull her and Olivia closer— then settled for just lightly patting her back. Until he was certain what the truth was concerning God and His expectations, he'd better play it safe. He didn't want to get his hopes up that God wouldn't mind him caring for his wife. He just hoped he hadn't set himself down the path to destruction concerning the reading problem. If Helen found out the truth about that, even God's approval might not be enough to make this marriage work.

Chapter Ten

The boarded-up windows left the kitchen and living room about as dim as Helen felt that evening. In her resolve to find love with her husband, how had it never occurred to her that they weren't connecting spiritually? Her parents had often talked about how praying together had been one of the things that had helped draw them closer during the first few months of their arranged marriage. They'd also encouraged her to read the Bible every day, which was a habit she'd somehow lost after she'd moved to Peppin. Hopefully, all of that would change now.

Reece's heavy sigh drew her attention as she checked on the batch of dinner rolls baking in the oven. "Did everything go well at school today, Reece? No trouble from Jake?"

"Nah. He minds Miss Etheridge because their pa told her to spank Jake if he gives her any trouble." He made one final mark on his slate then glanced up at her. "I'm done. Will you check it for me?"

"Certainly." She added a pinch of salt to the pot of

stew then left it to simmer on the back burner of the stove as she looked over the list of math problems. "You're doing great, honey. Look at the third one once more, though."

He glanced up with a sheepish smile after going through the steps again. "I forgot to carry the two, but I fixed it."

"Excellent." She gave in to impulse and kissed him on the forehead. He ducked his head a second too late to hide his smile. Helen glanced at Clara, who was working on her penmanship. The little girl must have been satisfied with her efforts, for a little smile curved her lips even as faint lines of concentration stretched across her forehead. Trent and Olivia imitated their older sibling by drawing on their own slates. Trent's strokes were slow and deliberate. Olivia's were pure abandonment.

"What?" Clara asked.

Helen blinked, realizing the older two were looking at her curiously. She grinned. "Y'all are so cute."

Clara giggled.

Reece groaned and made a face. "I'm not cute."

"Oh, yes, you are." She slipped into a nearby chair then leaned forward and lowered her voice to capture all of the children's attention. "In fact, I think you have about three seconds before the cuddle monster attacks."

All of their eyes widened. Clara and Reece exclaimed as one, "Cuddle monster?"

Helen nodded. Olivia's shoulders rose in anticipation at the playfulness in Helen's voice as she began to count. "One..."

Clara slowly backed her chair out from under the

table and edged toward the living room, whispering loudly, "Reece, you'd better get Olivia out of her chair."

"Two…"

Reece jumped out of his chair and removed Olivia from her high chair then urged her toward the living room. "Trent, run!"

Trent just stared at her with a serious look on his face that pulled at Helen's heartstrings. *Lord, please let him play. He needs it as much as the others, if not more.*

"Three!" She rounded the table, reaching for Trent. He slipped beneath the table and crawled to safety. She laughed with relief. "Clever boy! I'll get you yet, but first…"

Olivia was toddling toward her rather than away from her, so Helen lifted the girl into the air then kissed and tickled her until she screamed with laughter. Setting Olivia down, she managed to catch Reece next. He was too big for her to pick up, but she hugged him tight then blew a raspberry into his neck before tickling him until he went limp with laughter and ended up on the floor.

"What is going on in here?" Quinn's voice made everyone freeze. They'd been so noisy they hadn't even noticed him come inside for supper.

Clara rushed over to hide behind his leg. "Save me! Aunt Helen turned into the cuddle monster."

"She did?" Quinn lifted an eyebrow at her. Helen blushed and was ready to explain herself, when he gave her a quick wink. "That's funny. So did I."

Clara squealed as Quinn lifted her into his arms, spun her around, dipped her backward then kissed her cheeks. He set the girl down but kept ahold of her so she could regain her equilibrium. "Who's next?"

"Trent." Helen turned to find him slowly crawling toward the door. At the sound of his name, the boy picked up his pace. She was closest to him, so she hurried over to him. He tried to evade her grasp by wiggling like a little worm. "Oh, no, you don't."

She sank to her knees and dragged him back toward her. Trent let out a screech of laughter. She barely had time to pull in a silent gasp before Quinn was on his knees in front of her. Their eyes met, sharing a wealth of hope, desperation and disbelief in an instant. Quinn began tickling the boy, whose hoarse laughter echoed through the otherwise silent room. Then an equally hoarse little voice said, "Stop! Stop!"

Quinn froze at the sound then sat Trent up. Helen couldn't resist taking the giggling little boy's face in her hands to plant a few kisses and raspberries. When she let go, he turned his bashful face into Quinn's chest as his uncle wrapped him in an embrace. Helen felt a small hand on her shoulder and glanced up to find Reece staring down at his little brother. Clara sat beside Quinn, pulling Olivia down to sit in her lap. Trent peeked out curiously as if wondering why everyone was so quiet. Reece sat down beside Helen and captured his brother's gaze. "Trent, you talked!"

Trent froze. His eyes widened in shock then filled with fear. He buried his face in his little hands and began to sob. Helen reached over to touch his knee. "Don't cry, honey. That's a good thing. A very good thing."

Clara inched closer, disturbing Olivia enough for the girl to seek out Helen's lap. "Yeah, Trent. It's good. Say something else. Say my name."

"No, say mine," Reece insisted.

Quinn hushed them both before gently asking, "What's wrong, Trent? Why haven't you been talking to us?"

Between the hoarseness and the crying, it was hard to understand him. "I wasn't supposed to make a sound."

"Why?"

"Mr. Jeff said so."

Helen looked to Quinn. "Who is Mr. Jeff?"

Reece answered instead, clearly in full-on protective big-brother mode. "Jeffery Richardson. He was Pa's assistant. He's the one who brought us here. Why'd he tell you that, Trent?"

"I heard him talking about our inherance."

"Inherance?" Helen narrowed her eyes. "Do you mean inheritance?"

Trent nodded. "He said not to make another sound unless I wanted my brothers and sisters to go away like my parents did. So now…now, you're all going to die!" The last word ended in a wail.

Quinn frowned. "No, we aren't. He can't hurt you— any of you. I won't let him. Besides, he's long gone and good thing, too, because if he wasn't, I'd teach him a lesson he'd not soon forget."

Helen sniffed at the funny smell wafting through the room then gasped. "The rolls!"

She set Olivia on the floor then jumped to pull the baking tin from the oven. Grimacing at the burnt rolls, she set aside the few worth saving as Quinn joined in the kitchen. "What do you make of all of this, Quinn?"

"I don't know anything about an inheritance. It's

never been mentioned before. Not by Richardson or the children."

"I hate to say this, but my first thought was that this Mr. Richardson might have stolen it."

He grimaced. "Mine, too. Why else would he want Trent to keep quiet about it?"

"What should we do?"

"I don't know yet." He watched the children with a furrowed brow. His expression was so fierce, so protective, so loving that she couldn't look away. He glanced at her and his eyes widened before he reached into his pocket to pull out a thick envelope. "Oh, I almost forgot. I stopped by the post office today. They had this for you."

"It's from my parents. Maybe they sent my dowry." She opened the letter to find that a check had been included. She glanced at it before handing it to Quinn so she could investigate the rest of the contents. "It's made out to both of us, so you should be able to deposit it without any problems."

She heard him suck in a quick breath. "Helen, this is too much. Surely your father can't spare this."

"Nonsense. I told you they've been saving it for me." She was surprised to find one sheet of the letter was addressed to Quinn individually while the rest was intended for her. She spared a quick glance at her husband and seeing he was still somewhat dazed by the amount of the check, she scanned his page to make sure her parents hadn't given away her secret. She was relieved to find it was simply a newsy letter welcoming him to the family. They expressed the hope that he would correspond with them so that they could get to know their new son-in-law. It also asked if it would be possible for the family to come to Austin for a reception in Helen and Quinn's honor. "Quinn, they wrote to you."

"They did?"

"Yes, here. They want us to come for a visit." She handed him the page and realized there was another sealed envelope inside the original one. Her name was written on the front of it. She froze as she recognized the handwriting from the myriad little notes they used to exchange despite living in the same city. It was from Thomas Coyle, her ex-fiancé. Why would he write to her after all of these months and why would her parents include his letter with their own? She glanced at Quinn, who seemed engrossed in his own letter. "I'll be right back. I just want to read this really quickly."

"Go ahead." He tucked his part of the letter into his pocket. "I'll get the children to wash their hands and move their schoolbooks for supper."

"Thank you." Moments later, she closed her bedroom door and leaned against it to read her parents' letter for some explanation. She found it toward the end.

I know you will be surprised to find the other letter we've included here. Thomas came to us quite desperate to explain himself and begging for your address. We did not feel it wise to give it to him. However, we promised to include his letter with one of our own. You are, of course, under no obligation to read the letter, but I thought it might help on the off chance you needed closure as much as Thomas seemed to. If not, forgive us for interfering.

Helen set her parents' letter on the desk then sat in the chair to stare at her name printed in Thomas's succinct handwriting on the outside of the envelope. Were her parents right? Did she need to hear from Thomas to be able to put the past behind and move on? She broke the seal on the letter.

A knock sounded on her bedroom door. A hoarse little voice called from the other side of it. "Aunt Helen, we're hungry!"

She smiled. Tossing Thomas's letter in the desk drawer, she closed it firmly. She didn't need closure. The past was over. Her future was on the other side of that door and she wasn't about to ignore it.

Chapter Eleven

Anticipation thrummed through Quinn's veins as he watched Helen flip through the thin leaves of her Bible later that evening. He leaned forward in his chair by the fireplace when her finger trailed down one of the pages and stopped. She glanced up with a hint of nervousness in her smile. He returned it and, though he knew he was on shaky ground when it came to getting through this with his secret and his pride intact, he wanted to ease her mind. "No need to be nervous about this. I want to hear what you have to say."

Relief lowered her shoulders. "Thank you. It's just— I'm no expert here, so I may not have all the right words or the right answers."

"You don't have to." He gave her a supportive nod. "Go on now."

"First, I want to make sure that I understood you correctly when we spoke earlier. It seemed to me that you were saying God had punished you for taking advantage of a blessing not meant for you by sending that hailstorm."

"That's about right."

She nodded. "Well, then. Punishment only comes after someone is condemned, or in other words, judged to be guilty. Right?"

He frowned. "What do you mean?"

"Wouldn't you make sure that one of the children really did something wrong before punishing them for whatever they were accused of?"

"Of course."

"Keep that in mind as I read this. It's from John 3:17. Jesus is speaking and he says, 'For God sent not His Son into the world to condemn the world, but that the world through Him might be saved. He that believeth on Him is not condemned...' Now, you believe that Jesus is the Lord, don't you?"

"Yes, I do."

"Then God is not condemning you, which means you won't experience the consequences of condemnation."

His brain had a bit of trouble wrapping around that. "Why did the hailstorm happen right after I kissed you, then?"

"Quinn, that hailstorm would have happened whether we'd kissed or not. I'm sure the storm had more to do with the season changing from autumn to winter than anything else." Helen tapped the Bible. "God's word, on the other hand, never changes. It says He isn't trying to punish you. In fact, I think He's trying to show how much He loves you."

He gave her a doubtful look. "By allowing our crop to be ruined?"

"Perhaps." She lifted one shoulder in a shrug. "After

all, it did bring you here to this moment where you could hear the truth."

He tried real hard to think that through, but he couldn't help being distracted by the vision sitting across from him. There was something so beautiful about Helen in this moment. Perhaps it was the eagerness on her face, the soft upturn to her lips or the way her pink dressing gown brought out the same shade in her cheeks. Was it talking about the Bible that had put that sparkle in her eyes, or had it always been there?

"Oh, and by the way, Quinn…" She lifted an impervious brow. "I kissed you first."

He tensed as Helen moved from the settee to sit on the footrest in front of his chair the way she had the night of the storm. He really needed to move that thing. He tried not to stare at the Bible in her hands. Surely she wouldn't make him read it. "What does that have to do with anything?"

She gave him a look that made his heart ram against his rib cage. "It means 'the blessing' was not taken advantage of."

"You weren't?"

"No, and, if you insist on thinking of me that way, I won't complain, but there is something you ought to know about God's blessings."

"What's that?" Maybe if he kept her talking she'd forget about the book. Nope. She opened it and flipped a couple of pages over. His hand clutched the arms of the chair, his knuckles turning white. "Helen, you've given me a lot to think about. Maybe we should call it a night."

"One more verse then I'll leave you alone." She angled the book toward the light from the fireplace and began to read. "'Or what man is there of you, whom if his son ask bread, will he give him a stone? Or if he asks for a fish, will he give him a serpent? If ye then, being evil, know how to give good gifts unto your children, how much more shall your Father which is in heaven give good things to them that ask Him?' To whom does the Father give good things?"

"Huh?" He'd been too panicked to pay attention.

"Listen." She read the verse again and asked the same question.

"He gives good things to them that ask Him."

She closed the Bible, much to his relief. "Who asked God for a helpmeet, a mother for his children?"

"I did," he said quietly.

She responded in the same volume. "So to whom did God give good things?"

"Me. He gave them to me."

Silence stretched between them as they stared into each other's eyes. He wasn't at all sure at what point he'd leaned forward during their conversation, but his face was dangerously close to hers. Or, *was* it truly dangerous if God wasn't out to get him? Yet, how did that new information or anything else that Helen said account for the misfortune that had fallen upon his father and brother? He suddenly realized it didn't. They'd done it to themselves. It had been a consequence of reaching out for something they didn't deserve. He would be doing the same thing if he closed the distance between him and Helen.

He leaned back in his chair. Her lashes swept down to cover her eyes, so if she was disappointed it didn't show. Patting his knee, she stood and placed the Bible on the end table next to him. "Now I'm done. Good night, Quinn."

"Night, Helen."

She went to her room without looking back once, which left him free to try to rub at the warm impression her hand had left on his knee. His mind kept replaying that last verse, "how much more shall your Father which is in heaven give good things." It was a nice idea even if it was contrary to what he'd thought he'd known. Imagine—God going above and beyond on his behalf. Was that why God had given him a princess for a helpmeet?

If so, it wasn't fair to Helen or him. Quinn was no prince. Far from it. He'd lived much of his life dirt-poor. Now he made his living out of the dirt as a farmer who might not have made it to his next harvest without an influx of money from his wife's wealthy parents. He was a Christian man who apparently knew very little about his faith. If that wasn't enough, he was uneducated and illiterate.

He set the Bible on his knee. It opened to a place bookmarked by a thin red ribbon. His rough fingers smoothed over the delicate page filled with words. It was a code he'd never learned to crack. He'd always told himself he didn't mind, that it didn't matter. He could no longer pretend. It was torture having so much knowledge, life and truth at his fingertips yet totally unreachable.

At least he now knew that God wasn't waiting to strike him down for his next mistake. That was a relief. However, it didn't really change anything about who he was or what he should expect out of life. He

would never measure up to the man he wanted to be—
the man Helen deserved. That was the truth, too, and
there was no changing it.

"Mama."

*Helen turned her mount toward the distant call.
Peering through the thick forest surrounding her, she
waited for it to sound again. This time it came as a terrified scream. "Mama!"*

*The horse leaped forward as Helen galloped
through the trees, chasing the child's cry. Low-hanging
branches slapped against her face, painting angry
red welts upon her skin. The cries grew louder. She
was close. Suddenly, the ground disappeared before
her. The horse reared backward, searching for stable
ground and throwing her from the saddle. She sailed
through the air.*

*Crashing through prickly bushes, she rolled to a
stop at the base of a tall oak tree. Pain lanced through
her body. She couldn't move. She couldn't breathe. She
could only stare at the branches overhead that were
wide and thick as they entwined to block out the sky.*

*Footsteps crunched through the dead leaves and
stopped. Quinn stood over her. He was so tall, so strong.
His gaze bored into hers with an intensity that made her
shiver. His gaze trailed to her lips and stayed there as
he knelt. She thought for sure that he would kiss her.
Instead, his hands began to probe her abdomen with
enough force to make her eyes smart with pain. His
voice was rough, harsh, unyielding. "Damaged. Damaged. Damaged."*

"No," she whimpered. "Help me. Please."

His lip curled in disgust. "I can't help you. No one can. You did this. You brought it on yourself with your own recklessness."

She grabbed his arm as he stood. "Please, Quinn—"

"No." His gaze was steady. "I don't want you. I will never love you. Now, let me go."

Stunned, she released him. He disappeared, leaving her alone and broken in the silence.

Helen jolted awake, gasping for breath. Her shaking fingers searched the night table for a match. Lighting the lamp beside the bed, she turned it up as bright as it could go to dispel the murky darkness surrounding her. The light couldn't take away the memory of the dream as she lay in bed examining each aspect of it as one might pick at an old wound.

Mama. A child had called her "Mama." Tears pooled in her eyes and spilled down her cheeks. Not even in her dreams had she been able to reach that which she so longed for. Then to somehow confuse the sentiments of her family's doctor concerning her injury with Quinn's face, form and unspoken words. It was too much to bear.

A soft knock sounded on her door. No doubt it was Quinn coming to awaken her as he did every morning. Dashing the tears from her cheek, she called, "I'm awake. You—"

The door opened.

"—don't need to come in."

Seeing she was awake, Quinn stopped in his tracks. "Sorry, I didn't— Hey, are you all right?"

"I'm fine." She threw back the covers then splashed her face with water from the pitcher and bowl on her nightstand to remove the traces of tears from her face. "I just had a bad dream."

"It must have been pretty awful. You look…shaken."

She met his gaze in the mirror as she patted her face dry with a towel. For a moment, the whisper of his words from the dream seemed to fill the room. *Damaged. Damaged. Damaged.*

She couldn't seem to stop the tears from filling her eyes again, so she closed them. She felt his hand on her arm an instant before he turned her toward him and enveloped her in his arms. She rested her cheek on his firm chest, allowing the reality of his strong arms around her to chase away the sinking feeling in her stomach. Of course, if he knew the truth about her, his reaction might be closer to what it had been in the dream. Or, at the very least, closer to Thomas Coyle's.

"Do you want to tell me about it?" His deep voice rumbled in her ear. "That always seems to help the children if they have a nightmare."

She shook her head. "I'll be fine."

He pulled back enough to look her in the face. "You're sure?"

"Yes," she said, though she avoided meeting his gaze. "I'd better get ready. Are you putting in the new windows today?"

"Yep, Rhett is coming by to help me with it this afternoon."

"That's good." She gathered clothes for the day and saw her finished response to her parents sitting on the desk in the corner. Thomas's letter was still in the drawer where she'd tossed it. Perhaps that's what had brought on the dream. That letter she hadn't read. Well, she certainly wasn't going to read it now. "I'd like to mail the response to my parents' letter today."

He scratched the shadow he'd yet to shave from his cheek. "I, uh, haven't written mine yet. I probably won't have time to do it until after I install the windows."

"That's good. You can mail it when you pick up the children from school, then."

He nodded. "Well, I'll let you get dressed."

For an instant, she thought she saw a pensive look on his face. She turned to question it, but he was already out the door, so she let it go and focused her attention on getting ready for the day. Hopefully, it would only get better from here. How could it get any worse?

That odd feeling was back—the one he'd had after Helen had explained why she'd become a teacher. Of course, anyone who'd seen her after the nightmare she'd had this morning would have come to the conclusion that something was bothering her. Whatever it was, she wasn't telling. Not that Quinn had any room to be offended by her secrecy since he was currently holed up in the tack room with her parents' letter. Still, he was concerned and it was distracting him from a very important task.

"Anything else you want me to add to this letter?" Rhett sat on a stool in front of the thin workbench where he worked as a somewhat reluctant coconspirator in the mission to keep Quinn's illiteracy a secret.

"I'm not sure." Quinn left his post near the door where he was supposed to be keeping watch to look at the piece of paper his friend had been writing on. "You're using your best penmanship, aren't you? Helen's folks are fancy people. I want to make a good impression."

Rhett seemed genuinely confused. "I thought you wanted me to be as sloppy as possible so they wouldn't want to write you again."

"Not funny."

"You asked for it."

"Save the jokes for later. Can you read what you've written so far?"

"Sure." Rhett leaned his elbow onto the workbench for a closer look at the letter.

Dear Mr. and Mrs. McKenna, Thank you for the letter. It was kind of you to welcome me to your family. Helen and I accept your invitation to visit—

The distinctive sound of the barn door closing made them both jump. Quinn's heart skipped a beat then made up for lost time by pounding in his chest. He rushed to the partially open tack-room door to peer into the barn. No one was there…which meant someone had been. Maybe Trent had been wandering again. But if so, the boy would have come right into the tack room. That meant the person had probably been… "Helen."

"You don't know that."

"No, but I'd better find out." Quinn jogged through the barn then into the barnyard. The children were playing in the nearby meadow and Helen was walking at a fast clip toward them in a direct line from the barn. Dread slammed into his chest with enough force to ease the air from his lungs in a groan. The sound made Helen hesitate then stop. Slowly, she turned to face him. He swallowed hard, forced himself to close the distance between them, all the while controlling the urge to run the other way.

Use your head, man. Play it safe. Maybe she didn't hear everything. Maybe you can explain it away. He couldn't quite make himself meet her eyes, so he stared at the ground between them. "Were you in the barn just now?"

Her voice was soft. "Yes."

"Did you need something? I was in the tack room. You should have called out. I would've—"

She placed a hand on his arm, mercifully stopping his flow of word. Feeling his jaw tighten, he finally lifted his gaze to meet hers. The surprise and confusion lingering in hers told him she'd heard more than enough to know the truth. "Why didn't you tell me, Quinn?"

"I…I never tell anyone." He gestured toward Rhett, who was giving them wide berth en route to the children. "Well, I had to tell Rhett because I needed someone to read the Bachelor List for me."

"You couldn't read the Bachelor List." The tone in her voice and the widening of her eyes told him that she was finally beginning to understand the immensity of his limitations.

"No, I couldn't." He stepped backward out of her grasp. "Well, now you know."

Turning away, he strode toward the field. Be it pity, disgust, disillusionment or outright laughter; he didn't want any part of whatever might come next from her reaction. At least, not right now. Not while he felt so naked, so ashamed.

"Quinn, wait." That was all the warning he had before she caught his arm and slid in front of him. He stumbled into her and had no choice but to pull her close to keep them both from going down. She frowned up at him. "You've got to stop walking away from me when we have a problem."

He shook his head. "This isn't your problem. It's mine."

"It doesn't matter. We'll face it together. Please, don't walk away from me." Her plea ended in a near whisper as her eyes glistened with unshed tears.

He stared at her in disbelief. How could it be that after finding out the truth about him she had run toward him rather than away? It didn't make sense. Yet, she stood before him looking concerned and hurt. He wasn't at all sure how to respond. "Helen, I need to walk. I need to think."

She looked at him for a long moment then gave a single nod before releasing him. He walked a few steps alone then took a deep breath and did one of the bravest things he'd done since asking her to marry him. Turning toward her, he held out his hand. "Are you coming?"

Chapter Twelve

Without hesitation, Helen slipped her hand into Quinn's grasp. Relief softened his features, prompting a hint of a smile on his lips. She followed his troubled gaze to the wooded hills surrounding the farm. The trees bedecked in sable, orange and yellow leaves contrasted sharply against the somber gray sky. She knew neither of them was truly concerned with the view and merely needed time to gather their thoughts.

The wail of Rhett's harmonica sounded above the wind, reminding Helen of why she'd gone into the barn in the first place. She'd wanted to find out if the men would play together for the children. She hadn't been trying to eavesdrop. However, it had been impossible not to hear what Quinn and Rhett were saying as she'd approached the tack room.

Momentary shock had rooted her in place long enough to grasp a full understanding of the situation. Needing time to figure out what she should do next, she'd left the barn only to have Quinn follow her.

She had many questions but didn't want to make the

situation harder for him by asking them. She was relieved when he broke the silence between them, even if his tone was defensive. "I can't read. So what? Not everyone can. I've managed just fine until now."

If it didn't bother him that he couldn't read, he wouldn't have kept it a secret. She knew that from experience. However, it would hardly help the situation to make him admit his obvious fear and embarrassment. "I know that not everyone can read and write, but why can't you?"

The question seemed to catch him off guard, so she waited while he mulled it over. She saw the moment he settled on an answer, for his features clouded with pain then resignation. He stopped walking, took her other hand in his and looked her in the eye. His voice deepened in all seriousness and sincerity. "Well, Helen, the truth is…I'm just plain stupid."

Her mouth fell open. She stared at him, blinked, shook her head. "What? You don't really believe that."

"I *know* it. Granted, I've gotten pretty good at hiding it over the years, but I am not a smart man. That's just a fact."

"That is *not* a fact."

He released her hands to comb his through his close-cropped curls. "Look, you've got to accept—"

"No, I don't, and neither do you, because it isn't true." She started walking again. "No, there has to be another explanation."

He sighed as he caught up with her. "There isn't. I just couldn't figure it out."

"What do you mean? No one just figures it out. You have to be taught. Did you go to school?"

He grimaced. "Yeah, I went a couple of times. That was enough for me. I hated it."

"Why?"

"After my ma died, Pa couldn't seem to find the strength or will to take care of himself or his sons, so I was a ragged, dirty little thing when I first started going. The other children picked on me incessantly because of it. Meanwhile, the teacher seemed to take an instant dislike to me. Once she discovered reading didn't come as easy to me as arithmetic, she began making pitying remarks about my 'lack of intelligence.' She'd finish my lessons for me because I was 'too slow' even if I was going at the same speed as the others. The other children picked up on it and it only made the teasing worse."

"That's just…*abhorrent*. As a former teacher, I can't imagine doing that to one of my students." Helen shuddered at the thought. Yet, hearing his story gave her insight as to one of the reasons why Quinn had been so passionate about taking proper care of his nieces and nephews. He didn't want them to experience what he had as a child. That brought to mind Reece's attempts to protect Clara from being teased. "What about your brother? Did he try to stop them from teasing you?"

"My brother was six years older than me and had already had his fill of being teased at school himself by that point. After a couple of weeks, I followed his example in refusing to go. That worked until my grandmother came to live with us. She fussed some sense into Pa, cleaned us up and sent me back to school. Nothing at the schoolhouse had changed, so I started skipping again. Pa eventually figured out what I was doing and said if I didn't go to school I'd have to get a job, so I went to work."

Concern furrowed her brow. "How old were you then?"

"Eight or nine."

Her eyes widened. Their lives had been so different. At that age, her only concern had been what dessert the cook would serve at dinner or how to convince her parents to have a tea party with her. Meanwhile, Quinn had been taking on the responsibilities and work ethic of a grown man. "And you never went back to school?"

"Never set foot in one again until the children came to live with me. My brother taught me a bit more arithmetic, but I refused to even attempt the reading and writing. My grandmother tried to teach me when I was older. She couldn't see too well by that point, so I ended up more confused than I'd started out."

"See?" She lightly nudged his arm with her shoulder while not even attempting to temper her triumphant smile. "I told you it didn't have anything to do with intelligence. The problem is that you've never studied with a proper teacher."

It was as plain as the scowl on his face that he knew exactly where she was going with this. "I suppose you think you're the proper teacher for me."

"Well, I am certified to be a teacher even if I wasn't one for very long. As for being proper…" She tilted her head and shrugged. "I do believe you've described me that very way several times in the past."

He caught her arm and, with gentle force, turned her to face him. His pure blue eyes deepened as he searched hers—for what she wasn't sure. However, what she found in his was unmistakable. She saw the pain of old wounds hidden but unhealed, shame at a past foisted upon him then adopted as part of his identity and a desperate hope for something unattainable. In his eyes, she saw a reflection of herself. Yet, even in the face of his compelled honesty, she dared not reveal just how much she could empathize with his struggle, for there was one major difference. He had the ability to change his circumstances. She did not.

Still, he held back, though his scowl softened to a frown as he shook his head. "I appreciate the offer, but nothing doing."

"Why not?"

"It wouldn't work."

She tilted her head as she considered him. The decision to learn had to be his or he would have neither the confidence nor the will to succeed. "Quinn, not once in my weeks of knowing you and living with you has the word *stupid* even crossed my mind concerning you. Don't cheat yourself into thinking that's only because you were good at hiding it. I would have seen the signs of that just as surely as I did for this, even if I didn't know how to interpret them."

He frowned. "You were suspicious?"

"No, but I probably would have been soon enough." She paused, wondering if she'd been inadvertently giving away hints that she had a secret, as well. At least there was little chance hers would be revealed so long as Quinn continued sleeping in the living room. She displaced the thoughts with a quick toss of her head. "That is neither here nor there. What matters is that

I've seen you just as you said you'd seen me the night we— The night of the storm."

A worried look returned to his face. "What do you see when you look at me, Helen?"

"I see an *intelligent* man." She dared to smooth the worry lines from his brow. "A man who is steady, kind, self-sacrificing, talented and…"

He must have noticed the color she felt warming her cheeks, for he cocked his head and edged slightly closer. "And what?"

The word *handsome* hovered on her lips, but she replaced it with a secretive smile before settling on a different word altogether. "Brave. Brave enough to face the mountain of illiteracy and make it a mere stepping stone. I can help you do that if you'll let me."

Though obviously listening intently, he'd glanced away to stare into the distance while she spoke. He released a heavy breath. Finally, he met her gaze again. Reluctance had changed to a hunger she suspected would only be sated by knowledge. Whether he knew it or not, he'd just reached a decision.

If he didn't get his nerves under control, Quinn was sure he was either going to pass out or lose his supper. The sight of Helen spreading out her teaching supplies on the kitchen table sure didn't help his efforts to calm down. He reminded himself that he needed to man up if only because he couldn't take another blow to his pride after being found out yesterday. That on top of needing to ask Rhett for help again and needing Bible lessons from his wife… Well, come to think about it, he didn't really have much pride left to protect. What little was left probably wouldn't survive the night.

Helen had been eager to get their reading lesson under way once the children had fallen asleep. The reading lessons he'd agreed to for reasons he couldn't fathom. As if her knowing about his illiteracy wasn't bad enough. Now she was going to experience his lack of intelligence firsthand. Her words to the contrary had been sweet and inspiring if not entirely accurate. The ways she'd described him had bolstered his courage—perhaps a little too much. Particularly that talk about being brave, since he was pretty near sure she'd been about to say something else entirely.

He couldn't get that secretive little smile or her blush out of his mind. It wrestled for dominance with all the memories of the times he'd tried to learn to read and failed. Well, he hadn't tried that many times, but that was for good reasons. Reasons Helen seemed bent on discovering as she slid a piece of paper and pencil his way. He stared at them. Quinn hadn't asked God for anything since he'd been given Helen. Now might be a good time to try out what he'd recently learned about God's giving nature.

He closed his eyes. *God, I don't think Nana was wrong about You knowing my every thought, even if she was wrong about some other things. The Bible says You give good things to those who ask. It would be a real good thing if You could give me some help...or a way out. I'm not choosy. Please, Lord, I'm asking You to help me.*

He took a deep breath and felt his pounding heart begin to slow to a more relaxed rhythm. This wasn't the end of the world. It was just learning with a new teacher. He could do this. He *would* do this. At least until Helen gave up.

He opened his eyes at the sound of Helen dragging a chair closer to him. She squeezed his shoulder then settled in beside him. "Ready?"

"Yes." *No. Maybe.* He attempted a smile, which she returned eagerly. She was enjoying herself already and the lesson hadn't even begun.

"Before we start, you should know this is going to take time. Don't expect to learn everything overnight. Be patient with yourself."

He wasn't expecting to learn much of anything, so he'd have no problems there. He nearly groaned. Who was he fooling? He wanted to learn to read— desperately. That's why he'd agreed to this crazy scheme. He wanted to know once and for all if there was something truly lacking in him or if, as Helen had suggested, he only suffered from lack of proper instruction. "How much time would it take for me to learn to read?"

"As much or as little as you need. It also partially depends on what you know so far."

"I can write my first name." He demonstrated.

"That's good! Can you tell me the names of the individual letters that make up your name?"

He touched the pencil point to the paper beneath the first letter. "*Q-u-i-n-n.* Quinn. That's it. That's all I know. No. Wait. I don't know what this letter is called, but it's how your name starts. I remember because it sort of looks like a longhorn."

She laughed. "I've never thought about it before but you're right. It does. That's an *H*."

"How many other letters are there?"

"There are twenty-six letters in the alphabet. They look like this." She wrote them out across the top of the paper for him.

He gave a low whistle. "How am I ever going to remember all those?"

"You already know a few of them. Can you find the letters in your name among the others?"

"Yep." He pointed each of them out as he found them. "That's strange. The *Q* doesn't seem to be here."

"This is the *Q.*"

"Why does it look different?" He couldn't hide the alarm in his voice. "Have I been writing it wrong all these years?"

"You've been writing it correctly. Each letter comes in two forms—uppercase and lowercase. We usually use the uppercase form to start a sentence or a name. That's why these are both *Q.*" She wrote the uppercase letter directly over the lowercase then did the same with *H.* "These are both *H.*"

He stared at the paper, wondering what the other uppercase letters looked like. First... "Show me the rest of the letters in your name."

She did so, filling in the uppercase forms of those letters as she went. Then he asked her to do the same with the names of Reece, Clara, Trent and Olivia. There were still some letters to uncover, but he slid his paper toward Helen. "Can you write our family's name all together in one place?"

She smiled and slid the paper back toward him. "I think it would be better if you did. I'll spell them out for you. Remember that with names the first letter will be uppercase and all the rest will be lowercase. You already have your name written down, so suppose we start with mine."

It must have taken a while with her telling him the letters, him finding them on the list and then learning how to write them. However, before he knew it, he had all of their names written on his paper. The letters were big and a little misshapen. Yet he couldn't help feeling a sense of pride while looking at them. He sent a self-deprecating smile to Helen. "It's kind of sloppy."

She returned his smile with tears in her eyes as she shook her head. "It's beautiful."

"What about the other letters? There are still a lot of them I don't know and I want to see their other forms."

"Then let's go over them." She went through the alphabet, filling in their uppercase counterparts and teaching him how to write both forms of the letters.

By the time she was finished, Quinn felt himself drifting toward confusion. "I'm never going to keep them straight even if I manage to remember them."

"Sure you will, because I have a song that will help."

"A song?" He couldn't help perking up at that.

She winked. "I thought you'd like that. It's called 'The Alphabet Song.' As you sing, I want you to focus not just on the melody or sequence of the letters, but on remembering what each looks like. Got it?"

"Yes, but will I be able to play it on my banjo?"

She laughed. "I have no idea. Maybe. Now listen, repeat after me and do as I do. Ready?"

"Yep."

She touched the appropriate letter when she sang it. He repeated after her, copying the melody and her actions as she walked him through the song. They did the same thing twice more. Then they sang it together. Finally, he sang it on his own. She clapped for him when he finished, though she did so softly so as not to disturb the sleeping children. "Bravo, my good man."

He managed a small bow even though he was seated at the table. "Thank you. What now?"

"That's all for tonight. You've accomplished a lot and I don't want to overdo it on our first lesson. However, you should know that I am thoroughly impressed with you."

"You are?"

"Most definitely." She yawned and he realized that he'd been so involved with the lesson that he hadn't noticed how late it was getting. "You catch on quickly."

"I do?"

Her heavy lashes blinked drowsily. "You do. Now it's time for sleep. Morning will come early and you'll want to be rested for our lesson tomorrow. Good night."

"Wait." He stood with her then lifted her chin so that her gaze focused on his. "I said it earlier in jest. I want to say it again from the bottom of my heart. Thank you. I never thought I'd be able to learn even this much. Now I'm beginning to think that maybe I can do this, after all."

"Then you'd be right."

It would be so easy to taste the sweet smile blossoming on her lips, but he doubted that she'd want him to. Sure, she'd kissed him once before, but that had only been to shut him up. Besides, as wonderful as she had been about his illiteracy problem, it had to have lowered her opinion of him—even if she didn't show it. In fact, she probably *wouldn't* show it so as not to make him feel worse about himself. That was just the kind of thing she would do because she was smart and patient and far too good for him.

Pulling in a deep breath, he released her chin and let her retire for the night with nothing more than a softly spoken good-night. He sat back down at the kitchen table to stare at the papers on the table—papers on which he'd written letters he now recognized. Something within him quickened. He may not deserve Helen now, but if he could learn to read…perhaps he could earn her.

Why hadn't he thought of that before? Surely, if he made himself a better man, he'd deserve better things and he wouldn't have to worry about ending up like his father and brother. It would need to be more than just learning to read, though. He'd need to become a better Christian, father and husband. It wouldn't be an easy task. Yet, if it would give him a chance to earn Helen, then he had to take it.

Chapter Thirteen

Two weeks after Quinn's first lesson, Helen cleared the books and paper he'd been using from the kitchen table to make room for breakfast. She'd just set them on the end table by the settee when he clomped in from outside with an armful of wood for the stove. He stacked the logs in the wood box. "Sorry about that, Helen. I meant to move them before I left."

"No problem." She returned to the stove and began cracking eggs into a bowl. "How late did you stay up last night?"

He scratched his jaw. "I think I went to sleep about one."

"Quinn—"

"I know. It's just that I get caught up in practicing what you teach me, then I look up and hours have gone by." He gave her a confident grin that set his dimples winking. "Did you see my handwriting? It's improved a lot, hasn't it?"

"It certainly has." How could she chide him when he was so eager to learn and please? He was blazing through the process so quickly that she was afraid he'd burn out. Every spare moment not consumed by the children or the farm was spent in her teaching him or him reviewing what he'd learned. There seemed to be a lot of spare moments lately with the winter wheat no longer in the ground. He also hadn't made any mention of adding on to the house though there were plenty of funds for him to do so. However, rather than finding encouragement in that, Helen suspected it was only a side effect of his determination to conquer reading and writing.

Helen reveled in his every accomplishment and enjoyed seeing the confidence he was gaining in those subjects spread to other areas of his life. Yet she couldn't shake the nagging fear that she'd relegated herself to becoming merely a teacher in his eyes. She wanted to be more than that, but she didn't feel as though she was making much progress in that respect. She was getting impatient and frustrated with herself. After all, how long had they been married? Shouldn't they be further along in their relationship than this?

"I'll awaken the children."

She nodded, deep in thought as she whisked the eggs together with some seasoning. A month, she realized. They'd been married for one month today. It wasn't that long. Just long enough for her to become a little discouraged that she'd never be able to convince Quinn to love her. Maybe she needed a change in her perspective or just a change of scenery. She hadn't left the farm except to go to church on Sundays since she'd married Quinn. If she gave in to this sudden craving for a few moments to herself, would she be a horrible wife and mother?

She certainly felt like one during breakfast when she announced her plan to go to town alone. The children from oldest to youngest followed their uncle's lead in setting down his fork to stare at her. Quinn wiped his mouth with a napkin and frowned. "There's no need for that. I'd be happy to go to town to get whatever you want."

"I know you would, but I'd like to get it myself." Particularly since she hadn't decided on what exactly she'd be getting yet.

Clara leaned across the table with dancing blue eyes. "Will you bring us back a surprise, Aunt Helen?"

"I certainly will."

Quinn's acquiescence was a bit grumbly. "I'll saddle one of the horses."

"Actually, I'd rather drive the wagon than ride." The doctor had ordered her not to ride again after that fateful accident. Out of concern, her parents had enforced that rule. Helen wouldn't feel comfortable enough to ride to town alone on a horse even if she'd wanted to—which she didn't. Thankfully, Quinn didn't find the request odd. He just nodded and that was that. Soon Helen put on her hat and coat then kissed the children goodbye before walking to the wagon Quinn had readied for her. He helped her onto the seat then handed her the reins. "You won't be gone too long, now, will you?"

"I'll be back before you know it."

"We'll be waiting." He backed away to watch her go. She glanced back as she neared the turn that would soon hide the house from view. The sight of Quinn waving at her with the children lined up beside him made her want to turn the wagon around right then and there. How could she leave them, if only for an hour or two?

No, she was being silly. She'd cure her case of cabin fever and be back home in no time at all. She answered Quinn's wave with one of her own then focused on the winding road before her. It wasn't long before she strolled into Peppin's bustling mercantile. The owner's daughter, Sophia Johansen, welcomed her with smile. "Hello, Helen. What can I do for you?"

"I'll take twelve ounces of candy corn."

"Sure thing."

Isabelle sidled up to the counter beside Helen. "Sophia, do you have any of my mother's favorite tea in the back? There's none left on the shelf."

"I'll check." Sophia handed Helen the candy corn in exchange for payment.

"Thank you!" Isabelle turned to Helen as Sophia disappeared into the stockroom. "This is a nice surprise. What are you doing in town?"

Helen shrugged. "Cabin fever set in."

"You made it about a month. Not bad for a former city girl." Isabelle glanced around the mercantile. "Where are your husband and the little ones?"

"I left them at home."

Isabelle smirked. "She said guiltily."

"I feel awful." Helen grimaced. "You should have seen them when I left. It was as if they thought I would never come back."

Isabelle only had time to make a sad face in sympathy before Sophia returned with her order. At that instant, Helen felt a soft touch on her back and turned to find Ellie grinning at them. "So many of my good friends all in one place. Why didn't anyone tell me there was going to be a party?"

Helen laughed. "It wasn't intentional."

"Says who?" Sophia asked. "Whenever I'm bored, I pray for company then wait to see which one of my friends will show up."

Isabelle gestured to the busy counter where Sophia's father, Mr. Johansen, and brother, Chris, were dealing with customers. "It looks like you have a lot of friends, Sophia."

"That's why my father keeps me around." Sophia winked as Isabelle paid her bill. "What can I do for you, Ellie?"

"Not a thing. Lawson is the one with the list and I think Chris is helping him. Hey, all of us being in one place is too good an opportunity to pass up. Why don't we go across the street for some of Maddie's pie and coffee."

Helen and Isabelle quickly agreed. Sophia declined since she had work to do. After Ellie arranged to meet her husband later at his parents' house, they settled in at a table in Maddie's Café. Ellie's warm green eyes focused on Helen first. "So you're in town alone?"

"Yes." Helen shot a quick glance at Isabelle, who patted her arm.

"And she feels guilty about it. Ellie, tell her she shouldn't."

"Why don't you tell her, silly?"

"She's more likely to believe you because you've been married longer than her."

"Just a minute." Helen set her cup of coffee down

with mock indignation. "Ellie only beat me to the altar by a week."

Ellie waved off her protest. "Listen to some advice from a mature, married woman." She waited until they finished laughing before she continued. "Actually, it isn't from me, but from my sister Kate who's been married more than ten years. It's permissible to take some time for yourself every once in a while—healthy, even. Stop feeling guilty, Helen."

"Yes, ma'am."

Maddie brought them three slices of pecan pie and the conversation lulled as they dug into it rather enthusiastically. Ellie set her fork aside long enough to ask, "Helen, what's it like being a mother to four children from the get-go?"

She felt herself beaming. "It's more wonderful than I ever dreamed. It's also harder than I imagined. Just keeping up with all of them can be a challenge sometimes. Each one has their own little personality that's so fun to see developing. Reece is the protector. Clara is just a sweetheart to everyone. Trent is the deep thinker of the group, even at four years old. Baby Olivia is always a smiling little ray of sunshine."

Isabelle smiled. "They think the world of you. I can tell that just from seeing y'all together at church."

"Well, I think the world of them, too."

"Aw. That is very sweet," Ellie said, then tilted her head. "What about Quinn? How are things going with him?"

"He's doing well." Helen sorted through what she could and couldn't say since she wasn't sure he'd want anyone to know she'd been tutoring him. "We've been able to spend more time together recently, so that's been nice."

Isabelle shook her head. "It seems like everyone is getting married all at once. First, you, Ellie. Then Amy. Then Helen. All back to back. I have to admit, y'all have me curious as to what all the fuss is about."

Helen lifted a brow. "Curious enough to try it yourself?"

"Perhaps one day. Of course, there is a little matter of finding the right groom. None of the boys in town seemed the least bit interested in me when Amy was around. There was something about her that drew them like bees to honey."

Ellie nodded. "I think you're right about that, but she's gone now. That ought to change things."

"I think it did." Isabelle blushed.

Helen's mouth dropped and she exchanged wide-eyed glances with Ellie before turning back to Isabelle. "You've got a beau. Who is it? Rhett?"

"What? No! I don't have a beau. If I did, it certainly wouldn't be Rhett. Why would you guess him of all people? Everyone knows he was in love with Amy."

Ellie just smiled and ignored the protests. "Helen, what made you think of Rhett?"

"He drove Isabelle to my house once and I detected a certain something in the air."

Isabelle rolled her eyes. "Manure most likely."

"Methinks the lady doth protest too much," Helen murmured over her coffee.

Ellie shuddered. "Please, no Shakespeare. It brings back memories of a certain pig farmer who shall go unnamed."

Helen sent a sly grin to Isabelle. "Which is funny because the quote is from *Hamlet*."

"You, stop it." Ellie glared then turned to Isabelle. "Who did you mean if not Rhett?"

"I only meant that men in general seem more interested in me now that Amy is gone. Now, let's change the subject. So, Ellie, how is married life?"

"Beyond amazing."

"How so?" Isabelle asked with a laughing glance to Helen. They both knew Ellie wouldn't have let Isabelle off so easily if the conversation had changed to any other subject.

"I thought my relationship with Lawson was special when we were just friends, but it can't even compare to this. That isn't to say that it hasn't been an adjustment. Learning to live with someone, sharing everything, has been challenging at times. However, at the end of the day, there's nothing like being held by the man you love and knowing beyond a shadow of a doubt that you are loved in return."

Helen felt her breath hitch painfully in her chest. The pie might as well have turned to dust in her mouth. She washed it down with a sip of coffee. Isabelle's concerned look only made it worse. Ellie was oblivious in her dreamy state and kept going.

"The best thing is seeing how that has affected both of us. It's—" Finally realizing the mood had changed, Ellie stopped and looked back and forth between her friends before settling on Helen. Dismay parted her lips. "Oh, Helen, I'm sorry. I didn't mean to—"

"There's no need to be sorry. Why did you stop? I was listening." Helen realized she was fooling no one when Isabelle handed her a handkerchief. "I'm not going to cry. Or, at least, I wasn't until you gave me this silly thing."

"Lawson and I have been praying for y'all ever since my visit."

Isabelle nodded. "So have I."

Ellie tilted her head. "I asked a question earlier I think bears repeating. How are things with Quinn? Give us the real answer this time."

"It isn't bad. Truly, it isn't. At first, I thought that falling in love would be easy for us. After I found out he wasn't inclined to allow that to happen, I guess I thought I could make him love me. The problem is, I don't really know how to do that." She shrugged. "He cares for me, I think. That's about as far as it goes. I keep hoping that circumstances will draw us closer and they seem to in the moment, but there is no lasting change as far as I can tell. Like I said, I don't know what to do."

Ellie reached over to cover Helen's hand. "Will you take some advice from a fellow newlywed?"

"Of course."

"Stop trying." Ellie softened her words with a smile and shook her head. "You can't *make* someone love you."

Helen stared at her. "Then you're saying it's hopeless."

"No. I'm saying stop trying to do this on your own. God can and will help if you let Him. In fact, we can take our lessons of love from Him. He proves His love over and over, but He doesn't force anyone to accept it. He just…loves them. That's it. End of story. That's all you can do with Quinn. Focus your thoughts, attention and time on loving him. Stop trying to *make* love happen and *let* it happen through you."

Helen stared into her nearly empty coffee cup, trying to ingrain Ellie's words on her memory. "Stop trying. Let it happen through me. I think I understand."

Ellie tilted her head, then narrowing her eyes, she searched Helen's face. "*Do* you love him, Helen?"

"Do I..." Finding she wasn't ready to answer that question, she asked another instead. "Why do you ask?"

"Because it isn't fair to ask him for something that you aren't willing to give in return." Ellie's smile was gentle yet her words revealed a hard truth that Helen couldn't deny.

She didn't want to love Quinn. Not yet. For no matter how much she'd convinced herself love would make the difference, she'd never be completely sure until he did, in fact, love her. She'd been guarding her heart without even making the conscious decision to do so, waiting for Quinn to fall in love first. It was the smart thing to do. She now realized it was also selfish. What's more, it wasn't working.

Stop trying. Let love happen through you.

It was good advice, but was she brave enough to use it?

Quinn leaned forward in the church pew soaking in every word of Pastor James Brightly's sermon the next day. The man was less than ten years older than Quinn's own twenty-six years of age. Yet his style had a dynamism that reminded Quinn of a tent revivalist his grandmother had taken him to many years ago. Without the fire-and-brimstone flare, that is. The past two weeks

Pastor James had been preaching things that Quinn had never heard—or, at least, paid attention to—before.

"How does God see us now that we have been restored to him through faith in Jesus Christ? Are we still enemies of God as we read earlier in Romans 5:10? Not at all! If you'll turn with me to Ephesians 5:25, we find that he sees us as a groom might see his bride. It says, 'Husbands, love your wives'—now, I could teach a whole sermon on that."

While chuckles echoed through the church, Quinn glanced down the pew to where Helen sat with Olivia in her lap three little fidgeting bodies away. Loving her had never really been part of their deal. Yet he suddenly knew that was exactly why he'd been working so hard to be a better man. He'd wanted to level out things between them so that they could have a chance at love. *Turns out that's a pretty good thing since the Bible commands me to do it.*

Quinn refocused on the pastor as the man continued, "'Even as Christ also loved the church, and gave himself for it, That he might sanctify and cleanse it with the washing of water by the word.'"

Quinn flipped through the Bible clutched in his hands wondering where he might find the scripture. Ephesians started with an *E*. Was the next part an *F* or a *PH*?

"Notice it is Christ who is doing the sanctifying and cleansing. It isn't something we are able to do on our own no matter how hard we might try. It's by God's grace and comes through Christ with the washing of water by the Word. And what is the Word?"

"The Bible," Quinn called out before realizing this

wasn't a tutoring session with Helen and the question had been rhetorical. Folks turned to look at him while he shot a wide-eyed look at his wife. She looked just as surprised at his outburst as he was. Her shoulders lifted in tandem with her eyebrows as she tried to suppress her amusement by pressing her lips together.

The pastor had no such compunction on containing his grin as he moved from behind the pulpit to point at Quinn. "Exactly! The Word of God. Every time you read the Bible you are allowing Christ to wash you in cleansing water. But why? Is He doing this just for the sake of doing it? No! There is a purpose."

Pastor James took up his Bible. "It's revealed in the next verse. 'That he might present it to himself a glorious church, not having spot, or wrinkle, or any such thing, but that it should be holy and without blemish.'"

Quinn sighed, realizing he had a lot more Bible reading to do if he wanted to be part of the glorious church the scripture talked about. Still, he enjoyed hearing about God's free, all-encompassing love for him even if he was having some trouble adjusting to the idea—especially since he hadn't had much experience with that type of love before. Perhaps he'd seen shades of God's kind of love from Helen. Not that she loved him, but she accepted him and was helping him overcome his limitations. That had to mean something. Whether it did or not didn't change the fact that the Bible commanded him to love her. How was he supposed to go about that exactly? It wasn't as if he had much experience wooing a woman. All right, so he hadn't had any experience.

He was jolted from his thoughts when Pastor James shook his hand heartily on the way out. "Quinn, I sure do appreciate you participating in the sermon. It really helps to know someone is listening and as involved with what I'm saying as I am. I pray your enthusiasm spreads to the rest of the church."

Quinn wasn't sure how to say his participation had been more of an accident than anything, so he just murmured something in agreement as the man moved to the next parishioner. Seeing Helen's arms were free since all of the children had rushed outside to play, Quinn offered her his arm. She took it as they strolled toward the door. "It looks like you started something, Quinn."

He shook his head. "All because I forgot I wasn't at our kitchen table."

"I thought that was it." She laughed. "Maybe I've been testing you too much."

"No. It's good for me." He held the door open for her to precede him outside. It was warm for November. Quinn wouldn't be surprised if it was seventy degrees. His nieces and nephews seemed to revel in the fair weather as they played on the church lawn with the young Rutledges.

Helen paused. "Oh, there's Kate Rutledge. I'd better make sure Ellie told her sister she invited us all over to the ranch for dinner."

"Go ahead. I've been meaning to talk to the sheriff about what Trent said a while back about Jeffery Richardson."

"That's a good idea. You'll let me know what he says?"

"Of course." Quinn waited until she left before making a beeline for Ellie's brother.

His neighbor listened carefully as Quinn related

Trent's tale. "Hmm. That does sound suspicious. I'll contact law enforcement in Alaska to see if they have any information about Jeffery Richardson or what might have happened to your brother's estate."

"I'd appreciate that." Quinn took a deep breath then pushed aside his inhibitions. "This isn't related to what we've been talking about, but I was wondering if you could give me some advice."

"I can try. What do you need advice on?"

"Marriage."

Sean lifted a brow. "I don't pretend to be an authority on the subject since I've only been married about a year and a half. Still, I'd be happy to share what I've learned."

Lawson appeared at his brother-in-law's side. "Sorry for butting in. I was passing by and heard you mention needing advice on marriage, so of course, I had to stop. I figure I'd probably benefit from whatever Sean had to say, too."

Sean combed his fingers through his dark blond hair and grimaced. "Great. No pressure. So what's the problem, Quinn?"

"I wouldn't say there was a problem exactly. It's just that verse about husbands loving their wives made me think. Helen and I got married pretty quickly, so there was no wooing period for us. Now I believe that maybe there should be, only I don't know how to go about it."

Sean nodded thoughtfully, then said, "There are the general things like finding something that you enjoy doing together."

"I think we have that." He was pretty sure she enjoyed teaching him and he enjoyed learning from her. "What else?"

"You can do small things to show her that she's special and you're thinking about her, like giving her genuine compliments and giving her flowers."

Despite the warmer weather today, most of the flowers had long since faded. He wasn't sure simply saying she looked nice would have the result he wanted. "I can try those things, but I want us to become closer, more connected to each other."

Lawson tilted his head. "Chemistry. Is that what you're talking about? You want to build chemistry?"

"I think so."

Sean grinned. "That's a whole other animal. Lorelei and I had sort of a love-hate type of thing going on between us at first. We were both too stubborn and afraid to admit we were attracted to each other. We traded barbs whenever we were forced into each other's company. Once we fell in love, those barbs changed to banter. It can get pretty spirited at times. Anytime I want to spice things up I use that. It's always good for a kiss or two."

"Ellie and I started out from a completely different place than Sean and Lorelei since we'd been good friends for a long time," Lawson contributed. "I guess that's why she seems to get a kick out of flirting with me. Truth be told, I feel the same way."

"Banter and flirt." Quinn grimaced. "It sounds complicated."

Lawson shrugged. "My matchmaker of a wife once told me that every couple has a unique chemistry. You just need to find out what works for you."

"Remember, at the end of the day, a woman just wants to feel loved," Sean added. "There are a lot of ways you can show her you care. Have fun with it. Be creative. You may be surprised by what you can come up with."

Even as he agreed to try, Quinn wasn't so sure it would work. He was attracted to his wife. He just wasn't sure she felt the same about him. He might not know much, but he was pretty sure that mutual attraction was an important part of courting someone. She'd seemed open to deepening their relationship that night of the storm. However, a lot had changed since then.

He wanted the type of closeness he saw between these men and their wives now that he knew God wouldn't punish him for it and now that he was endeavoring to deserve her love—a love that didn't yet exist. It would go on not existing unless he did something about it. A sense of foreboding settled on his chest right there in the church yard. Was God trying to warn him that he was heading straight for trouble just like his brother and father before him? Had they felt this same way before they'd started their journey—excited and nervous all at the same time? If so, they'd pushed on, anyway…as Quinn intended to do.

Of course, they'd ended up dead. Quinn would just have to be more careful than them if he didn't want to get hurt in some way. He knew just how to do it, too. He wouldn't even broach the subject of love until he was certain he deserved her. Surely that would make things easier for both of them. Or, at the very least, safer for him.

Chapter Fourteen

As if Helen wasn't nervous and edgy enough from
her talk with Ellie and Isabelle yesterday, now she had
to deal with Quinn sending her inscrutable glances as
he drove them to the Rutledge ranch for dinner. Her
nieces and nephews had chosen to ride in the wagon
with the four Rutledge children, leaving nothing to fill
the air between her and Quinn except a rather uncomfortable silence. At least, it was uncomfortable to her.
She wasn't entirely sure whether or not Quinn noticed
since he seemed unreachably deep in thought.

She supposed she couldn't fault him for that since
she'd been doing more than her share of deep thinking
lately. She'd arrived at the conclusion that she would follow Ellie's advice and allow herself to fall in love with
Quinn. However, she'd also realized there was a big difference between deciding on a course of action to take
and actually starting down that path. To put it plainly,
she was scared out of her wits. What if she fell in love
and he didn't? Or, they both fell in love but it wasn't
enough? Or, what if love was enough for the meantime

but not enough later when the truth finally came out? It was impossible to know for sure that he'd never resent her for her inability to bear children.

"Helen, we're here."

She glanced down to find Quinn waiting to help her down from the wagon. She blinked. "Oh. I guess I was woolgathering."

Ellie appeared at Quinn's side with a large picnic basket in hand. "It's too nice of a day for that, Helen."

"Are we all going on a picnic?" Helen asked as she made it safely to the ground.

"No. You and Quinn are going on a picnic alone."

"Alone?" Alarm widened Helen's eyes. She had been counting on the company of the group to ease the tension within her. "But the children—"

"The older ones are already heading to the hay fort my brothers built in the barn and the younger ones will be inside with Kate and me. They'll have dinner with us later, so you two will have plenty of time alone."

Helen narrowed her eyes at her friend. "You were planning this when you invited us over here, weren't you?"

"Of course." Ellie's green eyes sparkled. "I'm just glad the Lord provided such good weather for it."

A hint of a smile tugged at Quinn's lips as he took the picnic basket Ellie offered. "Where is this picnic supposed to take place?"

"The creek probably has the best view. See that little break in the tree line? The path there will lead you straight to it. Go on now. There won't be many more days like this, with it being November." Ellie's wink encompassed them both. "Best make the most of it."

"Thanks, Ellie." Quinn caught Helen's hand and tugged her toward the tree line. "We'll see you later."

Helen sent him a suspicious sideways glance as she followed him. He seemed awfully eager all of a sudden, and he was holding her hand instead of letting her take his arm as he usually did. What was going on?

She hadn't figured it out by the time the path ended in a clearing where a thin veil of bronze leaves covered the ground. Water cascaded down a short waterfall to make the creek's surface a rippling mirror of the blue sky overhead. Meanwhile, an intermittent breeze set the leaves in the trees trembling as they provided a golden backdrop. Awed by the sight, Helen stood near the banks of the creek and pulled in a deep breath then wrapped her arms around her waist. "I had no idea this place would be so breathtaking in the daylight."

"Hey, this is where it started." Quinn came to stand slightly behind her.

"This is where what started?"

Warmth filled his deep voice. "Us."

She turned to face him and the gentleness in his eyes made her heart lurch, shaking the walls she'd built to guard it. She tilted her head. Allowing a smile to touch her lips, she lifted a brow. "You mean, this is where you dragged me into a freezing creek."

He chuckled as he eased even closer. "I thought you looked pretty all mussed up."

"I looked half-drowned which I was." She swallowed. Was that really her voice sounding all soft and breathless?

"No, I remember distinctly. You had a trace of mud

right here." His fingers traced a light trail across her cheek.

"I did not."

"No, I guess you didn't." He let his hand stray toward the loose chignon at the back of her head. "Well, I know for sure that your hair was more like this…"

She noticed the mischievous look in his eye only an instant before she felt one of her hairpins being tugged free. She batted his hand away and covered her hair while retreating a few steps from the creek. "Don't you dare, Quinn Tucker."

A lazy grin revealed his dimples. "You were the most beautiful woman I'd ever seen."

She froze and stared at him. "I was?"

"Yes, even though you weren't very nice to me that night."

"I was, too."

"No." He crossed his arms, which somehow only made them look more powerful. "You said I reminded you of a bear and desperately needed a shave and a haircut."

She kept her tone solemn even as she felt her eyes begin to dance. "But you *did* remind me of a bear and you *did* desperately need a shave and a haircut."

He growled.

She held up one finger. Widening her eyes, she glanced at the woods surrounding them in fear. "Did you hear that?"

"Hear what?" His entire body tensed while his boots spread into a protective stance as he scanned their surroundings.

"I don't know. It almost sounded like…a bear." She

waited for his gaze to snap back to hers, watched his eyes narrow and his jaw twitch. Her lips already curving into a smile, she pressed them together to keep from laughing. A giggle slipped out, anyway.

"That's strange. To me, it sounded like someone asking to be thrown in the creek."

Her eyes widened for real this time. She held up her hands, backing away from him as he stalked her every move. "Now, Quinn. Be reasonable. Don't do anything I'll make you regret."

"Oh, I won't regret a single thing, darlin'." He grabbed for her. She evaded him by dashing behind a tree. He ran around the other side to cut off her escape. She faked left then went right. He caught her arm then channeled her momentum to spin her around so that she ran right into his hard chest. The impact hardly rocked him as he locked his arms around her waist. "Better prepare yourself. It may be warmer today, but that water is still going to be cold."

She tilted her head back to search his face. He wouldn't really throw her in the creek, would he? Suddenly, she wasn't so sure. There was a playful glint in his eyes that she didn't trust. She worked her hands between them in an effort to push her way out of his arms. He wasn't cooperating, which made the task nigh on impossible. "An honorable man would allow me a forfeit."

"What kind of forfeit?"

"I'll let you wash the dishes for me tonight."

"I don't think you understand how forfeits work. You're supposed to do something for me." His voice deepened. "Or...give me something I want." His attention flickered down to her lips before returning to her eyes.

Her breath seemed to get lost in her chest. Perhaps he'd forgotten that he'd ordered her not to kiss him again unless it meant something. She hadn't forgotten. In her book, that meant the next person to do any kissing would have to be him. She lifted a brow. "I have a better idea. How about I apologize and you let me go?"

"Not a chance."

He said it so gravely that she had to smile. Sliding her hands up to his shoulders, she clasped them behind his neck and rose on tiptoe to place herself more securely in his arms. She took care to speak tenderly so as not to rile him as she whispered, "Please, Bear."

"No." He whispered, and then eased her backward in a slow dip that shifted her to the center of his embrace. He finished the smooth movement by lifting her just enough to meet his kiss. Her equilibrium, already struggling to compensate, was completely lost. She clung to him as the kiss deepened and intensified. She could feel the walls she'd built around her heart catching fire with her, tumbling into ashes, floating away on the wind that teased her senses with the faint scent of Quinn's bay rum aftershave.

She was left vulnerable and exposed as her fears melted away. They would return. She was certain of that because there would be no getting him out of her heart after this. He would stay there no matter what his reaction was to her secret. That meant she could potentially be hurt deeply—as deeply as she allowed herself to love him. She didn't want to get hurt, but it was too late. What she hadn't wanted to admit before was clear to her now. She was well on her way to loving Quinn already. In fact, she probably had been from the very beginning. Otherwise, she wouldn't have been so eager to accept his offer of marriage no matter how many children he had.

He allowed them both a free breath before he sealed his kiss with a softer, briefer one. When he released her waist, she stumbled a few dazed steps to stare at him. She pressed the back of her hand to her lips then trailed it upward to smooth her hair. She tried to speak, but what came out was little more than the last half of a sigh.

"That was..." Quinn slowly shook his head as he stared back at her in wonder. After a moment, determination set the angles of his chiseled jaw. "Now, for your forfeit."

"My—what was the kiss, then?"

"A kiss." His smile told her he knew it had been far from just an ordinary kiss. "You still owe me a forfeit." He chuckled as she set her hands on her hips and glared. "Don't worry, darlin'. All I want you to do is answer some questions for me."

She tilted her head and narrowed her eyes. "What kind of questions?"

"Questions about you. On the drive over here, I realized that you know so much about me—even down to my deepest darkest secret. Yet, I know hardly anything about you. Why is that?"

"I'm not that interesting."

He gave her a disbelieving look. "I think you are. What's more, you've helped me with all of my problems, from needing a wife, to finances, to reading. I'd like to help you like you've helped me, but you've never even mentioned having any problems except that time you had a nightmare."

Her heart started racing for an entirely different reason. "I guess I do tend to keep my problems to myself."

"Then you'll tell me more about yourself?"

"What do you want to know?"

He stepped forward to take her hands in his. "Everything."

"Everything?" She swallowed hard. She couldn't tell him *everything*.

He nodded. "Start at the beginning. What were you like as a child?"

She pulled in a calming breath. She could do this. She could tell him about herself without betraying her secret. She just had to be careful. Something akin to conviction pricked her conscience. She struggled to salve it. After all, it wasn't as if she was lying. She was just leaving a few things out…for now. She forced a laugh. "That may take a while. I'm sure you'll find out plenty about me when we visit my parents, but I'd be happy to tell you about the distracted little daydreamer I used to be. Why don't we sit down and have our picnic while we talk."

"I almost forgot what brought us here in the first place." He gave her a little wink that caused her heart to skip like a rock. "Come on. Let's see what Ellie packed for us."

He led her toward the picnic basket and she followed him—followed her heart even as it brought her closer to her day of reckoning. She tried to convince herself that she was making more out of this than she needed to

since they had four children already. Surely that would
soften the blow for him as it had for her. However, there
was still the possibility—or, perhaps, *probability*—that
he might resent being sold damaged goods as much as
Tom had. In that case, the best thing she could do was
enjoy these moments with Quinn so she would have
them to cherish later if things ever changed. What else
could she do now that she'd thrown down the shield
around her heart like a gauntlet to both love and heartache?

Ten days later, Reece and Clara had finished their
last day of lessons before the Thanksgiving break,
which, Quinn discovered, somehow gave them bound-
less energy. Trent and Olivia seemed to take their cue
from their older siblings, so he found himself blind-
folded during a fourth game of blindman's buff after
supper. A small hand tapped his leg. He turned toward
it slowly enough for whoever it was to get away, earning Olivia's giggle as a reward. A snicker that sounded
like Reece came from his left just as a breeze passed
by on his right. It stirred the air enough that he caught
Helen's scent.

She was close. He froze, listened carefully enough
to discover the almost-silent rhythm being beat out on
the floor. Of all the gall…she was dancing! In fact, she
probably had been for a while, though how she'd evaded
his searching outstretched arms all this time was beyond
him. She was too easy a mark now that he knew, but
he couldn't help joining in with a little jig of his own.

Laughter came at him from all sides while someone

gasped. It must have been Clara, because she spoke up from behind him. "He's been able to see all this time!"

"No, but I can hear real well." He spun toward her. She yelped. He gave her a head start as she dashed away. However, her steps were heavy with panic and she was easy to track down. He caught her arm and reeled her in. "Who could this be?"

"Cla—" Trent's yell was muzzled; probably by Reece, who'd been particularly frustrated by his brother's inability to remember the blind man had to guess his captive's identity correctly to win.

"I think it's Clara." He removed his blindfold to glance down at her.

She pouted. "You hunted me down."

"You bet I did, sweetheart, because I needed one of these." He lifted her into the air high enough to place a smacking kiss on her cheek before setting her down. "We'll pick up with Clara the next time we play."

The children's protests at ending the game were immediate and fierce. It was getting close to bedtime and they needed to calm down, so Quinn shook his head. "Sorry, that's it. I'm done. Y'all wore me out. See?"

He collapsed onto the rug. One at a time his family took their cue from him by wilting down to the floor. However, instead of landing on the rug, they all ended up on him or each other until he felt like the floor in a game of pick-up sticks. After more laughter and a few grumbles, they seemed content to relax, so Quinn didn't have any room to complain or to move. He didn't mind, though. Especially since Helen's head came to rest on his left shoulder.

Ever since that kiss at the creek, she somehow seemed

hadn't been able to make any progress
The local officials in Alaska seemed to
of outside interference. It was frustrat-
least. Meanwhile, Quinn wouldn't stand
essing with his family. The trespasser
at out soon enough. So would Richardson.
uldn't shake the feeling that he was miss-
ng important pertaining to that situation,
he answer came to him later that night just
ed reviewing Helen's reading lesson. Rich-
sent Quinn a letter notifying him of Wade's
as still in the desk where Quinn had put it be-
couldn't read. Well, he could read now. Surely
would offer some information about what had
d to Wade's assets even if what it said was false.
anted to be able to give the letter to the sheriff
reak, which meant he'd have to go into Helen's
while she was sleeping at some point. He might
l do it now. He'd just have to be quiet about it. He
ed Helen's door, wincing as it creaked. So much
eing quiet.

e found her pushing to her elbow with sleep lad-
her thick lashes. She spoke almost as slowly as she
ked. "Is it morning?"

"No, I—"

"Must be the children, then." She didn't even bother
ith her house robe. She just took the blanket with her
s she stood. "They were still a little upset when I read
them. I mean the book." She gave her head a minus-
cule shake. "What?"

He really ought to tell her to go back to sleep, but it
was hard to do anything other than watch her be adorable. "Are you asking me or yourself?"

even kinder and sweeter than she'd been before. He
hadn't kissed her again because he didn't want to pre-
sume too much, but he'd been thinking about it a lot.
Perhaps more than he should. To get his mind off of it
now, he asked, "Are y'all excited about our trip to Austin tomorrow? It sounds like Helen's parents have a lot
of fun things planned for us."

"Yes," Reece answered. "I just feel bad because we'll
have to leave Charlie all alone. Can't we take him—
Ouch. Clara!"

Quinn wasn't sure what Clara had done to Reece, but
her fierce whisper was easy to hear. "You weren't supposed to tell about Charlie. Now he'll have to go away."

Quinn and Helen sat up at the same time, which
forced the children to do the same. He barely got the
question out before Helen. "Who is Charlie?"

Trent was wide-eyed and obviously confused. Olivia
frowned at them all. The older two looked guiltier than
he'd ever seen them. Finally, Reece explained as if it was
the most natural thing in the world. "He's our friend who
lives in the woods."

"What woods, Reece?" Helen asked.

"The woods around our house."

Quinn frowned in concern. "What is Charlie? A
child? A dog? What?"

Clara shook her head. "He's a man. A full-growed
man."

"Full-grown," Helen corrected then shook her head
as though unable to process the children's meaning.
"Wait. So there's a strange man living on our property?
And y'all knew and didn't tell us? How long has this
been going on?"

Clara lifted her chin. "He isn't strange."

"Yeah, he's nice."

Quinn waved off their words. "Answer your aunt's questions. How long?"

Reece shrugged. "I don't know. We met him last week when we were playing outside. He gave us some cookies like our ma used to make. Our second ma, I mean."

Trent's little body stiffened. "You had cookies, and you didn't tell me?"

"Cookie?" Olivia looked around as though expecting them to materialize from thin air.

Clara patted Trent's knee. "I wanted to, but it was *supposed* to be a secret."

Reece grimaced. "Land sakes, Clara, I'm sorry. What more do you want from me?"

Trent glared. "I want my cookies."

Olivia held out her hands, with chubby fingers grasping the air. "Cookie!"

"That's enough." Quinn stood and set the three oldest side by side on the settee. With Helen at his side holding Olivia, he looked them in the eye one at a time. "I want y'all to listen to me very closely."

Trent looked near to tears. "I didn't do anything!"

"I know that." Quinn knelt in front of the settee and covered the boy's cheek. "I'm not angry at you. Or you, Clara. Or you, Reece. It's just important to me that y'all understand what I'm going to say. That's why I want y'all to stop bickering and pay attention to me. Understand?"

He waited until the three of them nodded then extended his hand to Helen. Once she took it, he turned

back to the c[...]
of you more t[...]
want you to be [...]
to watch out for [...]
people."

Clara frowned. [...]

"Tricky people a[...]
secrets from your aun[...]
tell you it's all right to [...]
sion. That includes taki[...]
places with them or doin[...]
to do. Grown-ups who as[...]
also tricky people."

Helen squeezed his hand in [...]
the children do if they think [...]
tricky person, Quinn?"

"Get away from that person. [...]
Tell us about it. Understand?"

They all nodded. Reece put a pr[...]
Clara's shoulders. She frowned. "[...]
person?"

"I'm afraid so." Quinn allowed Hele[...]
conversation. As she helped them deal [...]
tional part of it, he was already planning h[...]
of action. He wanted to take care of this be[...]
for their trip tomorrow afternoon. Since it w[...]
dark, he'd best wait for first light to start ca[...]
the woods for the trespasser. Perhaps he'd swir[...]
sheriff's place first to get his help.

During the past ten days, Sheriff Sean O'Brie[...]
been persistent in searching for information regar[...]
Jeffery Richardson and the children's inheritance. H[...]

198

The

ever, the sherif[...]
on either issue[...]
resent any kin[...]
ing, to say the[...]
for anyone [...]
would find t[...]
Quinn c[...]
ing someth[...]
but what?[...]
as he finis[...]
ardson ha[...]
death. It [...]
cause he[...]
the lette[...]
happen[...]
He [...]
at day[...]
room [...]
as we[...]
open[...]
for b[...]
ing[...]
bli[...]

"I'm not sure." She stared up at him until her eyes focused. "Which one of the children needs me?"

He aimed her back toward the bed when she tried to walk past him. "There's nothing wrong with the children. You go on back to sleep now. I just came in here to get something from the desk. I promise I won't disturb you again tonight."

She made a humming noise and was already sleeping by the time he grabbed everything out of the desk drawer. He spread his loot out on the kitchen table. He discovered that many of the papers he'd saved over the years on the off chance he'd learn to read were nothing other than advertisements for products he'd never use or need. He ignored everything except the letter on top with its seal flap facing up. He opened the envelope and sat down to read aloud in case he needed to sound out any words.

He went straight to the body of the letter, which was written in a smooth, precise script.

I never stopped loving you. I cannot tell you how much I regret letting you go the night of our engagement.

It took a second for the words to process. He read them again, frowned and glanced at the header. "Dearest Helen"? Was this a love letter? From whom? Unlike the rest of the letter, the signature boasted fancy curves in the cursive style of writing Quinn had yet to learn.

How long ago had it been written? There was no date on the letter. However, the paper had a stiffness to it that suggested it had been recently transcribed. Stranger still, there was no stamp on the envelope. Did that mean this person lived around here? Was that why Helen had insisted on going into town by herself?

He barely resisted the urge to crumple the paper in his fist. Instead, he folded it and slid it back into its envelope. He didn't want to read any more. Whatever was written there wasn't intended for his eyes. Besides, it was far too painful. He'd been trying so hard to be a better man so that he could be worthy of his wife's affections. He'd never considered he might also be competing for them.

He'd asked Helen to tell him everything that day at the creek. She'd told him about her growing-up years and the silly society gatherings she'd been expected to attend. She'd never once hinted at a former romance—certainly not a former fiancé. He'd been too involved with what he'd considered the beginning of their own courtship to even think to broach the subject. Well, he had questions now. Plenty of them.

He started to rise with the intention of going to Helen's room, then sat back down after remembering that he'd promised not to disturb her. Besides, it would be better to approach the problem with a cool head in the morning, so he'd let her sleep. Tomorrow, however, he intended to get some answers.

Chapter Fifteen

Quinn was gone when Helen awoke the next morning. A note on the kitchen table told her that he'd gone to get the sheriff and search the woods. She was supposed to bar the door until he returned. Bar the door? She'd been hoping to get her chores out of the way quickly so that she'd have more time to prepare the children for their trip. As much as she'd anticipated seeing her parents again, the date of departure had sneaked up on her. She'd had to make several arrangements at the last minute. One of them being arranging to have some formal clothes made for Quinn in Austin.

He had none to take with them, save the suit he wore to church every week. As handsome as he looked in it, it just wouldn't be enough for the events her family had planned. She'd told him about it, hadn't she? Maybe not. Everything had been so hectic. She'd make sure to tell him when he came in for breakfast. She'd better start fixing it now. She'd learned that the smell of it was often enough to awaken the children. Perhaps an early start for them would help her get a jump on the rest of the day.

After remembering to bar the door, she accidentally knocked over the stack of papers Quinn had left on the table in her haste to return to the kitchen. She bent to pick them up then hesitated, realizing that mixed among his assignments was the contents of what she'd come to think of as her desk. She suddenly remembered that he'd mentioned needing something from the desk as the reason for coming into her room last night. What could he have wanted with all of this junk? That's all it was, too, since she'd had the foresight to burn the letter with her mother's references to that dreadful night she'd almost become publicly engaged to Thomas. She gasped. "Tom!"

She'd completely forgotten about his letter. Dread filled her as she sorted through the papers looking for the note she'd never read. She winced when she found it. It had obviously been disturbed. Was that because Quinn had read it? Or was it simply from her knocking it onto the floor? Oh, why had she been so careless with it? If Quinn had read it, then she needed to, as well.

She set the other papers in a stack on the table then opened the letter to read it just as someone pounded on the front door. She froze. Thinking something might have happened to Quinn, she stuffed the letter into her apron pocket and rushed to the door. She was ready to unbar it before she realized it might not be the sheriff or Quinn at all. It might be Charlie. The pounding sounded again. She swallowed. "Who is it?"

"Quinn. I've got Sean with me. You can unbar the door. It's safe."

A wave of relief flowed over her then ebbed into tension as she realized she still had that blasted letter in her pocket. However, she couldn't leave the men out there. She moved the wooden bar out of the way and opened the door to let them in. Almost immediately, she wished she hadn't because Quinn's mattress was still on the parlor floor. There was no way the sheriff could miss it. It was too late now. At least the bed was made. "Come to the kitchen. I was just about to put on some coffee."

"Thanks, Helen," Sean said. "I may not have time to drink it, though. I've got to head into town soon. Quinn and I just wanted to let you know how it went."

"Y'all said it's safe? Does that mean you found Charlie?" Helen glanced up from adding water to the coffeepot in time to see Quinn move his stack of papers to the end table. Nothing in his expression told her whether he'd seen Thomas's letter or not.

Sean picked a chair that faced away from the parlor. "No. We found the place where he'd been camping, but the man himself wasn't anywhere on the property."

"Hopefully, he's moved on." Quinn settled at the corner of the table with a frown. "It strikes me as strange that he gave the children cookies, though. Usually vagrants don't just happen to have sweets around to offer children."

Sean frowned. "You think he befriended them for a specific purpose?"

"I don't know. I hope not."

"Well, I'll keep an eye on the place while you're gone. I was planning to, anyway. Meanwhile, I'll look into any new clues I can gather from the letter."

Helen whirled toward them. "What letter?"

"The one Richardson sent to notify me of my brother's death. I'd forgotten that I had it." There was something in his eyes that she hadn't seen before. An underlying steel. She had a feeling that meant he'd read Thomas's letter. What if that also meant he knew the truth about her?

The room swayed. Her stomach roiled. She leaned back onto the counter to steady herself. She struggled to sound normal "What did it say?"

"It said all of Wade's assets had been turned over to the state because he'd made no will."

Sean nodded. "That should be easy enough to check. I'd better head into town now. Y'all have a nice trip. Don't worry about anything."

After seeing Sean to the door, Quinn returned to the kitchen and held up the empty envelope with her name on the front in Thomas's handwriting. "Who is writing you love letters?"

She blinked. He didn't know who had written her. Was there a chance he also didn't know her secret? "You didn't read it?"

"Only enough to know what it is. The name was written in cursive. Who is this man?"

"His name is Thomas Coyle. He was my fiancé for a few days before he jilted me at our engagement dinner. Officially, it was never announced, but everyone knew."

"How long has he been writing you?"

"That was the only letter I received. He gave it to my parents and they enclosed it in their letter. I didn't answer it. I didn't even read it. I was going to just now, but you came in." She swallowed. If he didn't already know the truth about her, she didn't want to give it away. However, she had to know how much of her past Thomas had revealed. "Did he say anything you think is important? Anything we need to discuss?"

He stared at her for a long moment then shook his head. "No. He didn't say anything important to me. Although, I do think he was headed toward an apology."

The pressure building in her chest eased out with a long, slow exhale. Her secret was safe for now. Her relief came a moment too soon, for Quinn asked, "Why didn't you tell me you'd been engaged?"

"It only lasted a few days. It hardly counts."

His eyes narrowed. "Did you love him?"

She shrugged. "I thought so at the time."

"Then it counts. I'm not saying you had to tell me every detail because I don't expect that. Still, it would have been nice to find out from you and not from his letter." His jaw clenched. "Will we see him in Austin?"

She frowned. He didn't sound upset about the prospect. In fact, he sounded downright eager. Did he want to ask the man why he had jilted her or just punch him in the nose? "I doubt it. He ought to know better than to think I want to see him since I'm married and never responded to his letter."

Quinn turned the envelope over in his hands. "Why would your parents send such a thing to their married daughter?"

"I'm sure they didn't read it. They probably assumed he was apologizing, which I guess he did. My mother thought it would be good for me to have a definite ending to what happened between us." She shrugged. "For me, it ended with the engagement."

She found him searching her face as he approached

her, and she wondered if he could see the wariness within her. "So that's all there is to this?"

"Yes, that's all there is to the letter."

"May I have it?" He waited until she pulled it from her frilly apron pocket to place it in his hand. As soon as she did, she wanted to take it back. What if he read it again? He might have missed something Tom had written about her secret the first time, but he surely wouldn't miss it again. Her worries vanished an instant later when her husband tossed the letter and its envelope into the fiery belly of the stove.

Pure relief filled her as she erased the distance between them with a single step and slipped her arms around his neck for a hug. "Thank you for understanding and believing me."

"Well, I'm still a little confused, but I do believe you." He hugged her closer then released her, though he kept ahold of her arms. "What about Coyle? Am I going to have to compete with his memory?"

She stared at him in confusion. "Compete with his memory? For what?"

"For your heart."

"You…you want my heart?" Did he hear the awe in her voice? It must have been hard to miss, for he grinned.

"Seeing as I'm your husband, don't you think I should?"

"Oh." Happiness wrestled with disappointment. He wanted to win her heart. That was good. However, it wasn't because he loved her and wanted to be loved in return. It was only because he felt obligated to do so as her husband. "Don't worry about Thomas. He isn't going to be a factor. Now, I'd better get breakfast ready and the children up if we want to make it to the train on time. Austin awaits."

Quinn could almost feel the tension emanating off Helen as the train chugged to a stop at the station in Austin. It was easy to recognize her anxiety since he was more nervous than he'd been since Helen had discovered his illiteracy. That situation had ended far better than he could have hoped. He was resolved the same would be true in this case. It wasn't an altogether different situation, for he'd mentally designated this trip as a test of sorts.

Surely if he could make it through four days in a house, society and role so far above his means and come out unscathed, then he ought to be set for the rest of his life. He could stop looking over his shoulder waiting for trouble to catch up and just live his life. No, not just live it. Enjoy it. He wasn't there yet, but he could be soon. He just needed to get a little help from God, keep thinking on his feet and continue to find new ways to better himself.

He'd been doing well so far. The reading lessons were getting progressively more challenging. However, he was determined to learn as much as possible. The children seemed far less gloomy than they had been when they'd first come to him grieving their parents. That meant he and Helen had to be doing something right. Helen seemed more engaged with him, so his wooing must be having some effect. However, he had hoped for more of a reaction to the news that he wanted to claim her heart. Her excitement had quickly died. That wasn't exactly encouraging.

As for Helen herself, the longer he knew the woman, the more he was discovering that she was an enigma wrapped in warmth, beauty and fancy clothes. How many more mysteries did those deep brown eyes of hers hold? She revealed another one as they gathered their belongings in preparation to disembark. "Have I mentioned this is the first time I've been to Austin since I left only a few weeks after my engagement dinner with no engagement?"

"Apparently there's a lot you haven't mentioned." His comment brought them both up short. She paled. He grimaced. "I'm sorry. I don't know where that came from."

"I do. You have every right to be angry at me for not telling you about..." She let the sentence fade and he realized that the children's gazes were bouncing back and forth between them.

"I'm not angry." Even that came out a little gruff.

Of course, Reece had to call him on it. "You sound angry."

"No, he doesn't." Clara shifted Olivia to her other knee and patted Quinn's arm. "He's just grumpy because the train ride was long."

They began to bicker about whether Quinn was grumpy or angry. The truth was, neither. He was jealous. He had been since he'd found out that Helen had at one point thought she was in love with that city fellow. What would it be like, Quinn wondered, for Helen to think she was in love with him?

"I'm grumpy, too." Trent crossed his arms while Olivia covered her ears and frowned at Clara and Reece.

Helen sent him a panicked look. Suddenly, Quinn realized they were frighteningly close to someone having a temper tantrum. Deciding it wouldn't be him, he transferred Olivia to Helen's care and ushered the older three children into the aisle that had cleared during their tableau. "No one is angry or grumpy. We are all very happy. What's more, we are excited to meet Helen's parents and will be on our best behavior."

By the time he finished his speech, they had stepped off the train onto what might very well be Quinn's proving grounds. He checked to make sure they were all accounted for as Helen scanned the busy station for her parents. Olivia was in Helen's arms. Clara was holding his hand. Reece stood beside Clara. Trent was…

Quinn turned in a circle, dragging Clara with him as he raked the area with his gaze and came up empty. Panic tightened his throat. "Where's Trent?"

Helen whipped around to face him. "I thought you had him."

"So did I." Just then a porter moved a huge cart of luggage and Quinn spotted Trent down on all fours at the edge of the platform next to the train wheels. "What in the world? I see him, Helen."

Those last words to Helen were thrown over Quinn's shoulder as he raced back to the train. He snatched up Trent just as the boy reached toward the train wheels. Setting him away from the track, Quinn knelt in front of Trent. He ignored his still-racing heart to speak in a reasonable tone. "What do you think you're doing, son?"

"I wanted to see what makes it go." Trent made a vain attempt to dodge Quinn's efforts at wiping mysterious black marks off his face.

"You cannot get that close to a train unless your aunt or I are with you. You could have been hurt."

"How?"

"You could have gotten your fingers caught in the wheels or fallen on the track. Your aunt and I didn't know where you were, so we might not have been able to find you before the train started. Remember, we talked about this? You aren't allowed to go off on an adventure without permission from your aunt or I. Understand?"

While Quinn had been talking, the boy had gone from fascinated to appalled, to downright sober. Finally, Trent nodded. "Yes, but we need to go on more adventures."

"That's a deal." Quinn turned Trent to face the train and explained as best he knew how the steam-powered engine made it move, before herding the boy back to the others. Seeing that Helen's parents had joined the group, the nervousness he'd forgotten in his panic at losing Trent returned full force.

It did Quinn a world of good to see Helen smiling proudly as she introduced him. "Mother, Father, may I present my husband, Quinn Tucker?"

Helen's mother was the same height as her, though a bit plumper. She'd given Helen the shape of her large doe eyes, delicate bone structure and oval face. The woman's hazel eyes sparkled. "I am delighted to meet you, Quinn! You must call us Lucille and Robert."

"Thank you, Lucille. I've been looking forward to meeting you both." He turned to Robert, who had passed his dark hair and eyes on to Helen.

The man had a smile on his face. However, the look

in his eyes was not exactly friendly. His handshake seemed an attempt to assess Quinn's strength. "Not as much as I've been looking forward to meeting you."

Well, that doesn't sound the least bit threatening. He looked Robert straight in the eye to let it be known that he wouldn't cower before any man. Then Quinn gave a single nod to communicate his recognition, acceptance and respect of what the man was—a protective father. Not just any father, though. This was Helen's father and, by law, his own. It would be nice to have a father again. For now, Quinn would just appreciate not having this man as an enemy.

Quinn glanced down when Trent tugged at his hand. Following Helen's example of a formal introduction, Quinn said, "May I introduce my nephew Trent Tucker? Trent, this is Mr. and Mrs. McKenna."

Quinn stared in surprise as Trent wrapped one arm in front and the other in back to bow. "How do you, Mr. and Mr. McKenna."

Helen's parents returned Trent's greeting. Lucille waved her handkerchief. "Now, let's dispense with formalities because I am just dying to hold my grandniece. Do you think Olivia would let me?"

After Olivia went willingly, Robert ushered them all around the corner of the train station to the place where their luggage was being loaded onto not one but two waiting carriages. There wasn't enough room for all of them in one, so the men rode together in one and the ladies in the other. Robert made the ride enjoyable for them all by pointing out the interesting sights of the city through the carriage window.

The trolley cars, wagons, carriages and horses thinned

out once they passed the domed Capitol building to ride through quiet boulevards. Towering oak trees, spindly crape myrtle and yellow mimosas stretched out their branches to the mansions interspersed between them. The carriage finally rolled to a stop in front of a Queen Anne–style house of sea foam green with moss-colored embellishments. They followed a winding brick path leading from the curb to the house's wide porch steps, which, like the rest of the house, sat on the vast green lawn at a diagonal angle to the street. Quinn paused long enough to glance up to the turret on the third floor before pulling in a deep breath and steeling himself for what was sure to come next.

The entrance room was only a little smaller than the entire living room and kitchen area of his house. It had mahogany floors and archways that gleamed in the soft sunlight spilling from the windows. A grand staircase split to allow access to two sides of the upper floor. An antique grandfather clock that looked older than America itself clanged as though announcing the hour of his doom. No way would he ever deserve the love of a woman who grew up in a place like this. If this was just the beginning, he'd better turn around and keep on walking until he made it back to Peppin.

Escape became impossible when a man whom Quinn sure hoped was in the McKennas' employ obligingly and almost soundlessly made off with Quinn's hat and coat. Meanwhile, the children vanished up the stairs with Helen and her mother. Robert urged him to follow them with a rather strong slap on the back. "Better go up. The tailor is waiting to do a final fitting."

"Tailor?" His voice echoed through the corridor with enough grandiosity to match the surroundings.

A faint smile quirked Robert's mouth. "Our wives arranged for you to have a few things made so that you'll be comfortable during your stay here."

"Are you sure *comfortable* is the right word?" he asked, glancing at the man's current attire. It looked like a more fashionable, higher-quality version of Quinn's Sunday go-to-meeting clothes. He knew from experience that those weren't comfortable in the least.

He earned a chuckle from his father-in-law. "Believe me. Being inappropriately dressed at a society function would be a far more uncomfortable experience than wearing whatever clothes our wives deem necessary. Besides, don't you want to make Helen proud to be escorted by you?"

"Of course."

"Then up the left side of the staircase you go."

"Yes, sir." The echo made his heavy sigh sound excessively dramatic. Once he made it up the stairs, he followed the sound of voices to find his family.

Lucille was introducing the children to a nanny she'd hired to see to their needs during their stay. Quinn waited until his nephews and nieces followed the nanny into the nursery, which would function as their bedroom, before protesting, "You didn't need to go to the trouble of hiring a nanny, Mrs. McKenna. Helen and I can handle them and they're usually very well behaved."

"It's Lucille and I'm quite certain everything you said is true. I just thought this visit would be more restful and smooth for all of you this way. It was quite easy to arrange because the nanny was recommended by a dear friend of mine." Suddenly, dismay widened Lucille's eyes. "Oh, dear. I do hope I haven't offended you by hiring her. I know you and Helen are perfectly capable of seeing to them on your own."

He wanted to tell her that wasn't what he'd been thinking, but it was *exactly* what he'd been thinking. Why was he being so sensitive about everything today? He shook his head. "I just don't want you to feel that you have to go out of your way for us."

Now she looked offended. "Of course I'll go out my way for you, young man. You're family now, and that's how this family operates. Isn't that right, Helen?"

Helen grinned. "Yes, indeed."

"All right, then. Thank you, Lucille."

"You're welcome." She reached out to squeeze his hand and met his gaze with a smile. "Truly, you are welcome here. I hope you will come to think of this house as your second home."

"I'd like that." He relaxed a little and gave her hand a gentle squeeze in return. "By the way, Robert said something about a tailor?"

Lucille gasped. "Oh, dear. I completely forgot. He should be waiting in your room."

Quinn moved to follow the woman as she hurried down the hallway, but Helen tugged at his arm and moved closer to speak in a low tone, "I'm sorry. I meant to tell you about this. I realized a few days ago that you didn't have any formal clothes besides the ones you wear to church, so I sent Mother your measurements. She had a few things made for you by Father's tailor, who is one of the best in the city. Everything should be ready for the final fitting."

He nodded slowly as he processed everything. She was right about him not having clothes—at least, not the right kind for this setting. That much was obvious now. "I should have thought of it myself. It's a good thing you arranged it since I wouldn't have known how."

Relief softened her features before worry once more marred her brow. "I really did mean to tell you sooner…"

"Don't worry about it anymore." He stared at her hard to let her know he meant more than just the clothes. "I know you've had a lot to handle in making this trip happen. I appreciate that. It's all just a little…"

"Overwhelming?" she asked with a smile. "I imagine it must be akin to what I felt those first few days on the farm. I thought I'd never measure up to being the woman you and the children needed me to be. I might have seemed confident on the outside, but I was quaking on the inside."

"You measured up just fine, Helen."

"Thank you." She placed a comforting hand on his chest. "So will you, Quinn. I know it."

Her confidence in him meant more to him than her parents' fancy carriages, Texas-size mansion and expensive clothes. If she believed in him, then he had an honest-to-goodness shot at making a success of this visit. More important, he had a chance at becoming the kind of man he wanted to be. The kind of man who could win her heart.

Chapter Sixteen

In contrast to the cozy and immensely enjoyable Thanksgiving dinner Helen's family had partaken of on Thursday, Saturday's reception was a crush. Most of her father's associates had shown up, including the governor, a state senator, a few state representatives and many prominent businessmen. Their wives made up her mother's close-knit social circle. Each one of them made a point to welcome Helen back into their society's embrace with hugs, cheek kisses, compliments and an entire litany of the most recent gossip.

Her old circle of friends approached her a bit more cautiously, which she knew was no one's fault but her own. She hadn't corresponded with any of them after she left. Many had also been Thomas's friends, which added an undercurrent of awkwardness to their interactions. She didn't ask about him nor did anyone mention him. However, more than once a conversation suddenly hushed as she passed.

She'd been looking forward to this event if for no other reason than that she would no longer be thought of as a jilted fiancée but as a contented wife and mother. Now she found that their opinions meant little, their conversations were shallow and she longed for nothing more than to escape upstairs to the nursery. That wouldn't help, for the children were surely fast asleep at this hour.

Realizing she'd been standing alone for a few minutes, she glanced around in search of Quinn. She finally spotted him in a conversation with several men, including her father and the governor. Clad in a jet-black tailcoat with a white waistcoat and white necktie that accentuated the broad width of his shoulders and slim hips, he looked far more at ease than she'd expected him to be. He also seemed to be enjoying himself more than she was.

He caught her watching him and sent her a wink that made her eyes widen in panic. Polite gentleman simply did not wink at their wives in public. Thankfully, it had not been so brazenly done that anyone else noticed. She meant to send him a scolding frown but found herself smiling and shaking her head slowly instead. The governor placed a hand on his shoulder, stealing back his attention.

She decided to take a break from the crowd. Despite being one of the honorees at the reception, no one stopped her as she slipped out of her parents' ballroom. She told the butler that she'd be in the sunroom for a few minutes if anyone needed her. She went directly there after borrowing a candle from a nearby wall sconce. The circular room was chilly, but the view it provided of the night sky was worth the discomfort. She'd just placed the candle on an end table when she heard movement from the far corner of the room. "Who's there?"

A man stepped closer to the flickering circle of candlelight. He was dressed as though he was a guest at the party, although he most certainly was not. He toasted her with the silver flask in his hands but didn't bother to bring it to his smirking lips. "Good evening, Helen."

She gasped. "Tom."

He edged toward her, capping the flask in his hand with a bit of difficulty. His gaze raked over her dress. His speech was unmistakably slurred. "You look ravishing. That dark shade of pink was always my favorite color on you. Did I ever tell you that?"

"You're drunk."

He waved her comment away with a broad sweep of his hand. "Don't be rude."

"How did you get in here?"

"I—" his fingers made a crawling motion in the air "—sneaked in."

"Well—" she copied his motion "—sneak right out again."

"No." He rubbed his hands over his face, pulled in a sobering breath and shook his head as though to clear it. "I am in full possession of my faculties. What's more, I have things to say. I'm not leaving until I say them."

"Then I will." She rounded the furniture to head toward the door.

He cut off her escape path and her attempts to get around him. "Please, don't leave. I'm trying to tell you that I still love you."

"I don't care. Let—" She froze, stared at him in disbelief. "What did you say?"

"I love you. I can't stop thinking about you. All my life my father has ingrained in me the importance of passing our fortune to the next generation. I couldn't do that with you. However, I believe I might have been a bit hasty in ending things between us."

She shook her head as she tried to reconcile this with everything she'd told herself about love making the difference for her when Quinn found out. But if Tom had loved her, and still rejected her when she told him of her condition, did that mean that love wouldn't be enough for Quinn, either? "I don't understand. What are you trying to say? That my inability to have children doesn't matter to you now?"

He stepped closer. "No, it matters. So does my love for you."

"Actually, it doesn't, because I'm married to someone else." She swept a hand toward the ballroom. "It's sort of the reason we're having this little party."

"I know." He erased the distance between them. "That doesn't mean we can't see each other from time to time. You can't have children, so no one would know—"

He caught her arm when she would have slapped him. She tried to wrench from his grasp, but he wouldn't allow it. "How dare you even suggest such a thing? Let me go. If someone should see us like this—"

He jerked her closer. "You mean, if your *husband* should see us like this. Why do you care? You only married him for his children."

"That isn't—"

"Uh-uh." He shook his head. "That's the funny thing about lying, my dear. It doesn't change the truth. You're using him just as some common fortune hunter would use an heiress—to get something you couldn't have on your own. Money or children. What's the difference?"

He was right and she knew it. He must have sensed it, for he grinned. "Come now, Helen. Drop the righteous indignation. We both know you don't love him. How could you?"

She felt her eyes flash as his words illuminated the truth within her. "You're wrong. I do…I do love him."

His green eyes bored into hers, examining and recognizing her feelings for what they were. Hurt unfurled in his gaze then hardened into something vengeful. He tilted his head. "Ah, but have you told him? Have you told him what you told me? No, I can see you haven't. It's written all over your face. Perhaps I ought to tell him myself. Clear the field, so to speak."

Desperation and panic froze her in place. "Tom, you wouldn't."

"I might." His mouth tilted into a wry smile. "The funny thing is, I'm not sure if he'd care with the overabundance of children he already has. That was smart on your part. What worries me are the lies you must have told and the truths you must have covered up. That's what drives a man crazy. He'd wonder again and again what else he didn't know, what else you may have lied about."

Any fight she had left within her drained away. Her gaze lowered. She'd seen that very thing happening already.

"Poor fellow. I almost feel bad for him. Not quite so bad that I wouldn't steal his wife. Or, can you steal what never belonged to someone else in the first place?"

Her words came out in a near whisper. "He's my husband. Of course I belong to him."

"No." He smiled. "You belong to me. Always have. Always will. My only mistake was in thinking I had to marry you. You, my dear, are best suited for other purposes."

She gasped. Searching his face for the man she'd once wanted to marry, she found only resentment and anger instead. "How can you say these things?"

"I say them because they are true. I love you in spite of all your damage. No, *because* of it. That is something your husband will never do." He leaned closer to whisper in her ear, "When he rejects you—and he will—you know where to find me."

The moment he let her go, she ran for the door. She reached it just as Quinn entered the room. He caught her arms when she stumbled into his chest. Startled, he looked down at her then across to Thomas. Releasing her, Quinn crossed the room in two strides. One solid punch across the jaw sent Thomas stumbling backward until he hit the back wall of glass then slid down to rest on his backside. Quinn stood over him menacingly. "Who are you, and what have you done to my wife?"

Thomas didn't bother to get up. He moved his jaw to see if it still worked. Satisfied, he glanced at Helen with wicked mischief in his eyes. She held her breath. Would he go through with his threat to tell Quinn the truth about her? He smiled up at Quinn. "We were just talking, friend. Just talking."

Quinn's gaze fell to hers as she tugged on his arm. She needed to separate them before Thomas changed his mind. "Helen, did he hurt you?"

Emotionally and mentally? Yes. Physically? "No."

"Who is he?"

"Thomas Coyle." She felt Quinn's muscle bulge with tension beneath her hands. "Please, let's go. He's leaving now, too."

Quinn ignored her, growling, "What did you say to her?"

Tom lifted a knowing brow. "Nothing she'd want you to know."

"What is that supposed to mean?"

Helen answered before Tom could. "It means he told me he loved me. I told him I didn't care."

"Is that all?"

"That's all that mattered."

"May I get up now without you sending me right back to the floor?" At Quinn's short nod, Tom stood. He brushed himself off. Edging to the door, he paused long enough to smirk and lift his flask in a toast. "Many happy returns to the lovely couple and if not..."

She interpreted his meaningful glance to her to be an echo of his earlier words. *You know where to find me.*

For Quinn's benefit, he finally said, "So much the better."

This time he drank deeply of the flask as he disappeared. Her relief was momentary as she realized he might be heading straight for the ballroom. She grabbed Quinn's arm. "Make sure he doesn't go into the reception."

Quinn rushed to the door and peered out. "He went down the side hall toward the back door. You're sure you aren't hurt?"

"Yes, I'm sure."

"Did he take liberties with you? If so, I'll—"

"I'm fine. Please, don't ask any more questions. Not right now." He reached out a hand to stop her, but she evaded his grasp to walk out the door. "I don't think I feel up to returning to the party. Give my excuses to Mother."

His plea came soft and low. "Helen."

She shook her head and hurried up the stairs to her room with Tom's words nipping at her heels. They were waiting for her as she swept down the hallway to her bedroom. *When he rejects you—and he will—you know where to find me... I love you in spite of all your damage. No, because of it. That's something your husband will never do...*

His words wouldn't be so pervasive, so effective, if she didn't already believe them to be true. Nearly everything he'd said was an echo of a thought that had filled her mind at some point in the past. The others—the vile ones—she knew couldn't be true. Yet they felt true because they fell in line with all the others. Now she not only felt damaged but dirty.

A knock sounded on the door. Her heart began to pound. She couldn't face Quinn right now. Not in this state and not until she gathered herself. Her mother's voice filtered through the door. Helen hesitated only a moment before letting her in. Lucille closed the door behind her. "Quinn sent me to check on you. What happened? What did Tom do to you?"

"He said some pretty nasty things, which I'd rather not repeat." She moved to the vanity table to remove her earrings.

Lucille came to stand behind her. "It might help to tell someone."

"Not this time." She turned her back to her mother and placed her hands on her hips. "Will you unbutton me?"

"Yes, but how can you be so calm about this?"

"I'm not calm. Just a little numb, I guess." With the dress's back undone, Helen stepped behind the changing screen. "Besides, I refuse to cry over or because of some man who is not my husband." She froze as she buttoned the collar of her nightgown. "I can and *will* thank God in my prayers tonight that he isn't my husband. He might have been if he hadn't shown his true colors once he learned about my problem."

"Your problem." A frown filled her mother's voice. "I've been thinking about that lately. Maybe we should get a second opinion."

Helen rounded the changing screen to stare at her mother. "A second opinion from whom? I was attended by Dr. Whitley after my accident. He's the most respected doctor in Austin. Once he issues a diagnosis, all the others defer to it. That's why he is our family doctor in the first place, because he's the best there is."

"Yes, I know." Lucille sighed. "I just wish there was some way for me to fix this for you."

Helen sat at the edge of the canopy bed to take her hair down from its fancy chignon. "Some things can't be fixed, Mother. Things like me."

"You are not a thing," Lucille said fiercely as she sat beside Helen. "You are a person. You are my daughter, your father's little girl, Quinn's wife, an aunt to your nieces and nephews. That is what defines you, along with your faith, your spirit, your personality—not your problem. Not unless you let it. So stop letting it."

She stared at her mother in disbelief. "Do you think that I *want* to feel this way about myself? Do you think I would *choose* this? Choose to be the way I am? To pretend that I'm normal, all the time knowing there is something wrong with me? Knowing that the person I…" She choked on a sob. "The person I love more than anything could reject me for it once he finds out?"

"That isn't going to happen. Quinn isn't Tom. He's a different kind of man. A better man. He isn't going to reject you."

"You don't know that."

"Neither will you unless you tell him."

Helen pulled in a deep, calming breath. "I just…I wanted to wait until he loves me. I think he's close. It will be easier then."

Lucille shook her head even as her tone gentled. "Darling, he may grow to love you more, but you aren't going to love him any less, so it won't be any easier. You need to tell him soon. Do it for your own peace of mind, if nothing else."

"I know." She slid her fingers into her loose hair and sighed. "I will, but not tonight. I need to think, gather my courage…"

"Pray."

She nodded. "Pray."

"Meanwhile, I'll make your excuses to the guests and hint that it's time for everyone to go home. Get some rest, sweetheart." Lucille hesitated near the door. "One last thing to remember, Helen. Quinn already has four children. Four. That's enough of a handful for any man.

Unless he's expressly said anything different, he might not want any more. Good night."

That's what Helen had counted on in the beginning. Somewhere along the way she'd lost sight of that because she'd wanted him to love her for herself—not just accept her because having his own children made her tolerable. Yet, how could he truly love her if she'd never revealed how broken she really was? If he was falling in love with her as she hoped, then he was falling in love with the illusion she'd created.

She'd have to take the risk of losing whatever affection he may have developed for her by telling him the truth. She could see that now. Shutting her secret into a dark corner of her heart had only allowed it to grow and spread until its shame poisoned her thoughts and actions. Of course, bringing it into the light might only make it worse. How would she bear it every day for the rest of their lives if she saw pity in his eyes or disgust or disillusionment? She'd have the children's love. That would certainly help, but she wanted more. She wanted Quinn. She hadn't realized how much until tonight.

She burrowed under her blankets as though the extra padding could somehow insulate her from everything that had happened that evening and everything that would come. "I'll tell him, Lord, as soon as we return home. Will You prepare the way? Give me the right moment. Please work things out between us. I'm asking because You're the only one who can straighten out the mess I've made of my marriage, the mess I've made of me. Amen."

After saying goodbye to Helen's parents at the train station the next morning, Quinn made sure his family had settled comfortably into their seats before glancing out his window for what would be his last glimpse of Austin until they arranged another visit. The city had been Quinn's proving ground just as he'd expected. It had proven him to be a fool. In all of his efforts to measure up to the standard of what he thought Helen's husband was expected to be, he'd failed to be the husband she'd needed. He'd seen her staring across the ballroom at him, looking a little lonely despite the crowd of people. He'd seen the entreaty in her eyes for his attention. And he'd put off answering her silent call because he wanted to look important. He'd wanted to *be* important.

Somehow he'd gotten confused enough to think that meant swapping stories with the governor about the different places they'd each been in Texas. He wasn't confused anymore, but it was too late. Helen had left the ballroom by herself last night. If he'd been with her, she wouldn't have had to face Coyle alone, and whatever had passed between them wouldn't have happened. As it was, other than gaining favor with his in-laws, the only meaningful thing Quinn had received for reaching above his station was increased distance between him and his wife.

He glanced across the train aisle to where she sat in a smart sapphire-blue dress that served to make her large brown eyes look even richer. She was smiling as if everything was normal, for the children's sake, but there was a pensiveness lurking beneath the surface that she couldn't hide from him. She must have felt him watching her, for her gaze touched his then abruptly dropped away. He wished he was sitting beside her so that he could take her hand and try to bridge the gap between them. It would take some serious maneuvering of the children to manage it. He wasn't at all sure she'd appreciate his efforts, so he stayed put.

As the train began its sluggish crawl out of the Austin station, Reece gasped and lunged toward the window. "Hey, look! It's Charlie."

"What?" Alarm had Quinn out of his seat before the question made it past his lips. "Where?"

Quinn scanned the crowd as Clara squeezed in front of him to press against the window. "He's walking alongside the train, Uncle Quinn."

"I see him." The man was nothing if not average in height, build and looks. He wore a brown suit and matching bowler hat. The train picked up speed. Charlie didn't. Stopping at the edge of the platform, the man met Quinn's gaze and tipped his hat. Quinn watched him fade into the distance then sank down to his seat. "He just stood there and tipped his hat like he'd come to see us off."

His concern was reflected on Helen's face. "Did you recognize him?"

"I've never seen him before, which means he must have kept his distance on purpose."

"You think he's been following us around the whole time we were in Austin?"

"He must have been."

"But why?"

Quinn just shook his head, at a loss for any reasonable explanation. Trent climbed onto his lap. "I'm scared."

Too late, Quinn realized they shouldn't have been discussing this in front of the children. He wrapped one arm around Trent and pulled Reece closer to his side. Helen did the same to Clara and Olivia. "Hey, we're all safe. We're all together. Let's not worry about anything."

"Your uncle is right. How about each of us shares their favorite part of their trip to Austin? Who wants to go first?" Helen soon had them thoroughly distracted in reminiscing about the fun they'd had.

As the train ride lengthened, the younger two were lulled to sleep by the rhythmic clack of the rails, while the older two read the books Helen had brought along for them. Even Quinn was yawning by the time the train stopped in Peppin. Making sure everyone was accounted for once they exited the train was easier this time since Trent was sleepily clinging to his hand. He glanced at Helen, who had Olivia in her arms, while Clara and Reece stood close by. "I'll get the wagon from the livery and load our luggage in it then stop by the sheriff's office. Perhaps you..."

He faded off when he realized Helen's gaze was resting beyond him. "No need. I think the sheriff is coming to us."

He turned to find Sean approaching with his wife, Lorelei. The man reached out to shake hands. "Welcome back, y'all. I'm glad I caught you, Quinn."

Caught was probably a good word. It certainly appeared as though the couple had been lying in wait. Quinn glanced at Helen before sending a questioning look to the sheriff. Was something wrong?

"You're just the man I was hoping to see," Quinn said. "Do you have a moment to talk?"

"Sure thing. I've already arranged for your luggage

to be set aside. Why don't you let Lorelei take the children to my office while we take a walk."

Lorelei leaned down to whisper to the children conspiratorially. "We'll have some hot cider and sugar cookies."

Reece glanced to Quinn. "Is that all right, Uncle Quinn?"

"Sure. Y'all go ahead." Once the children were a good distance away, Quinn turned to Sean. "What's happened?"

Sean swept his hat forward to indicate they should leave the train station. "Let's head toward the courthouse and I'll tell you."

The sheriff had definitely been planning ahead for this conversation, but why? Momentarily forgetting Helen's earlier distance, he reached for her hand. Thankfully, she didn't pull away as they followed Sean down the street to the courtyard, where he slowed the pace to a leisurely stroll. "Did you want to tell me that you'd seen Charlie in Austin?"

Quinn exchanged a confused glance with Helen. "Yes, how did you know?"

"He sent a wire to let me know y'all were on the way." Sean veered onto the path that led toward the courthouse. "That's how I knew to meet your train."

Helen frowned. "Why would he do that?"

"Charlie is actually Charles Powell. He's a private detective who was hired to protect your family."

Quinn stopped to stare at the sheriff. "Protect us from what?"

"Hired by whom?"

"To answer Quinn's question, it was a preventative measure in case Jeffery Richardson doubled back—

which he didn't. He was caught by authorities in Mexico two days ago."

"That's great news." Quinn glanced at Helen to share a relieved smile before they started walking again. "What about the children's inheritance? Was it recovered?"

"Much of it was. However, that ties back to Helen's question."

Curiosity filled Helen's voice as she repeated it. "Who hired Charlie?"

Sean nodded toward the front of the courthouse, which came into view as they turned the corner. "There's your answer."

A couple rose together from where they'd been sitting on the courthouse steps. The man descended quickly at first, then slowed to a stop a few feet away. Quinn could do nothing but stare, frozen in place by the man's searching, deep blue eyes. A dimple appeared in his cheek. "Hello, little brother."

Chapter Seventeen

Quinn barely registered Helen's gasp behind him as he stared at the taller, broader version of the brother he remembered. "Wade, is it really you?"

"Sure is, partner. I'm a little worse for wear. You, on the other hand…" Wade's smile faltered with regret. "You're all grown up now. It's been a long time. Too long."

Quinn was having as much trouble as Wade in reconciling the boy he'd known with the man standing before him. Quinn had missed his brother fiercely those first few years after Wade and their father had left. However, with age, the memories of their time together had become something pleasant yet distant. He couldn't help feeling some of that distance now. Especially since no communication had passed between them and so much had happened after they'd said goodbye.

There had been Nana's death and their father's death. Wade had become a father through his first marriage then widowed and remarried. Quinn, of course, had gotten married, as well. Quinn struggled through his shock to find his voice again. "You're not dead. I mean I thank God you aren't, but how?"

"Believe me, I've been thanking God, too. I'd be happy to share the story with you and the children. First, let me introduce my wife, Charlotte." Wade held out a hand to the flaxen-haired woman who descended the last few steps with graceful ease. Her dark green eyes mimicked the color of her dress, which looked fancy enough that she could have borrowed it from Helen's closet in Austin.

"This is truly a pleasure, Quinn. After all the good things Wade has shared about you, I feel as though I already know you."

"Thank you. It's a pleasure to meet you, too." Realizing he'd never had occasion to introduce Helen before, he placed a hand at the back of her waist as he looked down at her. "This is Helen, my wife."

She blinked as though coming out of a daze at the sound of her name. She offered her in-laws a smile that was pure graciousness. "I'm so glad to meet you both and that y'all are alive and well."

She didn't look well. She looked pale. Suddenly, he realized why. Wade and Charlotte hadn't just come to visit him. They'd come to take the children away. As much as Quinn had come to think of his nieces and nephews as his own children—as much as he loved them as he would his own—they weren't. They belonged with their parents. Their *real* parents.

As glad as he was that his brother was alive and as wonderful as it was to be together again, Quinn's heart felt heavy at the prospect of the children leaving. Still, he knew what must be done. "Let's go tell the children."

* * *

Helen couldn't breathe. She could hardly think. If it wasn't for Quinn's hand at the small of her back guiding her toward the sheriff's office, she'd probably still be standing at the base of the courthouse steps in total shock. She rejoiced in the fact that Wade and Charlotte were alive. This was without a doubt the best thing that could have happened for her nieces and nephews. She knew that. Yet, somehow that didn't ease her heartache at losing them.

They'd decided on a similar plan to what the sheriff had done to break the news to the children, so Helen and Quinn entered the sheriff's office while Wade and Charlotte stayed outside. Sean waited right inside the door for his cue to open it. Lorelei offered a compassionate smile in greeting. The children glanced up from where they sat surrounding the sheriff's desk with their cups of cider and a cookie apiece. The sight of them was enough to fully pull Helen from the fog of shock that had fallen over her with Wade's first words.

"Thanks, Miss Lorelei." Reece swallowed the last bite of his cookie. "Are we going home now?"

Quinn mussed the boy's hair. "Actually, we have a surprise for you."

Clara's blue eyes widened with immediate interest. "What kind of surprise?"

"Where is it?" Trent asked, already pushing his chair back to stand.

Helen forced the cheery words past the lump in her throat. "It's the best kind of surprise there is. First, I want everyone to stand in the middle of the room and face me. Clara, you bring Olivia. Good. Now, we're all going to close our eyes and count to three."

With the children safely away from the steamy cups of cider, their backs facing the door and their eyes closed or covered, Helen met Quinn's gaze. "One."

He nodded to the sheriff, though his eyes didn't shift from hers as he came to stand beside her. His deep voice joined hers to say, "Two."

Helen watched the sheriff's door ease open silently for Wade and Charlotte to slip inside. Wade's chest swelled visibly in a gasp at the first glimpse of his children in months. Charlotte pressed a hand to her lips as tears filled her eyes. Helen swallowed. Quinn squeezed her hand and took over the count. "When I say the next number I want y'all to look straight at me. Understand?"

They nodded.

"Three." Quinn waited until their eyes were on him to grin. "Your parents are *alive*. Turn around. They're right behind you."

The children gasped and turned to run into their parents' waiting embrace. Pandemonium broke out between Trent's screams of joy and Clara's heartfelt sobs. Olivia's delighted giggles were punctuated by the occasional "Papa" or "Lotte." Reece kept murmuring, "I can't believe it." There wasn't a dry eye in the room or a face without a smile by the time the children calmed down enough to start asking questions.

Wade pulled one of the chairs over for Charlotte to sit. Clara immediately climbed onto her lap. Reece stood beside the chair and put an arm around the woman's shoulder. She, in turn, slipped one around his waist. Meanwhile, Wade sat in another chair with Olivia on one knee and Trent on the other. "I promised your uncle and aunt the story of what happened. If y'all listen closely and don't interrupt, most of your questions will be answered."

Trent nodded as he put an arm around his father's neck. "We'll listen good."

Wade smiled then turned to address Quinn and Helen. "My bride and I decided to spend our short honeymoon on our sailboat off the coast of Alaska. We left the children in the care of my assistant, whom until that point had been a close personal friend and a man I trusted to handle many details of my life. I believe you met Jeffery Richardson."

Quinn nodded but didn't interrupt, so Wade continued, "Our sailing trip was nearly over when we noticed the wind whipping up. Since it was earlier in the season than they normally occur, we didn't realize we were caught in a windstorm until we'd been completely blown off course. The mast broke and the ship began to sink, so we escaped into the lifeboat."

Charlotte shook her head as she gazed into Wade's eyes. "We nearly drowned many times that night. It was all we could do to keep the lifeboat out of the sea and try to keep warm. By morning, the worst of it was over."

"Yes, but we'd only had time to grab a few provisions. They barely lasted us past the first day. There was no sign of shore in any direction, so I could only row in the general direction of where it should be. On the second day we saw what appeared to be a shoreline. We thought we might be able to make it there by nightfall or early the next morning." Wade's frown turned into a smile. "We had just run out of water when we saw a small fleet of kayaks headed toward us. A tribe of Eskimos met us halfway and towed us to shore. We could only understand a little of what they said, which was about how well they could understand us. However, they welcomed us into their village where they took care of us for the next three and a half weeks because I had the misfortune of coming down with pneumonia.

"It took another five days for us to make it back home to Juneau by dogsled. Once there, we discovered that we'd been presumed dead, which I suppose is understandable since we hadn't been able to send word that we were alive. We were devastated to find out that our children had disappeared along with Jeffery. Apparently, he'd seized the opportunity of our supposed deaths to sell my fur-trading post and everything else I owned to the highest bidder. He took the proceeds along with all of the money I'd left to the children in my savings account." He shook his head and ran his fingers through his hair. "We're still in the process of trying to put our lives back together in Alaska."

Charlotte nodded. "Meanwhile, we managed to find out he'd talked about bringing the children to their uncle in Texas."

"The question was, where in Texas?" Wade focused his dark blue eyes on Quinn. "I've been searching for you a long time. I even hired private detectives to find you. They never could. You're a hard man to track down, little brother."

Helen glanced at Quinn, who gave a wincing grimace. "Sorry about that. I know I traveled a lot. Didn't leave much of a paper trail, either."

"You sure didn't. I finally decided to search for you

my own way since the professionals couldn't find you. By that time, I had children, so I couldn't just leave them or take them cross-continent to look in person. I spent several years investigating by mail and telegram. Toward the end, Jeffery joined me in the search. We built your history from the time I left and followed your path by contacting each successive employer. I knew we were getting close. He must have found you while I was gone. It took us a while, but we followed his trail to you. Then the authorities asked us to wait until they found and captured Jeffery before contacting y'all."

Quinn smiled. "It sure means a lot to know you were trying so hard to find me, Wade. I wish we'd been able to reunite earlier and under different circumstances. Then again, I guess this is pretty good, seeing as we found out that you and Charlotte are alive, after all."

Charlotte nodded. "God was looking out for us even when it didn't seem like it."

Helen waited until they'd told the children about Charlie's role in all of this and Jeffery Richardson's capture before asking Wade, "So what are y'all planning to do from here?"

"We're going back to Alaska."

Quinn placed a hand on her shoulder. "When are y'all leaving?"

"Our train leaves tomorrow afternoon. I know it's soon, but we need to arrive in Alaska before winter really sets in."

Helen had expected as much. Still, a protest rose up within her. Did they have to go so soon? Then again, why draw out the pain? The children were leaving. Whether that happened tomorrow morning or a week from now, it wouldn't change the inevitable. Dread pooled in her stomach as she realized the same principle applied to her secret. Yet, how could she find the courage to tell Quinn the truth after everything that had just happened? Then again, how could she not?

It was decided that they would all go to the farm to help pack the children's things. Once it became clear that the men would only be in the way until there was some toting to be done, Wade had requested a tour of the farm. Quinn was happy to oblige and spent the next twenty minutes showing his brother around and explaining all the improvements he'd made. Wade didn't seem to notice the cold breeze shifting through the trees as they stopped halfway up a nearby hill to look down at the farm spread out below them. "This is beautiful land, and you've done a great job with it. I'm proud of you, Quinn."

The words made Quinn stand a bit taller, and it was hard to hold back a grin. He suddenly felt like an eight-year-old again. Back then, he would have climbed to the top of any tree, jumped across any mud hole or captured a Texas-size toad to earn the attention and approval of his brother. Especially during the years their father hadn't been inclined to give it. He cleared his throat. "Thanks, Wade. It means a lot to hear you say that."

Wade's gaze shot to his. "It does?"

"Of course. I always looked up to you. You were smart as a whip, stronger than most of the boys we hung around with and you always made me feel important." Noticing the puzzlement on his brother's face, Quinn frowned. "What? Don't you believe me?"

Wade shrugged. "It's just…I got the impression that you resented me for leaving with Pa."

"As I remember, Pa didn't give you much choice in going with him. How could I resent you for that?"

"Then why did you refuse to write to me?"

"Wade, you know I couldn't read or write back then. I'm only learning now because Helen found out I was illiterate and wanted to teach me."

Wade frowned. "You mean, the tutor didn't help you?"

"What tutor?"

"The one I asked Nana to hire for you a few years after I left."

Quinn's jaw nearly dropped in shock, and it took him a minute to formulate a reply. "You wrote to Nana?"

"Sure, I wrote to her—not to mention sending money home every month." Wade narrowed his eyes. "You didn't know, did you?"

"I had no idea." Quinn sat down on a nearby log as his mind raced to keep up with the implications of what Wade was saying. "I'm sorry to say that I never saw any letters. I certainly never had a tutor. Although, Nana did try to teach me a little around the time you say you wanted her to hire one. The only money I knew of was what I brought in myself."

"I don't understand. Why would she keep all of that from you?"

Quinn sighed. "I can think of a hundred different reasons. Of course, we'll never know what motivated her. Maybe one. Maybe all."

"What kind of reasons?"

"She definitely resented y'all for leaving, so it could've

been her trying to punish you for that. She didn't want me to leave her like y'all had, which she probably thought I would as soon as I was old enough to follow if I knew you still cared about me, and that I'd be welcomed. She didn't want me to get any fancy ideas about what I could accomplish in life. She might have wanted to protect my soul from the influence of too much money. Need I go on?"

"No." Wade bit out the response and began to pace. "Pa and I couldn't send that much money at first, but it increased over time. Once he died, it dipped because I was the only one working. I knew I needed a better-paying job, which is why I jumped at the chance to go to Alaska when I heard how much I could make in the fur-trading business. I kept sending money until the letters came back saying no one lived at that address. It must have added up over the years. What did she do with all of that money if she wasn't buying food or hiring a tutor like she was supposed to do?"

Quinn smiled wryly. "Knowing Nana, she probably gave all the money to the church."

"I can't believe this!"

"I can." Quinn sighed. "I'm sorry she did it because we could have used that money. Although, now that I think about it, twice when things got desperate I came home to find a church lady had dropped off some groceries. Nana hated accepting charity, so I'm guessing that 'church lady' was actually your money at work."

"That's some consolation, but not much." Wade stopped pacing, turned to Quinn and stared as though trying to peer into his brother's soul. The anger in his tone was replaced with concern. "Forget about the money. What about you? How did you fare living with her?"

"Uh…good, I guess." At Wade's doubtful look, he shrugged. "It was difficult at times, but I loved her and I'm sure she loved me, even if she was a little flawed in expressing it."

"I'm not questioning that. You're a good man and she raised you, so she must have done something right. I just hope you realize that a lot of what she said about me, about God, probably even about you and the things you should expect out of life wasn't right."

Quinn stared at his brother. "How do you know what she told me?"

Wade sat beside him, straddling the log to look at him. "I know because she said the same things to me before I left. In fact, the last words she ever spoke to me were from Galatians 6:8. 'For he that soweth to his flesh shall of the flesh reap corruption.' It was as though she thought I was leaving out of rebellion to sow wild oats. All I did was obey Pa by going with him to find higher-paying work. We were trying to make life better for our family."

"She said y'all were going to look for gold."

"Where exactly would we find it? The last gold rush was way back in '59." Wade rolled his eyes and shook his head. "The point is, her words stayed with me for years until I read the last half of that scripture. 'But he that soweth to the Spirit shall of the Spirit reap life everlasting.' Don't let anything she said haunt you like it did me. Live your life based on God's truth—not our grandmother's."

Scratching his jaw, Quinn frowned. Did that include her warning about getting hurt or killed if he reached out for more than he deserved?

Wade placed a hand on his shoulder. "I can tell there is something bothering you. What it is?"

Quinn took a deep breath and explained what had been plaguing him.

"You think I went through all that trouble because I reached above my station for something I didn't deserve?"

"Can you find any other explanation? I mean, look at everything that happened. You got caught in an act of nature on your honeymoon and almost died. Your wife almost died. Your children were placed somewhere you might not have been able to find them. You lost everything you owned because it was stolen from you. Need I go on?"

Wade was quiet for a long moment. Just when Quinn thought he'd stumped his brother, Wade spoke. "I doubt I'll ever be able to say for sure why all of that happened to me. However, I know it wasn't some form of punishment."

"How can you be so sure?"

Wade pulled in a deep breath. "I'm alive. My wife is alive. I found my children. Everything else I called mine can be replaced or rebuilt. I didn't lose it all, Quinn. In fact, I found something I might not have otherwise."

"What's that?"

"You." Wade smiled. "I don't regret the trouble I went through. I see it as God's grace working through fallible man in a fallen world. Life is too short to live always looking over your shoulder for trouble. It's coming. It always is. But God's power and love and grace are already right there with you. That's what you focus on, little brother. Nothing else."

Quinn swallowed hard against the emotion building in his chest before giving a low whistle. "You should've been a preacher."

Wade laughed. "Stare death in the face a few times. You might find yourself thinking an unusual amount of deep, poetic thoughts, too."

"No, thanks. I'll just take it from you." Quinn would, too, because it was good advice. Especially since most of what Nana had said seemed to be a slanted version of what Quinn had been reading in the Bible lately. Why did he cling so tightly to that one adage of hers when he'd forsaken so many others?

Perhaps because it fit everything he believed about himself. It made perfect sense to him that a man who wasn't smart, literate, handsome or rich should have a life just as lacking as he was as a person. Yet Quinn wasn't that man anymore. He still had a long way to go with his reading and writing, but he'd made enough progress to prove to himself he wasn't as stupid as he'd always thought. While he may never be particularly handsome or rich, he'd discovered something of far more worth—a deeper relationship with God.

He certainly wasn't perfect. That had been made evident by his inability to protect Helen from whatever cruel words her ex-fiancé had spoken. However, he'd like to think that he'd made himself into a far better man than he had been when he'd first married her. Did that mean he could stop looking over his shoulder for trouble, as his brother had suggested? Would he actually be able to enjoy the life he'd been working so hard to deserve?

It was going to look different now that his nieces and

nephews would no longer be a part of it in the way he'd anticipated. Of course, different didn't have to be a bad thing. With the children leaving, perhaps Helen would be open to moving forward in their marriage. Surely, she could tell that he cared for her deeply. If she cared for him even half as much, maybe she'd be willing to start a family of their own.

Chapter Eighteen

This wasn't the final goodbye to her nieces and nephews. Helen knew that. Why then, was it a struggle to keep back the tears? She'd see them off tomorrow afternoon at the train station. That would be the real test. Now she should savor the last glimpse of them as they rounded the curve in the hillside that would take them out of sight after what had been a surprisingly enjoyable afternoon and evening.

She'd found a new friend in Charlotte, who'd expressed a desire to correspond often and promised to share news about the children. Wade's delight in finding his children and his long-lost brother in one place had been almost palpable in a way that Helen had found endearing. Watching the interaction of the reunited family had been as sweet as the applesauce cake Charlotte had taught her to make.

With a final wave and a heavy sigh, she returned to the house with Quinn trailing after her. He closed the door behind them with a slight thud that seemed to echo excessively in the empty cabin. She slowly became aware of the fact that she was well and truly alone with her husband. He had been a comforting and supportive presence during the day, but he had to know as surely as she did that everything had changed. She wasn't sure she was ready to deal with that within herself, let alone together.

Grateful for any distraction, since they would surely be few and far between tonight, she tied on her apron and went to work on the supper dishes. She fully expected Quinn to pull out his banjo or delve into his studies, so she was more than a little surprised when he chose to roll up his sleeves and join her at the sink instead. It had been Clara's chore to help Helen with the dishes. They'd talk about their day and share a giggle or two before reading or music time. Sharing the chore with Quinn was an altogether different experience.

He said nary a word as he took the sudsy dishes she handed him to rinse. The area in front of the sink was too small for both of them, so his arm kept brushing against hers. Each time, the urge to hide her face against his broad chest grew stronger. Would it be wrong to give in to that, knowing he might not want to have anything to do with her once she revealed the truth about herself?

When he rejects you... Tom's words whispered through her thoughts. The plate she'd just cleaned slipped back into the soapy water. She braced her hands on the side of the sink for support. In that moment, all she could see was the image presented in her imagination. The one from her dream where Quinn's hands examined her abdomen as the doctor had so many years ago while he pronounced the words she'd heard then. *Damaged.*

That's what she was. Damaged. With the children gone, there would be nothing to soften the news when Quinn found out. She'd been counting on love, but the word hadn't been mentioned between them since the night of the storm when he'd denied even the possibility of it happening. That meant there would be nothing to make up for her inadequacies.

She stiffened when Quinn stepped behind her, wrapped his arms around her waist and eased her back against his chest. Her breath caught in her throat as he pressed a kiss against her hair. The gentleness of that kiss released the sobs that had been building in her chest since she'd first realized she was losing the children, along with even deeper ones created by the awful encounter with Tom. Turning in Quinn's arms, she rested her cheek against his chest and let them all out.

Quinn rested his chin on the top of her head while he rubbed circles on her back. "I know, darlin'. I know."

But he didn't know. Not really. That only made her feel worse. She tightened her grip on the front of his shirt and pulled in a shaky breath. "Oh, Quinn."

"It's a hard thing to take." His deep voice rumbled in her ear. "We'll miss them terribly, but we can…" Leaning back slightly, he lifted her chin so that he could see her face. "We can start a family of our own someday, if you're willing."

She stared at him as her mind raced with the implications of what he was saying. He wanted a full, complete marriage. Did this mean…? Could he possibly love her, after all? Her hand instinctively covered his heart. "What are you saying?"

"I'm saying I think it would be good to have children of our own. I don't mean as a replacement to our nieces and nephews. They would be their own people." His eyes strayed from hers and took on a faraway look as if he could see into the future to the children she couldn't possibly have. "They'd be even more special to us because they'd be made up of you and me. No one would ever be able to take them away from us. We'll have as many as you want. If we have a boy, I'll teach him how to farm and we can expand—"

"Stop." The word came out in a near moan, but it was enough to capture Quinn's attention. She had to tell him. She had to tell him *now*. "There won't be any children. Not for us."

He searched her gaze. "You mean you don't want to have children with me?"

"I mean I *can't* have children, Quinn."

"I don't understand. Why not?"

"I had a riding accident when I was sixteen. The doctor said I'll never be able to have children. That's why I agreed to marry you. You already had four and…" She ran out of words when his face blanched. His arm dropped from around her. Turning away, he sank onto one of the kitchen chairs. She leaned back against the sink for support as raw, heavy silence stretched between them. Despair rolled over her in waves, washing away any trace of hope that he wouldn't reject her. Her voice sounded distant to her ears as she whispered, "Say something."

After a long moment, he glanced up with devastation written all over his face. "What do you want to do?"

She stared at him. Do? About what? Her condition? No. Their marriage.

He was asking her what she wanted to do about their marriage now that the reason they were together had been stripped away and she'd revealed the truth about herself. What *could* be done? They were legally married. That hadn't changed. "I'm not sure."

Something in his blue eyes hardened along with his tone. "Well, I'll not hold you here. You can go back to Austin if you like. Take the dowry your parents sent. I won't need it and it really belongs to you."

That was all she needed to know. She closed her eyes to hide the pain that cut through her chest. She forced her voice, her face, to remain impassive. "I suppose that would be best. I'll finish the dishes in the morning. Good night."

She closed the door to her room behind her but made no effort to get ready for bed. Instead, she sat on her bed with her hands buried in her hair and wept a silent torrent of tears. She tensed as she heard Quinn's footsteps in the hall, then relaxed when she realized he was retiring to the room where the boys used to sleep. She was physically, emotionally and mentally exhausted from everything that had happened, but sleep wouldn't come. Her tears faded as hurt slowly turned to anger. Soon she was pacing the floor of her bedroom with her hands clenched into tight fists. She paced until the walls seemed to close in on her, then she knew she needed to get out of the house and into the fresh air no matter how dark or cold that air might be.

She quietly crept from her room since another confrontation with Quinn was the last thing she wanted tonight. Or was it? She stomped into her boots while sending a glare down the hallway toward the room where he slept. She grabbed her coat and stepped into the night. The dark hills silhouetted by moonlight loomed around her. Innumerable stars shimmered above. A mockingbird's call drifted down from the woods. Yet, all Helen's mind could focus on was one question that continued to bother her. If Quinn didn't love her then why had he wanted to change their arrangement?

"He's just like Tom, that's why." Picking up a pinecone, she sent it spiraling toward a tree, which absorbed the blow with a satisfying *thwack*. Even as her words settled into the air around her, she knew they weren't true. Quinn was nothing like Tom, which was why his reaction had been so hurtful. She hadn't been sure what to expect from him, but she'd certainly hoped for more than just his silence. Once that had ended, all she'd gotten was a kindly put command to get out.

What she'd really wanted was for him to sweep her into his arms and profess his love. She'd wanted him to beg her to stay. She'd wanted him to tell her that he didn't think less of her because she'd injured herself in a moment of recklessness on a high-strung horse. She'd wanted him to contradict every word Tom had spoken and sweep away the self-deprecating thoughts that so often filled her mind. He hadn't done that. In fact, his action made her wonder if the doctor and Tom had been right all along. Perhaps it was time to fully accept that she was everything they'd said or intimated her to be: *permanently damaged.*

Something rose within her that she'd never felt before. Courage, strength, determination, temerity—whatever it was, it came out in one steely spoken word: *"No."*

Suddenly, a rush of what she could only describe as clarity overtook her. Let Dr. Whitley say her injury was caused by recklessness rather than pure accident. Let Tom try to convince her that she wasn't intended to be an honorable woman. Let Quinn return her to her parents as he would damaged goods to a mercantile. That didn't mean it was true. It certainly didn't mean she had to accept their view of her as something on which to base her identity, her thoughts or her plans.

She didn't need anyone to contradict words she knew weren't true. She couldn't wait for someone to come along who could clear her mind of cruel thoughts. She could—she *would* do it herself. In fact, it wasn't something anyone else could do for her. It was something she needed to overcome with God's help and Word and grace. He certainly didn't look at her and see damage. He saw His Beloved. How had she lost sight of the importance of that? The answer was simple. She'd focused on the opinion of others rather than God.

"Helen?"

She stiffened at the sound of Quinn's voice. The brittle scales of the pinecone she hadn't realized she was holding bit into her hand. She dropped it and pulled her coat closer. "Yes?"

"What are you doing out here? You'll freeze."

What did he care? She spun to ask him exactly that. The sight of him leaning against the door frame stilled the words on her tongue before they reached her lips. He lifted the lantern he held in what must have been an effort to see her better. For her, it only served to illuminate the concern marring his brow and the mussed curls that could only come from fitful sleep. His deep blue eyes were too tired to be guarded. She saw gentleness there, which was altogether confusing in the aftermath of their last conversation.

Her anger abandoned her, leaving her feeling vulnerable. It would have been easier to hold on to those feelings if she didn't love him so. Everything he'd done until earlier tonight had made her feel whole and even cherished. She'd thought he was beginning to care for her. Hadn't he said he wanted to win her heart? Could the truth about her really have changed that so quickly?

Afraid she'd do something or say something to reveal how close she was to throwing herself into his arms and begging him to let her stay, she lowered her eyes to the porch steps as she mounted them. Her intent was to quickly edge past him into the house, but he took his time in shifting his weight away from the door frame. His arm came up to block the entrance when she tried to move past him. Surprised, her gaze automatically locked with his, which was a mistake. Surely her tangled emotions were written on her face. Any hope that they weren't shattered as a frown deepened on his face.

Had she no pride? Just because she'd had a breakthrough concerning her condition didn't automatically alter Quinn's view of her. She was damaged in his eyes. Yet, she wasn't sorry for telling the truth. If she hadn't, she wouldn't have found the strength to face it or the courage to choose not to let it define her. She lifted her chin. "Excuse me, please."

A moment passed before his arm dropped. She edged by him and down the hall into her bedroom where she pulled in a heavy sigh. She wouldn't be able to sleep tonight, so she might as well start packing. It wouldn't do either of them any good for her to stay here longer than necessary. Yet what was the point of leaving? They'd still be married even if they were leading separate lives.

Didn't that mean that there was still hope for them? Perhaps he'd change his mind over time. Surely he'd get lonely out here all by himself. Eventually, he might ask her to return. She sighed. Was she truly prepared to spend months, years or even a lifetime waiting for such a thing to happen when he obviously wanted a way out of their marriage? Perhaps the only fair thing to do would be to let him go. She just wasn't sure how she could.

Quinn awakened the next morning feeling completely disoriented. Then he remembered he'd spent the night in the boys' room because the children had gone with Wade and Charlotte to the hotel in town. Children. Helen. He sat up in Reece's old bed and dragged his hands through his mussed hair as every painful detail of the past twelve hours rushed over him. Helen couldn't have children. The news had been disappointing in itself because he'd enjoyed being a father to his nieces and nephews. However, that hadn't compared to the devastation he'd felt when he'd realized how much more it mattered to Helen that she couldn't be a mother.

It had mattered enough that she'd married a man she didn't love—probably had no hope of loving—to obtain the children she wouldn't have been able to have on her own. And then they were taken from her. Now she was left with him. A man she'd never wanted in the first place. A man she must have known all along didn't deserve her. No wonder she was heartbroken.

He'd felt her pain along with his own. Yet he knew his wound had been inflicted by his own stupidity. He'd gotten so caught up in trying to be a better man, he'd forgotten that only one thing had truly qualified him to be her husband. It didn't have anything to do with him or the Bachelor List. It was that she'd loved his children. Now the children were gone, and he couldn't give her any more. He had nothing to offer that would be of any worth to her.

An image came to mind of Helen standing in the cold with her coat wrapped close around her. He still couldn't figure out what she'd been doing out there in the middle of the night and she hadn't deigned to explain. In fact, he couldn't recall that she'd said more than a few words to him during that exchange. She hadn't needed to because her eyes had spoken volumes—most of which didn't make a lick of sense.

Longing, hurt and something he might dare to call caring had replaced the pure apprehension that had stared back at him after she'd divulged the true reason she'd married him. The apprehension he'd understood. Why wouldn't she fear being stuck with him alone for the rest of her life? He'd done his best to let her know he had no intention of keeping her captive just because their names were on the same marriage certificate. He'd offered her a way back to the life she deserved. The one where she'd be able to live in a gilded mansion and never have to scrub dishes or milk a cow or avoid an ill-tempered rooster.

His plan had been to stay right here where he belonged. That would spare them both unnecessary pain—hers at being stuck with a man she'd never really wanted, and his at wanting a woman whose heart he'd never be able to win. However, the look she'd given him on the porch was not that of a woman whose heart was completely untouchable. He couldn't fathom why she'd want anything to do with someone who had nothing to offer, but what if she was amenable to changing her mind? Could there be some small part of her that wanted to stay?

The answer came to him as soon as he passed by her doorway and saw her struggling to buckle a nearly overflowing suitcase. Not only did she want to leave, but she couldn't wait to get away from him. The sight made him downright ornery even though he knew he had no right to feel that way. He felt a muscle in his jaw twitch. "Are you planning on leaving today?"

She jumped a little at the sound of his voice, then spared a quick glance his way. "I have a few things to do in town first, then I should be able to leave on the same train with the children."

Dandy. His whole family would be leaving him at one time. That ought to make things around here nice and lonely. Still, he could hardly protest since it was a smart plan. He crossed his arms. "Good. I don't like the idea of you traveling alone."

"Well, I won't be." The buckles finally snapped closed. "We'd better hurry if we want to finish the chores and make it into town in time to have breakfast with the other Tuckers."

The "other Tuckers" were already waiting for them at Maddie's Café—which meant the story of Wade and Charlotte's survival was probably winding its way through town with record speed. As soon as they finished eating, Charlotte took the children to the schoolhouse to say goodbye to their friends while Helen left to take care of a few things on her own. Realizing this would probably be the most privacy he'd get with his brother, Quinn decided to make the most of the opportunity. "Helen will be traveling as far as Austin on the train with y'all. Will you look out for her for me?"

"You know I will." Wade paused as Maddie refilled their cups of coffee before he continued, "You aren't going with her?"

Quinn felt a wry smile tug at his lips. "That would kind of defeat the purpose. She's going there to live with her parents."

Wade frowned. "You two are separating? For how long?"

"I don't know. Forever, I guess. I suppose I should have expected as much as soon as I found out you were alive." Quinn quickly explained everything to his brother from his original prayer for a helpmeet to the Bachelor List and all that came after.

"I had no idea," Wade said once Quinn had finished. "So you're just going to let her go?"

Quinn grimaced. "I can hardly force her to stay. That would be selfish since she deserves so much more than I can give her. Besides, I hardly think I'd stand a chance with her."

Wade shook his head. "That's Nana talking. Not you. At least, I hope you don't really believe that."

"I believe what you said about Nana's warnings not being true. In fact, I'm pretty sure most of what I learned from her was plain wrong. I've also read my Bible enough to know that God's promises for His children are good. It just doesn't seem like they're intended for me."

"Why not?"

"I'm not the kind of man who has great things happen to him. At least, not the kind that last. I thought that would change if I made myself into a better man. Well, I've changed a little, but not enough to make a real difference. Until I do…" He shrugged. "I don't deserve anything more than what I've always had."

"It kind of sounds like it's more about identity than anything else."

"Identity? What do you mean?"

"It's like this." Wade set aside his coffee and leaned forward. "You're saying because you're this person, you don't deserve certain things. This may sound strange and I know we've only recently reconnected, but I can already tell you aren't the person you think you are."

Quinn gave his brother a quizzical smile. It *did* sound a little strange, but Quinn was intrigued. "Who am I, then?"

"I'm afraid that's something you've got to figure out for yourself."

Quinn thought about it, then asked, "You wouldn't happen to have a Bible in town, would you?"

"As a matter of fact, I do." Wade settled the bill with Maddie then led Quinn to his hotel room where he placed a Bible in Quinn's hands. "I'm supposed to meet Charlotte at the mercantile. You'll have this room to yourself for a while. Make yourself comfortable."

Quinn wasted no time in doing just that, sitting in an armchair by a window that overlooked Main Street. The activity below faded away as he flipped through the pages of the Bible at random. The words seemed to jump out at him as they never had before. How had he missed this verse declaring him a new creature? Or this one saying that God would give him a double portion of honor in place of the shame he'd endured? Or another declaring that God wanted to give him a future and a hope? The more he read, the more he realized that his worth was based not on what he could do, but on what God had already done.

Even so, something about all of this didn't make sense.

Why would God do this for him? He leaned back in his chair to think over everything he'd read, everything Helen had shown him, everything he'd heard Pastor Brightly preach, and arrived at one conclusion. It was because God loved him. And that changed everything.

Well, perhaps not everything. Helen was still going to get on the train and never look back. After all, his newfound freedom didn't mean he should chain her to a life or a man she'd never wanted. She'd made her decision. He needed to respect that even though he prayed with all his heart that she'd change her mind.

Chapter Nineteen

Quinn grimaced as a hollow whistle announced the arrival of the westbound train. Steam hissed through the cold air while a few passengers disembarked and the large steel doors of the luggage car slid open to receive his family's bags. Quinn sneaked a sideways glance at Helen, who looked as proper and composed in a cranberry-colored traveling suit as she had the first time he'd seen her standing at the front of the schoolroom a few months earlier. She was clutching what appeared to be a scroll wrapped in brown paper and tied with string. Whatever it was had garnered more of her attention than he had since she'd joined the rest of them for a quick dinner at the hotel.

Wade clasped him on the shoulder. "Everything is loaded up. It's time to say goodbye."

Quinn's heart sank as everyone turned to look at him. Helen's goodbyes to Wade, Charlotte and the children wouldn't be necessary until she reached Austin. He pulled in a deep breath to steel himself. This was going to hurt. He had no doubt about that. Clara stepped forward and he lifted her into a hug. She threw her arms around his neck. "You're the best uncle in the world and I love you."

"You are a precious young lady and I love you, too." He held her tight then kissed her forehead before setting her down.

Trent was already tugging on his leg for attention. "I've got something important to tell you."

"Is that right?" Quinn swept the boy into his arms. "What do you have to say for yourself, young man?"

Trent hid his face on Quinn's shoulder with a sudden attack of shyness, which made his words a bit muffled. "You're my second-bestest buddy besides Reece."

"I am? Well, 'second-bestest' is good enough for me, cowboy." He jostled the boy slightly so they could grin at each other before they exchanged a hug. Charlotte handed him Olivia next. He told the little girl goodbye with a kiss on the cheek that she promptly returned, much to everyone's amusement. Reece was next. As they hugged, the boy admitted, "I'm going to miss you and Aunt Helen something awful. I wish we could all be together."

"We'll miss you, too, Reece. You'll be in our thoughts and prayers no matter how far apart we are. Distance doesn't stop family from being family." Quinn glanced up to find Wade watching and smiled. "Your pa taught me that."

After saying goodbye to Charlotte, Quinn offered his hand to his brother. Wade brushed it aside and went for a hug instead, which ended with them both pounding each other on the back. When they stepped apart, Wade put a hand on Quinn's shoulder. "I hate that we're saying goodbye again when it seems we've just said hello."

"So do I." A lump made its way into his throat even as his eyes began to smart. He fought back the feeling with a smile. "I can't tell you how much this has meant to me or how much you've helped me in the short time you've been here."

"It's meant the world to me, too. I only wish I could have been here a long time ago. We've missed so much." Wade shook his head and swallowed hard before turning away. "Charlotte, children, let's get on the train. Helen, we'll save you a seat."

Quinn pulled in a deep breath then slowly turned to face his wife. She offered a tremulous smile that soon vanished. He cleared his throat, rubbed his jaw and tried to form the words to say goodbye. They wouldn't come. He slipped his hands into his pockets. "Your parents will be waiting for you in Austin?"

"Yes."

He nodded. "Send me a wire to let me know you've arrived safely."

"I will."

"Good." Silence stretched between them until it was broken by the conductor's call of "All aboard." Quinn's heartbeat ratcheted up in his chest. This was really happening. She was actually going to leave. "I guess this is it."

"Yes, I suppose it is." There were tears in her eyes when she met his gaze for the first time all afternoon. "Thank you, Quinn. Thank you for giving me the chance to be a mother even if it was only for a short time. It was everything I dreamed it would be. Now, all you have to do is sign this and return it to Judge Hendricks. He'll take care of everything else."

"What are you—"

She rose on tiptoe to kiss him deeply. Startled, it took him a moment to respond, and when he reached out to pull her closer, she was already disappearing onto the train. All she left behind was the package she'd been so fascinated with all afternoon. Was this what he was supposed to sign and return to the judge? He ripped the brown paper away to reveal the official-looking document inside. "'Petition for an-nul...annul-ment.'"

Everything within him froze. He couldn't seem to breathe as he examined the pages that would legally make it as though his marriage had never taken place. Helen had already filled everything out and signed her name on the last page right next to the blank spot where his was supposed to go. This was far different than just letting her live with her parents in another city. This would mean letting go of her and any hope of reconciliation. It meant he'd most likely never see her again. *This* was what she wanted?

His hands fisted, crumpling the papers in them as he stared at the train that hissed out more steam as it began a slow chug out of the station. Well, annulment wasn't what he wanted. He was sick of this. He was sick of living his life expecting the worst then letting it play out right in front of him as though he had no choice or strength to change things. If God wanted him to have good things, an abundant life, a hope, a future, then why should Quinn be content to settle for anything less?

Helen was the best thing that had ever happened to him. He didn't deserve her. That was true. He didn't deserve God's love, either. That didn't mean that it didn't belong to him…just as Helen did in the eyes of God and the law. She was his wife. He was her husband. He suddenly realized that meant it was no longer a question of whether he deserved her. The true question—the only question that mattered was, did he love her?

The answer was undeniable. Yes, he did. He just hadn't dared to accept it or acknowledge it for fear that something would happen to take her away from him. Now what he'd feared was happening. Still, he had a choice. He could let her go or he could fight for her. It might not change the outcome of what would happen. However, for the first time in his life, he intended to try.

The train bellowed a whistle that sounded like an outright challenge, causing Quinn to realize his deep thinking had allowed the train to ease out of the station. It was gaining speed in an effort to leave Peppin behind. Without a second thought, Quinn jumped from the platform onto the track. He took off running after the train, ignoring the yells from the folks at the station questioning his sanity along with every misgiving and fear that rose up to tell him he was being a fool.

Quinn Tucker was chasing after more than he was entitled. What's more, he planned to catch her. Once he did, God willing, he'd never let her go again.

Helen rested her head against the train window and fought back tears as the train picked up speed. Her seat's window faced the opposite side from the center of town, so she'd have no last look at the place she'd called home or the man she'd called her husband. Perhaps that was for the best. Her conversation with the county judge had yielded a way of escape for Quinn. Maybe he would find someone else in time. Someone he wouldn't think of as damaged.

Meanwhile, she'd find a way to be content on her own while cherishing every memory of the eight weeks she'd been his wife. She could only imagine what Austin society would say when she turned up only a few days after her wedding reception husbandless. Right now, she really didn't care. The only thing that mattered was that she'd left her heart back in Peppin with a man she'd probably never see again.

Helen slid forward in her seat as the train abruptly slid to a stop. Her hand shot out to keep Trent, who sat next to her, from doing the same. She exchanged an alarmed look with Charlotte as Wade stood to peer out the window. He spoke over the confused murmurs coming from the other passengers in the train car. "Maybe there's something on the tracks."

Reece squeezed in between his father and the glass. "Maybe it's outlaws."

That brought Trent out of his seat. "I don't see anything."

"Boys, sit down." Charlotte's voice was commanding enough to make even Wade comply. Meanwhile, the folks across the aisle began opening their windows, allowing the cold to seep in along with the conductor's irritated voice. "That brake is for emergencies only. This does not constitute an emergency."

"It does to me."

Helen felt her eyes widen at the sound of the deep, familiar voice. A gasp eased through her lips and her heart thundered in her chest as she hurried down the aisle toward the door. It eased open from the outside and she found herself staring down at Quinn. He froze, with his hands braced on either side of the doorway as though ready to jump inside and...do what exactly?

Hope battled with alarm and uncertainty as they stared at each other for a long, drawn-out moment. His searching gaze traced her every feature before returning to hers. He must have seen something he liked, for his blue eyes deepened while his dimples flashed in a reckless grin she'd never seen before. A strange weakness filled her knees. His strong hands caught around her waist and hers automatically braced on his shoulders as he swung her down to stand in front of him. Her fingers slid from his shoulders to push away from his chest once she found her bearings. It did little good since he didn't release her. "What is going on? What are you doing here?"

He ignored her questions completely. "Helen, please don't go."

She was dreaming. She'd fallen asleep on the train and was dreaming. "What did you say?"

He spoke louder, as if that would somehow help her understand. "I want you to stay."

Before she could think of a response, a collective "aw" sounded above her head. Helen glanced up and her eyes widened. All the passengers on her car had crammed together at the open windows. They weren't the only ones. People were hanging out the windows down the length of the train to watch. The engineer had climbed down from his station to stand in the tall grass with his hands on his hips. Even a few folks on the platform of the train station a good distance away had stopped what they were doing. "Land sakes, Quinn. You stopped the train."

"Yeah, I sure did." He didn't look the least bit repentant about it, either. Nor did he seem fazed by all the attention they were garnering. He led her a short distance off and positioned her so that she faced away from the train. Suddenly, it felt as though it was just the two of them beneath the wide Texas sky. His gaze had lost none of its intensity. "Did you hear what I said, Helen? I don't want you to go to Austin. I want you to come home with me."

It was exactly what her heart was aching to hear. Well, not exactly. Still, it was the closest he had ever come to a profession of love. Even so, it didn't change anything. She slid out of his one-armed embrace and took a step back. "Quinn, as much as I would like it to work out between us, I don't think it will. It's better that you file the petition for annulment. Where *is* the petition?"

His jaw tightened at the mention of the annulment before his lips settled into a smirk that was entirely too distracting. "Don't know. Don't care. Why wouldn't it work?"

She glanced away, rubbed the nape of her neck and pressed her lips together.

"Helen." That one word issued a command impossible to ignore.

"It's going to be hard enough to stop thinking of myself as damaged. If I was living with a husband who saw me that way, it would be nigh on impossible. I can't do that to myself."

A blank look was followed by one of pure confusion. "What are you talking about? Damaged how?"

"The accident. I can't have children." She frowned when his confusion didn't ease. "Quinn, I told you this."

"I know you told me. I just don't understand where you're getting the idea that any of that matters to me. I never said that made you damaged. I never even thought it."

She stared at him in disbelief. "Then why did you look so devastated?"

"I thought you were saying you had no use for me. You married me for the children. The children were gone and I couldn't give you any more. You thought it was because...?" He shook his head. "Not at all. I mean, sure I'm disappointed that we won't be able to have any children. However, if I looked devastated, it was because I knew I was about to lose you."

"It was?"

"Yes, it was. It seems we've both been a little confused. Let me clear something up for you right now. You are not damaged." He eased closer, his hands cradling the loose fists she hadn't even realized she'd made. "You are intelligent, beautiful and caring, among so many other qualities, all of which make you an incredible woman. So much so that I almost let you go because I know I have no hope of ever deserving you."

"What changed your mind?"

"I fell in love with you. I'm pretty sure it happened the night of Ellie and Lawson's shivaree. If not then, it might have been when you thought I wanted you to milk the chickens, or when your kiss caused a hailstorm, or seeing your determination and patience in teaching me to read, or the time you called me Bear. I'm not sure. However, as I stood on the platform with that petition in my hands, watching as you rode out of my life, one thing became clear. I love you, Helen Tucker. I'm asking you to give me a chance to show you how much. I'm asking you to come home."

Those were the words she'd been longing for him to say. Hearing them spoken was like stepping into a daydream. She was afraid she'd blink and all of this would vanish. She'd find herself back on the train, staring out the window wishing for something she'd never have. Yet, he stood before her with his heart in his eyes confirming his words. She couldn't contain her smile. It started in the depths of her soul and spread until it reached her lips. He traced the upturned corner of her mouth. "Does this mean yes?"

"It means I love you, too."

"You—" Surprise gave way to searching. "You really love me?"

"With all my heart."

A grin spread across his face. "And you'll come home?"

She nodded. "And I'll come home."

He whooped. Catching her waist again, he lifted her into the air and whirled her in a tight circle, much to the delight of the onlookers, who let out a cheer of approval. She laughed and clung to Quinn's hand as he led her back toward the waiting train. Wade stood beside the conductor with a grin on his face and her luggage sitting in the grass at his feet. Her nieces and nephews raced toward her. She knelt down to receive their hugs, kiss their cheeks and tell them goodbye. Her in-laws each gave her a hug before ushering their children back onto the train. The conductor gave them one last scowl that reluctantly changed to a smile as he shook his head. Mumbling something about Peppin being a crazy town, he signaled the engineer and hopped back on the train.

Helen waved at the children and shouted, "Thank you!" in return to the strangers calling out well-wishes as the train lumbered down the tracks then sped away. A quick glance at the station told her most of the folks had gone about their business. Awareness rushed over her and she turned to find Quinn already watching her with an expectant smolder in his eyes. A blush warmed her cheeks. He might be ready for a kiss or two, but she had important business to take care of first. Placing her hands on her hips, she tilted her head and lifted a brow. "Quinn Tucker, what is that you said about not deserving me?"

"No idea."

She narrowed her eyes. She erased the distance between them until they stood toe to toe before poking him in the chest. "Hey, focus for me here. This is important."

"I'm listening." He caught her wrists and guided her arms up so that they encircled his neck before wrapping his arms around her waist.

She gave him a doubtful look but continued, anyway. "You said you were going to let me go because you didn't think you deserved me. Why would you think such a thing?"

"I may be a little smarter than I originally thought. Still, I'm not rich or handsome or…" He must have realized it would not be wise to continue. Perhaps her glare clued him in.

"How dare you say those things about my husband? You certainly are smarter than you think. Book learning is not the only measure of intelligence. While you are excelling at that, you are also intelligent in other areas such as practical wisdom, life experience, human nature, musical ability. I could go on and on." She leaned back in his arms. "As for finances, you don't give yourself enough credit for going from a child with a hungry belly to a man who owns his own land. Besides, I've lived rich in money. I'd a thousand times rather be rich in love."

"I believe you. Now you don't have to tell me I'm handsome."

"You make my knees weak."

He lifted a brow. "I make your knees weak?"

"Remember how I sort of stumbled the first time I saw you with your new haircut and a shave?" She smoothed the collar of his gray coat even though it didn't need fixing.

"Yeah."

"Well, right after that I…" She bit her lip then shot a glance heavenward before letting out a small sigh. "Truthfully, I sort of swooned. Just a little."

"I made you swoon." He grinned, looking all too pleased with himself.

"And when you gave me that look just a minute ago I could hardly breathe."

"What look?" he asked. She gave him her best rendition of his earlier smolder, which only made his blue eyes darken. "I see what you mean. So…what happens when I kiss you?"

"Now, that's a hard one." She gave him a mischievous smile. "I can't seem to remember..."

Recognizing her invitation for what it was, he lowered his forehead to hers. "I do. Lightning."

Then he set out to prove it.

Epilogue

One year later...

Helen was certain she must be dying. There was no other way to explain the peculiar way she'd been feeling of late. She'd tried to downplay her illness to Quinn, but there was no mistaking the mounting concern in his eyes. She'd come to town alone today, hoping a visit to the doctor would provide her some insight and tell her things weren't as hopeless as she feared. Tension filled the air as Doc Williams finished the examination. "I'd say you have about seven months left."

Dread filled her sensitive stomach. Tears filled her eyes. Her mind began to race. How on earth was she going to tell Quinn? They'd been married—truly married—for little over a year. They'd thought they had an entire lifetime to spend together. She'd had no idea that lifetime would be so short. "Seven months. That's such a small amount of time."

"Yes, and it will go by even faster than you think." He was far too intent on flipping through a calendar to notice the quiet sob that caught in her throat. "That puts your due date around the end of July."

She blinked. "Due date? I thought that term was only used for women who are expecting, not someone who is…" She couldn't say the word. Not yet. She swallowed. "Someone who has so little time left as I do."

Doc Williams straightened in his chair and peered through his glasses at her as alarm filled his distinguished features. "Mrs. Tucker, I never meant to give you the impression… I thought you already knew about your condition and were just coming to me for confirmation."

"I was."

"No. I don't think you understand." He removed his glasses and took her hand. "Seven months from now you're going to deliver a baby."

"A baby?" The world spun. If not for the man holding her hand, she might have toppled right off his examining table onto the floor. "That's impossible."

"I assure you it is not only possible but inevitable."

"No. There must be some other explanation." She told him of her riding accident and the doctor's prognosis afterward.

He listened intently, alternately nodding and frowning until she finished. "I see. Well, your body doesn't lie. It has all the symptoms of a woman in the family way. I am quite sure your family doctor's prognosis has been proven most decidedly wrong."

"I don't understand how that could be possible. He was so certain. As certain as you are now."

"The female body remains mostly a mystery to those practicing medical science. Unfortunately, that can breed a level of what I can only describe as ignorance in even the most respected of doctors. Some think that recklessness or personal misbehavior is the main cause of infertility in ladies. It would seem that your family doctor subscribed to that school of thought."

"You don't think that's the case?"

He shook his head. "The numbness and pain you described that took place following your accident aren't unusual for such trauma. From your description, it sounds as though those feelings went away with the rest of the bruises you acquired in your fall. You've never missed a month until recently, right?"

"Right."

He shrugged as though that settled everything. "It seems to me that everything is progressing normally. We'll keep a close eye on you to make sure there aren't complications. However, I don't anticipate there being any. You are a healthy young woman who is about to welcome her first child."

She couldn't seem to catch her breath, couldn't seem to get past the shock. "I'm going to have a baby."

Doc Williams grinned as he helped her down from the examining table. "Congratulations, Mrs. Tucker."

"Thank you." She walked from his office into the waiting room in a daze. She blinked, realizing Charlotte had rushed forward to meet her. "I'm sorry, Charlotte. Did you say something?"

Helen's in-laws had returned to Peppin with the children only a week after their train had pulled out of town. Wade said they'd realized if they were essentially going to have to start over, they ought to do it here in Peppin with their family. Quinn had been ecstatic and so had

Helen. The two families were constantly in and out of each other's houses, sharing meals and laughter. Charlotte had become one of Helen's dearest friends. That was why Helen had asked her sister-in-law to accompany her to the doctor without revealing the reason for the Saturday-morning appointment.

Charlotte watched her in concern as she looped her arm through Helen's and guided her out the door. "I asked if you were all right. You looked so scared when you went in and now you look sort of stunned."

"I am stunned." They paused beside the wagon Helen had parked outside the doctor's office. "I'm fine, though. Better than fine. I...I need to go home. I need to tell Quinn."

A knowing smile slowly tipped Charlotte's lips. "I see. Are you sure you're up to driving right now?"

"Yes. Oh, Charlotte." She hugged her friend tightly then left her in the dust. Helen barely made it out of town before she let out a very unladylike squeal of joy. "I'm having a baby. I'm having a *baby*! Thank You, God! Thank You! Thank You! Oh, I can't wait to see Quinn's face when I tell him."

There was another squeal, some laughter and a hundred more "thank-Yous" before she set the brake outside her house. She forced herself to pull in a calming breath, which had absolutely no effect before she flew up the porch steps into the cabin. The door shut behind her with a bang. Pulling off her gloves and shrugging out of her coat, she tossed them aside. "Where, oh, where is my Bear?"

"Right where you left him," Quinn called back.

She followed his voice to the girls' old room, which

had been converted into a study with an ever-growing library. He'd added a fireplace to the wall the room shared with their bedroom so it was nice and warm. As usual, rather than sitting at the rolltop desk or in one of the two comfortable chairs, he'd stretched out on the thick rug in front of the hearth. Before he could stand to greet her, she knelt behind him and wrapped her arms around his shoulders in a quick hug. "Have you been reading all this time?"

He caught her arm to keep her there as he sat up then glanced at the clock on the mantel. "I guess so. With no need for a winter crop, since the fall harvest went so well, I have a lot of time to improve my mind. Besides, what else was I supposed to do left all by my lonesome for ages?"

She rolled her eyes. "I've been gone little more than an hour."

"Felt like ages." He lifted her hand to his lips for a kiss. "Listen to this. It made me think of you. It was written by a fellow named Marlowe. 'Come live with me and be my Love, And we will all the pleasures prove, That hills and valleys, dale and field…'"

It wasn't very surprising that a man who loved music would find an affinity for poetry. Still, it was a delightful development. Speaking of delightful developments, she had one of her own to share if she could just get his nose out of that book. She leaned forward to kiss his cheek, hoping it would make his dimple appear. It did, so she did it again. He snapped the book closed, snagged her waist and brought her around so that her back rested against his propped-up knee. He'd perfected the smoldering look that had originated almost a year ago and had no qualms about using it on her now. "You are *the most* distracting woman."

He kissed her and she got a little distracted herself until he finally let her breathe again. She sat up but didn't go far. "Quinn, I went into town to see the doctor."

The fire in his blue eyes banked in concern. They'd both been afraid to speak of the frequent episodes of what she now knew was merely morning sickness until now. "What did he say?"

"He said…" Her fingers traced the curve of his jaw as her lips betrayed her serious tone with a smile. "You and I are going to have a baby."

His mouth dropped open even as his brow furrowed in confusion. He shook his head. "That can't be right."

"That's what I told him." She filled him in on Doc Williams's explanation for her previous diagnosis and his expectation that she'd have a normal pregnancy.

Quinn still looked a little stunned when she finished. He blinked, searched her gaze. "Are you serious? We're really going to have a baby?"

"I'm serious. You're going to be a father."

Shock faded to awe. His mouth opened and closed without him finding any words. Standing, he lifted her up with him then tugged her into his embrace. She tried to pull back to see his face, but he wouldn't let her go even that much. She mumbled into his chest. "Are you happy?"

She felt him nod.

She giggled. "Are you sure?"

He caught her face in his hands and kissed her. Cradling her cheek, he stared into her eyes with a look so joyful, so loving that it took her breath away. "I love you."

"I love you, too."

"I can't wait to meet our baby." He pulled her close again. His tone turned deep and reverent. "I don't know what to say except thank You, Lord, for answering my prayer and blessing me beyond anything I could have imagined."

She joined in from the depths of her heart. "Amen."

* * * * *

Dear Reader,

Welcome back to Peppin, Texas! I hope you're feeling at home here. This is the fourth book I've written in this sweet little town. Be sure to look for the other three if you haven't read them yet. There will be more to come as the Bachelor List brings love, trouble and a whole lot of adventure to every hand that holds it. If you don't know how the list started, you'll find its origin in Ellie and Lawson's story, *A Texas-Made Match*.

I hope that Helen and Quinn's story ministered to you as much as it did to me while I was writing it. This wasn't an easy story for me to tell because it hit close to home. Like Quinn, I struggled for much of my life under the weighty misimpression that I was, as he might say, "not a smart person." I worked hard in school to try to prove to myself over and over again that it wasn't true. That hard work paid off when I graduated summa cum laude after receiving awards for being an "Exemplary All-Round Student" at the university and the "Outstanding Student" in my major. I thought surely all of that would be enough to prove to myself that I wasn't dumb. Imagine my surprise when it wasn't.

Suddenly, I realized I was allowing the bad thoughts running through my head to tell me who and what I was, so I stopped buying into them. I no longer need to prove my intelligence to anyone—including myself—because I found out the truth about my identity. It is not based on the lies I accepted, my efforts to prove those lies wrong or accolades from others, no matter how grateful I still am for them. My identity is based on one thing—God's love for me. He sees me through that love along with His grace and forgiveness. How He sees me is who I am. End of story. The same is true for you. I hope this story was an encouraging reminder of that.

If you'd like to share your thoughts about the story, you can email me directly at author@noellemarchand.com. You can also check out my website at NoelleMarchand. com for updates and a list of my backlist books. Or connect with me on Facebook, Goodreads, Twitter or Pinterest. I'd love to hear from you!

In His grace,

Noelle Marchand

COMING NEXT MONTH FROM
Love Inspired® Historical

Available April 7, 2015

WAGON TRAIN REUNION
Journey West
by Linda Ford

Abigail Bingham is reunited with former flame Benjamin Hewitt when she joins a wagon train headed west. Will the Oregon trial offer a second chance for the socialite's daughter and a charming cowboy?

AN UNLIKELY LOVE
by Dorothy Clark

Marissa Bradley is drawn to Grant Winston, but his livelihood is to blame for her family's destruction. Can Grant find a way to maintain the family business and to have Marissa as his wife?

FROM BOSS TO BRIDEGROOM
Smoky Mountain Matches
by Karen Kirst

What starts as a strictly professional relationship grows into something more between boss Quinn Darling and his lovely employee, Nicole O'Malley. Until Quinn discovers Nicole's been keeping a secret that could derail their future together.

THE DOCTOR'S UNDOING
by Allie Pleiter

Doctor Daniel Parker doesn't want a fiery nurse telling him how to run his orphanage. But Ida Lee Landway's kindness—and beauty—slowly chip away at his stubborn exterior.

LIHCNM0315

REQUEST YOUR FREE BOOKS!

2 FREE INSPIRATIONAL NOVELS
PLUS 2
FREE
MYSTERY GIFTS

Love Inspired

HISTORICAL
INSPIRATIONAL HISTORICAL ROMANCE

YES! Please send me 2 FREE Love Inspired® Historical novels and my 2 FREE
mystery gifts (gifts are worth about $10). After receiving them, if I don't wish to receive
any more books, I can return the shipping statement marked "cancel." If I don't cancel,
I will receive 4 brand-new novels every month and be billed just $4.74 per book in the
U.S. or $5.24 per book in Canada. That's a saving of at least 21% off the cover price.
It's quite a bargain! Shipping and handling is just 50¢ per book in the U.S. and 75¢ per
book in Canada.* I understand that accepting the 2 free books and gifts places me under
no obligation to buy anything. I can always return a shipment and cancel at any time.
Even if I never buy another book, the two free books and gifts are mine to keep forever.

102/302 IDN F5CN

Name	(PLEASE PRINT)

Address	Apt. #

City	State/Prov.	Zip/Postal Code

Signature (if under 18, a parent or guardian must sign)

Mail to the Harlequin® Reader Service:
IN U.S.A.: P.O. Box 1867, Buffalo, NY 14240-1867
IN CANADA: P.O. Box 609, Fort Erie, Ontario L2A 5X3

Want to try two free books from another series?
Call 1-800-873-8635 or visit www.ReaderService.com.

* Terms and prices subject to change without notice. Prices do not include applicable
taxes. Sales tax applicable in N.Y. Canadian residents will be charged applicable taxes.
Offer not valid in Quebec. This offer is limited to one order per household. Not valid
for current subscribers to Love Inspired Historical books. All orders subject to credit
approval. Credit or debit balances in a customer's account(s) may be offset by any other
outstanding balance owed by or to the customer. Please allow 4 to 6 weeks for delivery.
Offer available while quantities last.

Your Privacy—The Harlequin® Reader Service is committed to protecting your
privacy. Our Privacy Policy is available online at www.ReaderService.com or upon
request from the Harlequin Reader Service.

We make a portion of our mailing list available to reputable third parties that offer
products we believe may interest you. If you prefer that we not exchange your name with
third parties, or if you wish to clarify or modify your communication preferences, please
visit us at www.ReaderService.com/consumerschoice or write to us at Harlequin Reader
Service Preference Service, P.O. Box 9062, Buffalo, NY 14269. Include your complete
name and address.

LIH13R

Love Inspired HISTORICAL

*On the wagon train out West, will Ben Hewitt find love
again with Abigail Bingham Black—the woman who
broke his heart six years ago?*

*Read on for a sneak preview of Linda Ford's
WAGON TRAIN REUNION,
the exciting beginning of the new series
JOURNEY WEST.*

Benjamin Hewitt stared. It wasn't possible.

The man struggling with his oxen couldn't be
Mr. Bingham. He would never subject himself and his
wife to the trials of this journey. Why, Mrs. Bingham
would look mighty strange fluttering a lace hankie and
expecting someone to serve her tea.

The man must have given the wrong command
because the oxen jerked hard to the right. The rear wheel
broke free. A flurry of smaller items fell out the back. A
woman followed, shrieking.

"Mother, are you injured?" A young woman ran
toward her mother. She sounded just like Abigail. At least
as near as he could recall. He'd succeeded in putting that
young woman from his mind many years ago.

She glanced about. "Father, are you safe?"

The sun glowed in her blond hair and he knew without
seeing her face that it was Abigail. What was she doing
here? She'd not find a fine, big house nor fancy dishes

and certainly no servants on this trip.

The bitterness he'd once felt at being rejected because he couldn't provide those things had dissipated, leaving only regret and caution.

She helped her mother to her feet and dusted her skirts off. All the while, the woman—Mrs. Bingham, to be sure—complained, her voice grating with displeasure that made Ben's nerves twitch. He knew all too well that sound. Could recall in sharp detail when the woman had told him he was not a suitable suitor for her daughter. Abigail had agreed, had told him, in a harsh dismissive tone, she would no longer see him.

It all seemed so long ago. Six years to be exact. He'd been a different person back then. Thanks to Abigail, he'd learned not to trust everything a woman said. Nor believe how they acted.

But Binghams or not, a wheel needed to be put on. Ben joined the men hurrying to assist the family.

"Hello." He greeted Mr. Bingham and the man shook his hand. "Ladies." He tipped his hat to them.

"Hello, Ben." Abigail Bingham stood at her mother's side. No, not Bingham. She was Abigail Black now.

Don't miss
WAGON TRAIN REUNION by Linda Ford,
available April 2015 wherever
Love Inspired® Historical books and ebooks are sold.

www.Harlequin.com

Hannah edged closer to her. "I don't like storms."

Mary slipped an arm around her daughter. "Don't worry. We'll be at Katie's house before the rain catches us."

It turned out she was wrong. Big raindrops began hitting her windshield. A strong gust of wind shook the buggy and blew dust across the road. The sky grew darker by the minute. She urged Tilly to a faster pace. She should have stayed home.

A red car flew past her with the driver laying on the horn. Tilly shied and nearly dragged the buggy into the fence along the side of the road. Mary managed to right her. "Foolish *Englischers*. We are over as far as we can get."

The rumble of thunder became a steady roar behind them. Tilly broke into a run. Hannah began screaming. Mary glanced back and her heart stopped. A tornado had dropped from the clouds and was bearing down on them. Dust and debris flew out from the wide base.

Dear God, help me save my baby. What do I do?

She saw an intersection up ahead.

Bracing her legs against the dash, she pulled back on the lines, trying to slow Tilly enough to make the corner without overturning. The mare seemed to sense the plan. She slowed and made the turn with the buggy tilting on two wheels. Mary grabbed Hannah and held on to her. Swerving wildly behind the horse, the buggy finally came back onto all four wheels. Before the mare could gather speed again, a man jumped into the road waving his arms. He grabbed Tilly's bridle and pulled her to a stop.

Shouting, he pointed toward an abandoned farmhouse. "There's a cellar on the south side."

Mary jumped out of the buggy and pulled Hannah into her arms. The man was already unhitching Tilly, so Mary ran toward the ramshackle structure. The wind threatened to pull her off her feet. The trees and even the grass were straining toward the approaching tornado. She reached the old cellar door, but couldn't lift it against the force of the wind. She was about to lie on the ground on top of Hannah when the man appeared at her side. Together, they were able to lift the door.

A second later, she was pushed down the steps into darkness.

Don't miss
AMISH REDEMPTION by Patricia Davids,
available April 2015 wherever
Love Inspired® books and ebooks are sold.

www.Harlequin.com

Love Inspired

JUST CAN'T GET ENOUGH OF INSPIRATIONAL ROMANCE?

Join our social communities
and talk to us online!
You will have access to the latest
news on upcoming titles and special
promotions, but most important,
you can talk to other fans about your
favorite Love Inspired® reads.

www.Facebook.com/LoveInspiredBooks

www.Twitter.com/LoveInspiredBks

Harlequin.com/Community

LISOCIAL